And Then One Day

Tom Yarbrough

Inspiring Voices®

Scripture quotations marked HCSB are taken from the Holman
Christian Standard Bible®, Copyright © 1999, 2000, 2002,
2003, 2009 by Holman Bible Publishers. Used by permission.
Holman Christian Standard Bible®, Holman CSB®, and HCSB® are
federally registered trademarks of Holman Bible Publishers.

Scripture taken from the New King James Version®. Copyright ©
1982 by Thomas Nelson. Used by permission. All rights reserved

Inspiring Voices books may be ordered through
booksellers or by contacting:

Inspiring Voices
1663 Liberty Drive
Bloomington, IN 47403
www.inspiringvoices.com
1 (866) 697-5313

ISBN: 978-1-4624-1225-9 (sc)
ISBN: 978-1-4624-1234-1 (e)

Print information available on the last page.

Inspiring Voices rev. date: 5/10/2018

Chapter 1

I could not believe the pain that shot through my neck and shoulders then traveled up the back of my head. It was like electrical wires attached to my spine squirting electricity through one wire at a time.

Besides that, a putrid acid boiled in my stomach. You know that stuff you burp up that tastes like hot soapy water. Because I sat at my desk, I pushed myself up, shuffled over to open the oak door just in time for a middle-aged woman to skulk past me, out of my office, like a frightened rabbit. I couldn't help but stare at her.

She had been a successful writer, having published and felt embarrassed about her situation. She kept her eyes on the floor as she moved. I watched as she fumbled with her purse, found a handful of tissue and dabbed her eyes. Just outside my office, she glanced over at the church secretary, ducked her head trying to avoid any embarrassing talk from that staff member, and bolted out the side door of the church offices.

I shook my head because I knew the truth down deep. Hearing people's problems never was my favorite part of ministry, but in Restoration Church, Oklahoma, with its 700 members, I received more than my share of individual matters. Some members called me Dr.

Sellers, some Rev. Sellers, some just plain Jerod. By nine o'clock this Tuesday morning, I'd already heard a young couple about to marry, and now, it appeared, an experienced woman about to UN-marry. I felt exhausted, like a squeezed sponge with no more absorption.

Quickly, I shut the door to my office. In our conversation, the woman mentioned in passing, An independent kind of Christian woman writer and I was curious. I walked to a shelf of my abundant library and pulled down a book of history about the first century Christians. Sure enough, there was a short item about a noblewoman named Perpetua who died in 203 A.D. She had written and published a diary about her last days. History suggested she was killed during a persecution time.

I slapped the book shut, sat it on my desk and moved to stand in front of a full-length mirror attached to the back of the door. I needed to see if I looked as bad as I felt. Small dark pouches under eyes looked back at me, but I felt those didn't show much if I kept my summer tan. I still stood six feet, broad shouldered, keeping the same physical conditioning, I'd had at twenty. Yet, my head ached and acid boiled in my stomach to remind me of my fallibility, but I threw back my shoulders and sucked in my stomach, heels together, chin out and glared at the mirror image. I looked at the top of my hair, parted on the left, full dark brown, laced slightly with those sneaky small grey hairs peeking back at me. I kept it somewhat long, halfway covering my ears and combed back.

I was one of those fortunate ones. Since I kept active, I could eat what I wanted and not gain weight, but this ability did not keep the acid away. I bent closer to the mirror and stared a second time, peered closer, looking to see if any other outward sign gave hint of my fatigue. How could I stay in such good shape and yet feel so tired? How was I supposed to be God's man and be so exhausted? I shrugged and moved to my desk. Easing myself back into my old high-backed chair, I glanced at pink slips, phone messages, some snail-mail and other paper work piled in middle of my desk. I didn't have the heart to deal with any of it.

I sighed so big, I blew some paper across my desk. I stared at the stuff and thought back to my youth. I remembered my strong ambition to get ahead. I'd rushed my teens, breezed through my twenties, fast-stepped my thirties. I was driven by some urgent nature. But, it seems I'd come to a shin knocking, knee burning halt in my forties. I couldn't help but grin and think, *if my advice-giving mother had told me one day I'd pastor a large church, be married with no children, be a very tired, forty-three-year-old with headaches and heart burn, I might have reneged on my anxious desire to grow up.*

I twirled my index finger toward the ceiling, as if pointing at anyone looking down on me now, shook my head and reached in my desk drawer for the antacid tablets and aspirin. Of course, both bottles were nearly empty.

Suddenly, I jumped as my hidden private land-line jangled. It was like a screeching drag against every nerve fiber. Only a few people knew this special number. Left over from the early days before cell phones, the land-line stayed hidden in a separate drawer-nook of my desk. I just never used it much. I slid open the drawer and jerked up the receiver.

A voice gurgled like running water. "*Dr. Sellers, my name is Ruben Michael. I'm a collector of sorts, mostly of antique books and rare manuscripts.*"

"How in the world did you get this number?" I demanded.

"That's not important. What's urgent is I have something I must show you." Came a regular voice.

"I'm pretty busy right now. If you could just. . ." I paused, hoping to get rid of the caller.

Michael's voice purred. "*I am no crank*. I assure you **Dr.** Sellers; you will want to see what I have. It will shock your life."

"Oh yeah, well . . . ok, if it's that urgent." I yielded.

Ruben continued, "I assure you what I must show is much more than some book of a long forgotten, undiscovered genius."

"Ok," I murmured.

"No one has seen all I have yet. I'm supposed to show only you. I need you to come to apartment 10 at those Riverside apartments. And pay close attention to watch out for an odd door number."

Breathing sharply, after a moment, I felt hooked. "Ok, I guess I'll come when I can."

"I was sure you would," Ruben hung up.

After I put down the receiver, I stared at the phone and wondered why I'd committed to this strange caller. I was used to weird phone calls, weird people and weird happenings, but this call made me extra curious. I began to think. *Maybe it's what I need to get out of a slump. After all, I like old books of theology.* I still had a good collection from seminary days. *Why not see this Ruben Michael and see what's up? It's probably some hustle but who cares?*

Just then, the church secretary tapped on the study door, opened it meekly and peeked in.

"Pastor . . . the hospital called. They want you to come right away if you can. Benny Sapp appears to be worse. He's in room 202."

"Oh, no . . . ok, I'll go right now if the calendar's free, thanks Betty."

I knew I had to go, even though I didn't want to really, but Benny was an old pastor friend I could not ignore.

■ ■ ■

I left the office, grateful to get out, and drove straight to the hospital. Arriving at my destination, I parked in minister-only parking, rushed to an inside elevator, punched #2 and hurried up to the second floor where private rooms were located. I went to room 202 where Rev. Benny Sapp, retired pastor, lay dying. The doctors were at a loss to diagnose his illness, watching as his major organs failed.

Quietly, I eased into the room and glanced down at the frail body in the hospital bed. I know some ministers thrived on hospital visits and I think that takes a special gift. But I could never get used to the setting. I was supposed to be there and offer some strength, some hope, but I always left a situation depressed. And now that I was so tired, I dreaded any hospital visit. Others might criticize me for this, but I just must be honest and admit, I just did not like hospitals. To me, they stay places of pain and besides, too many die there.

I stared again at the body lying captured by tubes

and bed. Benny Sapp was well known and generally well loved in his ministry. He and I had been ministerial friends for years; that is, we'd sat on committees and community functions together. Sapp spent most of his adult life as an active local pastor, until his health began to fail when he reached his sixties. His last pastorate ended in retirement, rumor said by agreement with the congregation. Soon after his duties at church ended, Benny's body began this mysterious decaying, needing intense medical care.

I braced myself against the alcohol smell and looked at the IV tubes in Benny's arm. As many times as I'd seen this, I still couldn't get over the idea that the plastic reminded me of an invasion.

In my younger days, I would have thought of the many science-fiction scenes where tubes ran in and out of some arm like highways carrying colorful fluids. Still, I reached down and stroked the old man's thin, blue-veined hand. I thought: *how many lives had that hand touched? How often had it been the transmission of God's healing power? Physician, heal thyself.*

"Benny," I whispered, "Are you awake?"

Sapp fluttered his eyes open with great effort, as if having to draw impossible strength from other parts of his body. Then he smiled, swallowed hard and spoke.

"You came. I knew you would. I sent the rest of the family home for a while."

I took a deep breath and said, "I know this sounds stupid, but how are you feeling?"

"Well, you see, Jerod . . . I'm going to die soon, I know it. I don't mind that so much . . . but I had to talk to someone without family being around. I sent for you, but I don't want anyone else hearing." Benny let loose with a ragged cough.

The smell of decay assaulted my nose and I almost gagged. I was afraid the smell signaled the truth of Benny's words about death. I turned my head to get a fresh breath, then said,

"Aw, an old workhorse like you will outlive us all, Ben. You take it easy . . . You can beat this thing." I felt stupid as soon as the words came out of my mouth.

Ben's voice broke in an obvious struggle to speak. "I don't know that I want to beat anything. That's beside the point. I've got to ask you something. . ."

Benny sighed and continued, "You know I respect you as a person and your whole life. Tell me true now. What's it all about anyway? I mean, what's the real use of it all?"

For a moment, I felt stunned. The question penetrated all my defenses and opened my own reserve of recent doubt. The room became uncomfortably hot. I felt my senses shut down and for a second, I went numb. I stood there dazed, not sure how to answer. Finally, I used the oldest technique in any minister's handbag of tricks.

"You just don't feel very good right now, Ben. It's natural to have some doubt when you're physically down."

Suddenly a racking cough, one sounding deep and wet, interrupted Benny's words. He pushed a tissue over his mouth. He lowered it and spoke out from reserve strength. "Bull chips, Jerod . . . I know I'm dying and I'll ask God about some of this when I get there, but I want to hear from the living."

I snatched another tissue from its holder and held it

to Benny. Sapp took the tissue, wiped his lips, breathed a raspy breath and continued.

"I mean I've spent my life preaching, teaching, supposedly bringing comfort to the world and I end up my days being unhealthy and bitter."

Every word stuck like pins along my spine. *Why indeed, God? Why this?* No scripture came to mind. No poetry. No stream of untapped wisdom came forth. I stood like the proverbial pillar of salt. Where was my taste, my flavor, my savor?

"Man, Benny, you sure hit a guy where he lives," I said.

"Yeah, yeah, I know . . . but I don't get it. I've gone over and over my life. I can't say I'd change much; oh, I've made mistakes, sins, and I wished I could undo some things, but I wouldn't trade my vocation for anything. Yet, here I am. I feel no use to anybody. I wonder if I've ever been any use. What went wrong? Where's the joy I'm supposed to have? It's not that I'm scared. I'm perplexed!"

"Heck, Benny, I don't know. I always thought you were one guy that had it all together."

Ben strained at his plastic shackles, rolled his body some and shifted in bed with great effort.

"Come on, son, talk to me. You can't hurt my feelings or say anything wrong. I just need flesh and blood communication."

"You know I have doubts too, Ben. And I'm like you, I don't have many to confide in either."

Sapp began slapping the bedside with his free arm, as if to hammer home some point. "Come now Jerod, this is my time. God seems unusually silent these days. You've got to give me some word. Lately, I think about

Jesus on the cross. Did He feel what I'm feeling? On that fateful day, did He look up to the Father and ask: *'Where's the joy?'"*

His voice rasped on. "Is this world so confusing that even the son of God left it perplexed? Or is it just us? Do we make things so complicated that we end by asking what's it all about? If so, Jerod, you'd better change your message and tell everybody to simplify life. Cut out everything. Be hermits and live like John the Baptist on nuts and grasshoppers. I don't know . . . even John must have felt perplexed some when the sword came down and severed his old head."

Benny shifted again and pointed to the water glass. Thankful to do something, I hurried to pour fresh water and held the glass still for him. He took small sips through the flexible red and white straw. Moisture dribbled down one corner of his stubby face. He spit out the straw and continued.

"I know how I sound to you. Remember, I was on the other side of this bed most of my life, standing where you're standing. And no one, in all those years ever gave me a chance to be totally honest. No one let me bare my soul in a time like this. Come on, let down your collar. Talk to me. You can't hurt one blessed thing. I'll be on the other side soon and I'll tell God I asked for it. You aren't accountable."

I moved slowly over to one side of the room and pulled over a chair, placing it close to the bed. I sat down and loosened my tie, trying to relax. Some random thoughts flooded my mind on how to answer Benny, but all seemed inadequate.

"What do you want me to do, Ben, be like Job's friends and say, 'curse God and die'? I'm not going to do that. Goodness, I still have my doubting days too. Doesn't everyone?"

"Now that's more like it. I knew a real heart beat under that pastoral suit of yours." Ben coughed again, choking. He pointed a bony finger to the water. I jumped up and gave him another drink, feeling a momentary reprieve. Ben smacked his dry lips, settled back and his cracked voice began again.

"I don't want to curse God. I don't figure he's to blame. In fact, I still praise His name for all that's happened to me. It's not God I'm concerned about. It's more on the human level, like we're missing something vital." Sapp waved his arm around, pointing like he singled out people everywhere.

He continued. "I know humans have always been a mess and I guess I'm just bitter about people. I didn't have the education you did, if that mattered, but in all those years of serving people, while I cared about folks in the name of the Lord, I don't know if I ever received anything back. I mean, it seems to me there ought to be at least one person I feel a special closeness to. Out of all those people, I can't point to one individual who I feel really close to."

"Aw, Benny, you've got lots of friends I'm sure," I fumbled.

"Oh, I had surface friends, like you do, but no one really knew me, not even my wife and kids. Isn't that sad? Doesn't that puzzle you? What happened? If Jesus really lives in us, and I truly believe He does, why can't people form close relationships like that, too? I don't think it's just us pastors either. I mean, I don't think we're supposed to take on a special loneliness just because of our role."

I stared hard at the thin frame before me. I didn't know if I could offer any answer or not. Besides, I sure didn't feel a good response now. Maybe Benny just needed a listener, a time to spit out verbally some of his inner pain. But in my deeper self, I knew he wanted something more, some magic word of reassurance that humanity was worth it all.

"Take it easy, Ben, you need to save your energy."

"I've got to cut bait and fish while I can," he blurted.

Just then, the door swung open. A short, skinny nurse breezed in, nodded to me, and went ahead to check the tubes and connections of her patient. Benny responded by closing his eyes. The nurse checked an IV bag, rushed over and looked at the numbers on the machine monitor. She fluffed Sapp's pillows, threw away tissue and replaced fresh water in a pitcher. She never said a word. All her motions were so fluid; she appeared to accomplish her tasks without interfering with us at all.

Finally, she looked around the room, glanced back at me, shook her head no to show her patient wasn't doing so well, and scurried out the door. The activity happened so quickly that I wondered if it occurred at all. I glanced at Sapp's face as tired eyes opened slowly. There was light in them yet.

"I don't mean to say anything bad about my loved ones," Benny continued, "my wife, bless her soul, is as good as they come. She's put up with a lot. But she's too fragile to talk like I'm doing now. I feel this distance from her. Maybe that just happens with mates. I mean, you go through so much crud together it becomes too hard to accept everything in another's life. You end up tolerating a lot of stuff that never gets resolved. You just somehow endure."

"Well, isn't that a good kind of friendship? I asked.

"Oh . . . she's the best friend I have, probably. Yet, it's not enough. Deep friendship should be a different matter. There should be a special bond. I think Jesus hinted at it when He talked about dying for a friend. Man, it's awful. I can't think of one person, except maybe you. My family might but I'm not sure of them, who'd die for me . . . either literally or symbolically. Where'd I miss it, Jerod? Was it something I did or didn't do? Am I reaching for something that isn't there?"

I thought about my wife, Jill, and the people of my congregation. Often, I felt alone and needed a sympathetic ear. Maybe that was it. I knew myself well enough to know I was tired enough most days to need some pity. I began to wonder if Ben was as bad as he thought. Maybe this illness did bring out these questions because the man needed sympathy. Perhaps he only needed a good listener whether good advice happened or not.

I sucked in some air, bolstered courage and spoke. "Look, I've got to be honest with you. I don't have all the answers. Oh, I could give you the usual platitudes, but that's no good here. For a lot of my life I've defended the Biblical principles of hope, faith and all that, but lately, those things seem very far away. I have many days when I'm so exhausted, those principles are only words. They're like whistling some old familiar tune you really get tired of but keep whistling it anyway."

"Maybe you're just tired," I continued, "and your sickness has certainly pulled you down and that's where all the doubt comes from." I looked deeper into the man's eyes and thought I saw sparks.

"You think I'm stewing in the juice of self-pity, don't ya boy?" Ben raised an eyebrow and stuck out his chin.

"Well . . . yeah, a little I guess. But I'm certainly not judging you, if that's what you mean. No man can know another's pain or real thoughts. It's probably a good thing too. Just like the other day. I had this funeral of one of my oldest church members. If people had been reading my real thoughts, I mean, they were ludicrous and my words were stale, dry routine, especially at the grave side. It was like whistling the old tune again. No **real** life in it. Just motion. See, I'm not a perfect minister either."

An impish smile passed over Ben's face. "By the way, Jerod, I've requested the family get you do my funeral."

"Thanks a lot, brother. Here, in so many words, I tell you I'm tired at funerals and you say, **good,** have another."

"I told you I was perplexed. I might as well share some with you." he grinned broadly.

At that instance, I felt the old man was a living picture of some playful sprite, some lesser naughty elf, and spreading mischief among the Christian populace. I was forced to smile and felt a warm kinship to this fellow struggler.

Ben raised his brows in perfect arches as if they'd been drawn on his forehead with crayons, then he widened his eyes.

"I've been thinking about loneliness. Seems like I've harbored a lonely spot, way deep . . . all my ministry days. I know Christ has been the only one to fill it sometimes, but surely, human beings ought to be able to get in there, too. It's not that I want some person to be a god and replace Christ. But, it just feels like good old flesh and blood in there would help, especially now I'm about to depart. . ." His words trailed.

"Maybe I'd better go, Benny. I'm afraid I'm tiring you too much," I reacted.

"I just want to be able to look inside and really know one person knew all my shortcomings, then loved me and accepted me anyway. This may sound odd to you, but in some way, it would make life more worthwhile . . . and death make more sense." Benny gasped, stopped abruptly and closed his eyes.

I moved in closer to the bed, bent down to investigate the man's breathing. Short jerking gulps came from the upper chest. I touched his arm and whispered, "You ok Ben?"

Ben's eyes popped open. "Yeah, sure, I'm having a heck of a time. Why are you whispering? Dang it, Jerod, are you going to admit I'm dying or not?"

His words sent fire in my gut. Strange emotions flooded me, like embarrassment, humiliation, weak self-confidence— all wrapped themselves in a stranglehold around my inner self. I still avoided the fact that flooded every one of my senses. My friend was indeed dying. Reality covered me like a net.

"Ok, Ben, you're dying." I blurted.

"There, now," he smiled, "we're getting somewhere. I don't know how much strength I've got left, or time for that matter, but talk to me, one living man to one not so living. I want to hear an honest human voice."

"You're sure something, Ben. I sure admire you. Somehow, you can sound bitter, which by the way, seems natural to me, yet you still love God and in the next breath talk about your own mortality. If I'm honest, and it's not easy to admit this out loud, I think I've been a coward about death. I don't even like the idea of facing it here with you. And I sure don't like thinking about my own. I don't know. Maybe I wouldn't mind dying if I knew for sure it wouldn't hurt so much."

"Well, buddy, there's no guarantee about that, is there? Pain is pain, but my pain now seems more emotional. Hang it all, Jerod . . . I'm so perplexed and can't shake it. And to think I might leave this world this way really grates on me. I think I could go easier if I could experience some peace about people, but it just won't come. God must have a good reason for leaving me like this. I accept that. And yet, it's like I can't relax or let go until I get peace. No schooling in the world trained us for this, did it?"

I moved closer, leaning on the bed. I truly admired this man. I wanted to touch him, embrace him, swoop him up and somehow soothe him. I yearned to relieve Ben's doubts even if he couldn't his own. I didn't know what to do. I glanced over at the water pitcher again and thought I'd offer some.

Suddenly, Benny hacked out a violent cough, filling the whole room with a decayed smell. He jerked his head to one side and stared at me. A strange look of wonder spread across his entire face. He reached a shriveled hand up and grabbed the lapel of my coat jacket. He pulled me close, face to face. Tears began running down his cracked face. Gulping for air, a slow eerie groan rose from his chest, finally erupting through his mouth.

"Jerod . . . I . . ." Benny Sapp lay back in slow motion, eyes rolling to the ceiling. Still twisting my lapel with one hand, he lifted his other hand—palm up—as if greeting some invisible source. One long, exhaled breath and his uplifted hand fell to his side; a slow smile grew in one corner of his mouth.

I reached and pulled the still clinging hand from me. The hospital monitor screeched behind me. I lay the limp arm across his chest and from some hidden reserve within my soul, I knew Benny was gone. Nothing else to do so I prayed: *Father, into your presence, I commend his spirit. Treat him kindly. Let it be so. Amen.*

I hesitated a moment, allowing the sense of void to wash over me. The machine beeped its message of death. Of course, I'd seen people die before, but this time was different. I looked at the ceiling, as if straining to hear above any hospital noise. Would God answer? Would He send some angel to say something? I waited for that one, tangible word from heaven. It did not come.

I glanced at the flat line of the life systems monitor. The screeching sound raked my nerves. The staff would know what had happened. I sighed and reached for the button to summon the nurse anyway. I pressed it hard and walked out the door. Let others feel their own loss. Let others take care of Benny now. I went straight to my car, passing people and buildings as if they existed in another dimension.

Driving zombie-like back to the church's parking lot, I switched off the engine and sat staring out the car window. Would anyone, even my wife Jill, learn the secrets I keep? Could I ever be truly real to anyone except God?

Outside, the electronic church bells chimed twelve o'clock noon. I tightly gripped the steering wheel, then laid my head down on my knuckles and felt the warm tears run down my cheek.

Chapter 2

White crinkled paint peeled from the outside door. I grabbed the brass knob and jerked twice to open the old wood mount. The moment I stepped inside, a thick musty smell hit me in the face.

After I left the church parking lot, I decided to visit the mysterious Ruben Michael character to get my mind off the death of Benny Sapp. The caller's name Michael was unfamiliar to me, but something about the winsome nature of his phone call intrigued me. Mr. Michael's plea to come see the merchandise in question was probably a ruse, but I began to rationalize that if nothing else, I would meet someone new and invite him to church. So, I proceeded to follow his detailed instructions to the apartment, feeling all the while, this might be an interesting needed diversion.

As I entered the hallway of the apartments and walked up two flights of soiled, brown carpeted stairs, I felt an extra shot of adrenalin coursing through my system and welcomed it. When the challenge of uncertainty buzzed through my veins, I considered it as adventure, a kind of medicine for my tiresome routine. Obnoxious smells attacked my nostrils—dirty diapers, mingled with furniture polish permeated the stairwell. I flinched and hesitated.

I didn't consider myself a snob, but I wondered why all these places smelled the same. Even though old, couldn't owners clean them up? Resigning myself to the task, I shook my head and continued up the steps.

Arriving at the top floor, I walked down the hall, looking right and left for apartment number ten. I remembered, Ruben instructed to pay close attention for the number and as I checked, I saw why. Number 10 had the zero missing with only a vague outline of the number 0, indented in old walnut colored varnish. Someone quickly glancing at it would think it apartment # 1.

I knocked on the door. Faint music floated from the old apartment . . . *Bach or was it Beethoven*? The door opened slowly and the music softened. A stooped old man stood in the doorway, holding his index finger to bleached lips in a shushing motion.

The man wore an old brown suit, with narrow red tie and old scuffed shoes. His complexion was wrinkled; in fact, all about him looked worn. He waved me enter with his other hand, then motioned me toward a chair while he lowered himself into a bright orange recliner. The music grew louder, reached its finale and stopped abruptly. I looked around for the source of the music and saw none.

"Do you like classical music, Reverend Sellers?"

"Well . . . uh . . . yes, some of it." I mumbled.

"Bach always puts me in the right mood for showing my latest discoveries," Ruben smiled and I could have sworn the man's face looked twenty years younger, complexion and all.

"Oh, I see." I said. Of course, I knew I'd flunk any test on classical music, though modern jazz was something else.

"Would you care for hot tea?" Ruben asked.

"Not really," then I thought maybe I should be polite on this first visit and changed my mind. "Well, on second thought, yes, if you have sugar."

Mr. Michael moved smoothly over to his kitchenette where hot water was waiting for its dose of tea bag. He loaded a neat silver tray with the tea and additives and placed them expertly on a small coffee table in the center of the little apartment. His movements were those of one who'd done this many times before. In fact, I thought he had the grace of a well-trained butler.

I supped the steaming brew, burned my upper lip and decided to put it on a small table beside me for cooling. Nothing irritated me more than a hot drink that was too hot to drink. I noticed Ruben supped the hot brew without a flinch.

"Mr. Ruben Michael. I'm just curious. Is that a Hebrew name?" I asked.

"Does it really matter? Today names don't mean much, but please call me Ruben."

"That's fine. Most people call me Dr. Sellers. I have an earned seminary degree and I don't particularly care for Reverend."

I noticed an unusual glint in Michael's left eye. It was as if it changed color from blue to brown.

"As you wish, **Dr**. Sellers. But now down to business. First what I am going to show you is genuine. I have it on the best authority and you may challenge its authenticity any way you choose. As you will see, the point of its uniqueness resides not so much in antiquity as in the surprising content and rare circumstances under which it appears."

"What is it you've discovered, some new book of the Bible?" I chuckled and began looking around the room.

Ruben sighed deeply, then spoke with a new authority: "I know all this sounds like something from a bad movie, but indulge me **Dr.** Sellers. I will explain later why I'm approaching everything as I am. The truth is I have been instructed to show you this material."

I jerked my attention back to his face. "Instructed . . . what do you mean? . . . and by whom?"

"Please, use some of your **doctoral** patience while I retrieve the item."

I cringed at his sarcasm and decided I'd been a little snooty myself. I reached for my tea. Took another sip. It was just right.

Slowly, Ruben rose from the bright orange chair like a man fighting every joint in his well-worn body. He moved to retrieve a small briefcase from behind an old stack of books and magazines.

I watched and considered. No one interested in valuables would look in so obvious a location, which because of its untidiness hid any sign of value whatever.

Ruben moved back to his chair, opened the case and pulled out a bundle, wrapped in rust colored velvet material, tied together with cheap mailing cord. Delicately, he unraveled the twine, as if the package held a fragile piece of china. From the bundle came a layered stack of old brown parchment. The bundle looked square, 10 by 10 inches, about two inches thick. Layered pages were separated with a kind of wax paper so each page could be removed one at a time without sticking to any other.

I watched and groaned to myself, *"Not the old lost scroll game."*

"Before you judge this as some forged parchment a hustler is trying to pawn off on an unsuspecting nit, listen to what I must say. After all, you can always count me as one of your church visits if I do not catch your interest at all."

I felt my ears redden, but glanced down at the first page Ruben held and saw little squiggles of letters. I recognized some of the Greek symbols.

"What you see before you," Ruben continued, "is a page from the first century house church era. It is written in Greek and Aramaic, a very crude street language. The fragments have been dated by experts by the carbon process and I have unquestioned certification the date is around 60 A.D. It is not to be considered scripture as you know your Bible, although it is evidently a record of events that transpired about the time the book of Acts occurred. A full translation is not available to you yet, but will be when I am so instructed."

There it was again. I was dying to know who instructed this weird little man. I started to interrupt. Michael stopped me with a raised hand and kept talking.

"The first page is dynamite itself. I have an English translation for you but let me give you the gist of it, then see what you think. Please hold your comments until I finish, at which time you may ask anything you want and I will do my best to answer you. This must all go in stages, you see."

I didn't see, but sighed and suppressed my inner desire to verbally attack this guy. I crossed my legs from left to right and crossed my arms from right to left. I leaned back and out of politeness, resigned to hear the man out.

"The first sentence identifies the author. The writer

is Clarissa, a **woman**, cousin to Priscilla and Aquila, from the house church in Antioch." He paused, smiled and waited.

I raised one eyebrow at hearing the writer to be a woman that early in history. But of course, any serious Bible reader had probably heard about Priscilla and Aquila, a married couple loyal to the Jesus movement. So, I asked, "I just read in a church history that the first woman Christian writer was Perpetua around 200 AD. Is that, not right?"

Ruben just smiled and carefully lifted the parchment, leaning it toward the overhead light, as if to get a better view and continued his talk.

"Clarissa explains she learned to read and write from a scribe employed by the household of one Ananias. Evidently, he taught her in secret as a kind of joke on his wealthy friends. He must have been a character because in those days—as you know— not many women knew how to read and write. They were mostly considered servants or vessels to raise children. Anyway, the time basically covers some persecution of the house church Christians by the pompous Sadducees and the haughty Pharisees through the spread of the Gospel to the Greeks by Paul and Barnabas. The facts check favorably with those in the book of Acts and I assure you, these are authentic documents."

To say the least, I was suspicious, but also felt curiosity awaken toward that part of me wanting to believe in new found parchments or discovering lost secrets. Whether it was the adventurous little boy in me or merely healthy curiosity, I sensed I needed the virtue of restraint. So, I swallowed any excitement.

"Mr. Michael, ah, Ruben, you really don't expect me to buy all this at face value, do you?"

"No, I suppose not, but Dr. Sellers, do you believe in special revelation, actual mystical experiences, visions or whatever you call individual inspiration?"

"Well, of course I believe in individual revelation like when I preach, but I guess I'm a doubting Thomas when it comes to most testimonies strangers offer up about their mystical events. I can usually explain most of them with natural phenomena rather than supernatural. I know the Bible gives us examples of unusual miracles and such, but that was a different day."

Michael interrupted. "You mean like the Apostle Paul's experience of being blinded on the road to Damascus?"

"Yes, that's right. That is certainly a miracle example but they did not have technology like today to explain things, I mean we very seldom say God sends the weather anymore, we have weather people who scientifically explain where the weather comes from and it makes sense. We have television, satellites, internet and books to explain those things to help avoid too much hocus pocus stuff."

"What I am about to tell you is going to be another jolt to your system, I am afraid but it is imperative." Ruben smiled the most benevolent smile I had ever seen. I wondered what new thing had come over the man.

"Dr. Sellers, I have had a personal commission from Christ himself to show you these parchments. I'm not talking about some inner impression, but an audible voice that gave me specific instructions. You are here today because of that divine commission. I understand this is an extreme amount to digest. I am not clear why you were chosen either, but it is not my place to judge."

He paused but bore into me with eyes that reminded me of those old movies of aliens that had x-ray vision.

I sat mesmerized. I wasn't sure if I wanted to call the mental health authorities, just run to escape this loony, or wait to see if this were some elaborate prank.

"Here's what I want you to do." Ruben placed the original first page of parchment and his translation in a large manila envelope and handed it to me.

"Take this with you, along with the translation. Do all the thinking and research you want. In one week return to me with your conclusions. You see, I will begin our relationship with an act of trust."

My mind whirled with arguments to refuse Ruben. Why not just say thanks but no thanks? It sounded too ridiculous anyway. I could just excuse myself, feigning some responsibility. I could express polite refusal and just walk out.

Then, without much warning, a more creeping emotional curiosity tugged at me. It surprised me because I'd been so tired lately and my interest level was usually very low.

Rather than be perplexed at this ridiculous event, my stimulated curiosity felt good and I found myself reaching for the parchment. I thought about my old Seminary professor who knew both Greek and Aramaic. He could check the original page and the translation.

"I'll do what you say, Ruben, but I'm not promising anything. You must understand, because I'm a pastor, I've been approached by all kinds of hustlers wanting money for their schemes and I really don't know you. I mean you seem sincere and you are willing to trust me. But I'll tell you one thing: by the end of the week, I'll know all I need to know." I took the envelope and rose from my chair.

I started for the door. "I can see my way out and thanks for the tea. I'll contact you in a week or less."

As I moved toward the door, I again heard music floating from somewhere. I stepped into the hallway and just before closing the door, I glanced back into the room and saw Ruben smiling like he'd won the lottery or something. In slow motion, he lowered himself onto the old orange chair, balancing himself with his arms like the best of athletes.

I got goose bumps on my arms for a moment. Something about Ruben's smile and that whole scene made me wonder. But then I shrugged and shut the door, hurrying down the stairs, trying to hold my breath until I reached the better outside smells of city traffic. To me, the fumes of city air were like fresh flowers compared to the stench of the stairwell. But right now, I had other pressing matters.

Chapter 3

Hurriedly, I drove to pick up my wife, thinking for a moment about what'd just happened at the apartment. The whole scene with Ruben Michael seemed a little bizarre. I wasn't sure if Ruben was a hustler, a crusty old scholar, or some lucky old book seller who just happened to come across a rare parchment. Either way, I felt excited to have that first page.

I thought about tentative plans to go visit my old seminary professor and the obvious reason I'd better keep this entire secret because I sometimes felt I lived in an open display case, totally vulnerable to the observations of my congregation. They always wanted to know all about my business.

I stopped at a red light. I looked across the intersection and realized I was only one block from the small strip mall where I'd pick up my wife Jill. I thought about her life for a moment.

I felt Jill Marie Sellers liked her life. She relished being a devoted wife, completely committed to her role as pastor's wife. Since childhood, she'd felt the call of God to do something special. At first, she wasn't clear about any special goal but she'd breezed through college constantly assured God would show her some personal destiny.

One day, out of nowhere, she felt the divine call to become a preacher's wife. This too seemed confusing because Jill learned early in her life she was unable to give birth. Disturbed by this in her early years, she tended to avoid close relationships with men who wanted children, but then she met me.

In our relationship, she correctly interpreted I was more interested in giving myself to ministry and wanted a wife dedicated to the same thing. The courtship was somewhat jarring to say the least. For one reason, she was much more socially minded than I was. She liked fellowships and I liked to sit and read. So, she had definite ideas about life, some of which did not agree with my thinking. But we felt the small issues like money or how we spent time, would solve themselves because we would be dedicated to each other. We were not an ideal couple but the relationship grew and soon married anyway. It was hard for me to believe, but that had been fifteen years ago.

After a while, Jill did discover the lack of her own children gave her much more opportunity to spend time with all people in God's work. Her role demanded much at times, especially in the two pastorates we'd experienced, hinting wives should be busy about all church activities. So, Jill always gave herself fully to the tasks and when people really got to know her, they saw she was perhaps one person who should not have offspring.

Sometimes Jill felt a hint of emotional pain from her barrenness, but she felt vicariously any child became hers since she could mother them unconditionally. Many crossed her path and she ministered to them wherever the need presented itself. She also seemed to love me dearly, serving alongside as an equal partner in various tasks of the church.

Still sitting at the red light, I thought about how Jill had a mind of her own and how we did have our disagreements. But I appreciated how she always used discretion in public, saving the juicier arguments for inside the home.

I smiled as I remembered Jill had been the one to create our mutual give-and-take relationship and I loved her for it. But I also wondered if she put too much of her own hope in me and I shuddered to think what might happen if we somehow parted. Still, I felt truly glad she would go with me on tough errands, like having the up-coming visit with Benny Sapp's now widow.

Just then a car honked behind me to move on through the green light. I pressed the gas pedal and soon swerved to a corner parking to pick up my wife.

"How was your morning? What took you so long?" Jill puzzled as she slid into the car, swooshing in a fresh cosmetic smell I always liked.

"Oh, just stuff, I guess, just as I was leaving to see Benny Sapp at hospital, I got this strange phone call from a guy named Ruben Michael. But before that, I've got to tell you." I machine gunned her about my conversation at the hospital.

"Benny had some real puzzling questions before he died that touched some of my own doubts." I blurted.

"What? Benny died?" Jill puzzled.

"Yeah, but listen. Then I drove after the Benny conversation and visited with this Ruben guy. He wanted to show me some old parchments. Anyway, I know

I'm jumping around but I've had quite a morning. And I'm afraid I'm not up for this grief visit. You know how tired I've been lately, so I sure hate to face Mrs. Sapp. She's probably going to want us to help plan the funeral arrangements since her kids are coming from a long way off."

Jill patted my arm softly. "Relax, relax. That's ok, hon. I'm here to help."

I stared over at Jill and felt the warmth of her support. I loved when she responded with such positive reassurance, giving me a chance to relax my feeling responsible for everything. I knew she was good with people, things like saying the right things to people no matter what the circumstance. But I still couldn't resist teasing her about it.

"What makes you so cheery today?" I asked.

"Haven't you figured out yet? I always enjoy things better when I feel like I've done a 'one up' on you." Brown tiger eyes darted at me, flashing good humor as the light bounced off them.

"Great! How about you pastor a couple of weeks and I'll stay home and keep house."

"You wouldn't last two days," she responded smiling, her chin thrust out as if nothing could shake her positive direction this day. Then she encouraged me to go to Benny's house right now. I shrugged but knew it was the right thing to do.

Soon, we arrived at Benny Sapp's home, a small two-bedroom, white framed house, nestled neatly among other small white framed structures, all in a row.

I knew the Sapp family could only afford this modest house because Benny pastored small churches his entire ministry and often lived in parsonages owned by the churches. When he reached retirement age, he did not own a home of his own and when his last church asked him to resign; he hadn't saved much money, but had enough for the little house. All his life he'd helped others, yet he ended with little security in his declining years.

I thought about my own financial situation. Of course, I kept a much larger church and salary. I did live in a house the church owned, a brand-new one just built, but Jill and I had saved enough to put a substantial down payment on a house if we wanted. We'd decided to keep our savings growing for retirement years because we wanted to travel some and not be tied to a house. I began to wonder if Benny's doubts had anything to do with finances. I started to daydream. *I'm better off financially and I still have some doubts. Would I someday leave this world wondering who I was no matter how much money I have?*

When we entered the Sapp house, we found Mrs. Sapp sitting in an old rocking chair. Next to her, sat her older sister who looked herself like she wasn't long for this world. I had never really known much about Benny's family. I certainly didn't know about Mrs. Sapp's sister and what her story was. I viewed the two women and wondered who was taking care of whom.

As soon as we approached and were introduced, the older sister shuffled off into another part of the house. I felt she did this when she heard I was a pastor. Maybe she wanted to withdraw, allowing me space to perform whatever magic I'd brought for the occasion.

Unfortunately, I felt no magic, no power, and no strength beyond the normal. I really wanted to run out of there, be anywhere besides here, experiencing anything besides this hollow emptiness while others expected miracles from me. I thought, *what can I say to this grieving woman*? From the looks of things, she's endured much more than me. She's the real saint here. I wanted to ask **her** help. I wanted to know more about Benny, especially what happened to him in those last days. A gnawing urge spread over me to fall on my knees in front of her and beg some explanation for Benny's lonely death, but, that's not what I did.

Jill and I sat down on a much worn, green velveteen couch close to the widow's rocker. The room smelled dusty, intermingled with various aromas of food that Sapp's last church members brought, either out of guilt or friendship. The smells drifted from somewhere out of sight of the small living room. I pictured a tiny kitchen piled high with food enough to last weeks, an absurd abundance now someone was dead. I glanced at the walls. Something seemed amiss. The strangeness of those walls held my attention, then, I realized what was different. There were no pictures, no mirrors, and no little plaques of art. Just dull white walls stared back at me. I wondered if she'd removed everything recently or never bothered to hang things. Glancing at the bleakness, I felt any minute those walls would start closing in to squash me, like in an old horror movie. I started to speak, but instead, stared at Mrs. Sapp, a solidly built woman who obviously took solace in her eating habits.

She sat with her right-hand palm up, resting on her thigh. With her left hand resting on her other thigh, she folded and unfolded a laced handkerchief. Her gaze was fixed on the handkerchief and her own hand movements as if waiting for others to speak. She didn't appear numb from grief, merely removed from any responsibility to entertain.

I opened my mouth to speak but my jaws snapped shut. I sat gritting my teeth, feeling every jaw muscle extend and contract.

Jill darted a look in my direction and quickly felt my mood so she spoke. "We're here, Mrs. Sapp to offer any practical help we can." Her voice was so rich in tone and control, I began to relax.

Mrs. Sapp looked up, never missing a fold of her hanky. "There is something," she blurted.

Jill waited for me to speak, but I sat transfixed and silent.

"Uh . . . we mean it," Jill continued, "what do you need?"

"Plan the services for me. I just want a graveside service. Pick the music, the scripture, and the order of service, anything you want. I don't want to do none of it." Mrs. Sapp's lower eyelids narrowed, her eyes dilated like big gray marbles as she stared at Jill.

I looked at Jill to see her response. I felt at ease to keep silent.

Jill said, "We'll be happy to take care of things for you. Now let me make sure I understand. You don't want an in-church service and you don't want anything to do with planning the content at graveside. What about your kids? Let's see, you have two boys, don't you?"

"That's right. They don't matter. They broke much contact with us a long time ago. I'll figure how to get them here. You folks just guide me through. I figure since your husband there was the last to see Benny alive and was asked to do the funeral; you'd know what's what. Just get it done. I don't care." She leaned forward in the rocker, turned her head to one side and called to her sister in the other room. "Claudel, bring us out some of that coffee, will ya!"

In my mind, it was as if our business was concluded and coffee signaled the mental signing of an agreement.

Jill rose and said not to worry, everything would be taken care of, and then she refused the coffee for us, explaining our tight schedule. We shook hands all around and Mrs. Sapp never left her chair, as if she'd finally gained the right to do as she pleased.

"May we say a short prayer," Jill muttered.

"If you want." Mrs. Sapp said.

Jill and I held hands. "*Lord, we know death hurts, especially for those left behind. Guide all of us in days to come, particularly Mrs. Sapp and family. In Jesus Name. Amen.*" Jill prayed. She and I looked up and there stood Claudel with coffee cups.

Sister Claudel clumsily placed the cups on a little table, then, ushered us to the door and whispered a casual '*thank you*'.

Back in the car, I finally got my tongue. "Thanks honey, for taking over back there. I don't know what came over me. Well, I do know. It was just too sad to see how these people ended up. I just couldn't pull out the words. You sure saved my bacon. It makes me feel good to know you're in my corner."

"I know, Jerod. But don't you think I thought they were sad too? Yet we still had to minister to them. I'm a professional too. Sometimes I think that you think I just like to be home with my pots and plants." Jill stared out the window.

"Whoa, wait a minute; I don't think I'd go that far." I spouted

"Well, lately, it seems like it. You've tended to leave me out. Oh, you finally tell me some things, but you don't really let me get involved right along beside you like you used to. It's more like you want to do stuff alone. Maybe you think it's quicker. I don't know. But remember, I'm still around."

"Mercy, Jill, you sound irritated or tired as well."

"Maybe both. I just know I'm a person too. I need to feel needed. Maybe Mrs. Sapp felt like she did because her husband left her out of things. I need to feel my own self-worth, more than just being the pastor's wife and handmaiden. When I took charge back there, it made me feel good too. It's like **I**, was doing something, not just the pastor's wife . . . I, me, did something. Can you understand that?"

"Wow . . . what happened to the person who first slid into the car with me?"

"I'm still here and I'm not angry or whining either. I'm simply talking how I feel. You know Jerod, lately when I try to discuss something a little painful, you back off and run."

"What do you mean, I run?"

"It's like you don't want to be bothered, like you want me to keep in my place and not cause you any extra effort. I'm not exactly angry, but I'm tired too. I know you're exhausted most days. I sympathize with that, but I don't know what your problem is. You never really talk to me anymore. I just know I can't stand much more of this."

"Goodness, Jill, all this because of what happened at the Sapp house?"

"No, not really. It's been building a long time."

"Well . . . what should we do about it? I'm not running

now, as you put it. Feeling unrest and tired. Yes. A lot on my mind. Yes. Sometimes, I feel I've stagnated and God is far away, but I don't see myself running." The very minute I finished, something didn't quite ring true. In trying to defend myself, I'd slipped over the line of absolute truth because I wasn't sure what the truth was. Overstating my case was the natural result.

We drove in silence. Outside the air was dry and the sun shone clear. Jill just sat and watched the trees, buildings, and scenery pass, lost in her own thoughts. Soon, we pulled into the driveway of our house. I shut off the engine and turned to speak to Jill again.

"You didn't answer; who's running now?" I asked.

"Jerod, I don't want an argument and I don't have an answer. Sometimes I wish I had a personal pastor to talk to, but I only have you to give me answers."

Her words jolted me more than I wanted to admit. I **was** supposed to be her spiritual help as well as my own. Yet, here I was feeling like I couldn't even take care of my own spiritual exhaustion. I glanced out the car window at the rose bushes Jill had planted in the front flower beds. I thought, God may have made a flower more beautiful than King Solomon and all his array, but He sure made a wife more complicated. I experienced an uneasy parting between us, a kind of rift that scared me because it seemed to question the spiritual quality of my marriage. I knew I had no answer for my wife now. And, I never did live very well with non-answers. What would happen next, I wasn't sure.

Chapter 4

I was involved in death, whether I wanted to be or not. Although Jill and I planned this occasion, because this was the only time, I still wondered why anyone would want to have a funeral on Saturday and mess up a perfectly good weekend.

I sat at my office desk, rubbing the back of my neck. The tension from looking down so much felt like the pain of a sunburn, a raw scratchy irritation just inside my shirt collar. I fumbled in a drawer for an aspirin, took three quickly. *Oh man, now I must go to the funeral with a throbbing headache* . . . just one more agitation to my day. I wadded up an old telephone message and threw it at the trash can across the room and of course, missed.

In a short time, Reverend Dr. Jerod Sellers, pastor of Restoration Church, Oklahoma would leave my personal sanctuary office for the grave side service, performing my pastoral duty of burying the dead. I would pronounce the sacred words over the departed Benny Sapp. My words were supposed to be freshly scattered flowers of memorial, but lately, they seemed more like dead phrases over unsuspected decaying fodder.

I glanced at the time. My bloodshot eyes lingered on a gold trimmed, china desk clock, given to me by one of the deacon's wives, Doris Butler. I loathed the fat, grinning little cherubs painted pink, especially since they rolled their wide eyes every hour on the hour, as if to say, 'I caught you again...I see you'. I thought, too many artists think angels look like cherubs, innocent children, yet most in Scripture are adults. They probably appear just like grown humans. Maybe it's not this clock design that bugs me, but the fact time told me I'd been sitting here too long, looking at my sweaty hands. Now, I've got to rush to the grave site. *No . . . no. It's this clock that really gets me.* Of course, as a pastor, I must receive a gift of mediocrity no matter where it comes from.

I jumped up, started to leave, then turned back to reset my answering machine. Also, at times like these, I always turned off my cell phone. Let the machine do my work some. As I hurried out the door, the land line began ringing. I hesitated but kept going, although it always bothered my sensibilities to leave a phone unanswered.

I rushed to my freshly washed, four door auto and drove to the grave site. I'd just stepped out of the car when something wet spattered my face. I wiped my cheek with the back of my hand, hoping it wasn't bird and saw gray moisture. I threw my head back and squinted at the sky. *Come on, God, must it always rain at funerals, especially this muddy rain? All this is hard enough . . . aren't you controlling the weather anymore?* A dark cloud burst back with wet, large pelting drops like liquefied gray hail. Quickly, I grabbed my trusty umbrella from the car and hunched my shoulders and tried to run, but decided I'd better use a more dignified, pastoral march step. Then I shook my head and hurried to the grave side where the coffin lay in repose under cover.

I stepped under the faded green canopy that sheltered the grave, family and friends. I folded the umbrella and leaned it by a post. As I positioned myself near the head of the casket, a gust of wet air sprayed my face as if God answered my earlier question about rain. Then I smelled the muskiness of the old canopy, the earthiness of freshly dug dirt and above all, the sour fragrance of people jammed close together with their variety of mixed colognes, emotions, and sweat. Everything assaulted my senses with rank familiarity. I felt insulted and tired of the sameness of it all.

I drew out my small New Testament from an inside coat pocket. Inserted in it was a small 2 x 4 card, listing the survivors. I was thankful the funeral home directors offered this little convenience of accurately listing family names. It was lodged in the Bible at the place of my favorite funeral passage, 1 Corinthians 15:55, "Oh death, where is thy sting...."

After the scripture and a short prayer, I slipped mental gears and scanned the group of mourners. The immediate family members sat next to Mrs. Sapp, under protection of the small canopy. All sat in neatly lined, metal-back folding chairs, all facing the uplifted casket awaiting its descent into earthly depth. Mrs. Sapp looked much as she did when we'd visited—same simple dress with handkerchief, same unconcerned expression on her face. Mrs. Sapp's two grown sons sat as stoic as she. Her sister, Claudel, seemed the only one showing normal grief.

Out beyond the arched canopy, the overflow crowd braved the weather in a tight semicircle, dutifully gathered under their umbrellas like some small mini-church. Jill stood among them. She'd ridden with the funeral procession to the grave side and now, along with the others, endured the finale. Multicolored flowers were arranged in a semicircle behind the immediate grave site. Various ornate stands held their floral masses as expressions of someone's concern, absence or guilt.

I pursed my lips, tasting God's malicious moisture as fleeting thoughts moved through me. *What else is there to say about Benny? He seemed to have a full enough life. I suppose he did his best. I sure can't tell them of his doubts about relationship. Did you get your questions answered, Benny? Are you somewhere watching all this?*

Over to one side, the funeral director gave a nod to signal me to complete the event. I cleared my throat and raised my voice level above the outside noises. "Dearly beloved, we are gathered here to pay our last respects to Rev. Benny Sapp, who faithfully followed his Lord all his days. Death has no victory today in the grave, for Christ is risen and taken us with Him . . . Benny is with Him now."

After the closing prayer, I walked down the front row, shaking hands with each family member saying: 'The Lord is with you'. Then I quickly moved back to my original position, folded my hands in front of me, looking like a natural part of the funeral home team.

One event was unusual. The family had requested an open casket viewing at the gravesite. Slowly, the family stood and filed by the casket for one last gaze. Mrs. Sapp stared at the hollow frame that was once her husband. She just kept shaking her head **no** with a stern look of disapproval behind dry eyes. Then she shuffled off, ignoring everyone around her. The two boys kept serious expressions on their faces also, as they walked by placing their lapel flowers on their father's chest. Claudel approached the open casket and wept bitterly.

Slowly, others walked viewing the body. Soon, the funeral director closed the two lids, one for the bottom and one for the top and stood at attention at one end of the casket. As the rain slowed to a bare drizzle, he motioned to the crowd they could move away. It was his policy to never allow anyone to watch the casket lowered into the earth.

I turned to the funeral director and muttered, *good job boys*. Quickly, I retrieved Jill who waited to one side and headed for the car. I jerked the passenger side of the door open and almost shoved Jill in.

"I'm sure glad that's over." I said.

Jill turned her whole body toward me, cocked her head to one side and glowered at me with cat eyes. I knew something more was going to happen. It wasn't over yet.

Chapter 5

The funeral and other busy church events kept me occupied. One week passed since I'd received the translated parchment page from Ruben Michael. It wasn't that I ignored his time limit, but small issues caused me to forget about the parchments. But the main reason was how to tell Jill my desire to pursue the authenticity of the material. I wasn't sure how she was going to take any involvement. Besides, I'd almost decided to dismiss the whole event as some plea of a lonely destitute old man, making his play for the big buck.

Then after the funeral, later in the week, an overwhelming inner dialogue kept running through my head: *I **should** keep my promise.* In the past, I had done business with legitimate book dealers and perhaps I might miss out on something by not responding. After all, my book collection could always grow and in my values, my personal library could get as large as it wanted.

Finally, one evening Jill and I sat in our den, a place with no phone and our reading space. I got up my nerve and spoke.

"Ok, you remember me telling you about that strange book guy that wanted me to check out a parchment?"

Jill looked up from her book. "Yah, I think so."

"Well, I've been thinking and praying some. I think I should go make the three-hour drive and visit my old professor in Texas so we could check out the first page of the parchments and its translation. The diversion would be restful for me, getting to visit the Seminary professor and all. What do you think?"

Jill dropped her book in her lap. "Why do you even ask? It sounds like you've already made up your mind. It's probably a wild goose chase."

I looked at the ceiling, then my hands. "I know but something just says I ought to go."

She picked her book back up. "Go ahead, if you must. God forbid if I go against your ought to. Just make sure your ought to is not just your want to!"

We finished the evening in pretty much silence. Jill read her book and I contemplated what would happen next.

■ ■ ■

Early the next morning, I punched in the number at the seminary in Texas and shortly had my old professor on the line.

"Dr. Sturgen, this is Jerod Sellers from Oklahoma."

"Hello, there. . . It has been ages since I heard from you. How are you?"

I told him briefly about the manuscript page and asked if he could visit with me later. I explained the story of the parchments, and my thoughts that the work might have some interesting old Aramaic language or it could all be a fake. Sturgen hesitated but agreed to see me, explaining that classes were still in process and nothing could interfere with that. I assured him that precious time for both of us would certainly not be wasted.

As I hung up the phone, I smiled as I envisioned old stonewall Sturgen frowning, looking at his phone, and wondering what kind of nonsense or trouble was headed his way.

The day was young yet, so I told Jill I thought I'd go on and drive to the Seminary.

"Please don't be mad about this, ok?" I toned. "I'm really sure I ought to do this."

Bless her heart, she'd already predicted me. "I packed you an overnight bag just in case. That's too hard a drive in one day. And I'm not mad, just a little perplexed."

My heart leaped a little and I kissed her right on the mouth. She nodded and gave me a smirk. I grabbed a bottle of fresh water from the fridge and my bag and headed out the door. I jumped in the car and began non-stop driving to Texas.

Along the way, I thought about my old professor. Everyone knew Dr. Ralph T. Sturgen operated every day the same routine in his office at the Theological Seminary, shuffling through his yellow worn lecture notes just before starting his early morning classes. He'd taught anthropology and archeology at the Seminary for thirty years and students and faculty alike knew him as "Solid Sturgen", always the seminarian and always fastidious about his work.

I knew my professor prized teaching, but down deep, the man loved the few hands-on experiences in his weekend archeological digs much more than the classroom. Professor Sturgen liked digging around the old Native American Indian burial grounds on the Brazos River in Texas, where he displayed a modicum of success. In addition, in another country, he'd been invited to take part in the unearthing of a site, once connected to ancient Troy.

I smiled as I thought about Dr. Sturgen and his wife Millie. They'd raised two boys, both pastors now in different parts of the state. They had four grandchildren, but didn't get to see them often, since their parents were always so busy. Ralph and Millie liked their quiet, sedate life, built around Seminary faculty and students. Millie cooked and gardened, spending most of her days occupied with their large four-bedroom, stone house nestled just off Seminary campus. Ralph taught, worked his languages and translations and occasionally went on his digs. They were not yet ready for retirement and felt they could go on like they were for the rest of their lives. I envied the professor's family life. However, I respected more the man's ability with languages because Sturgen was self-taught in Aramaic.

Finally, I arrived at the seminary, parked my car and preceded to the faculty offices. I looked at my watch, seeing I had a little time before my meeting. As I strolled through the large hallway of the classroom building, something caught my eye. I moved over to a display case next to the entrance of the professor's office. A full-sized display was off to one corner, resting in a special case with glass enclosure. Stepping closer, I looked down into the exhibition at an astonishing archeological find.

Behind a 6x12 feet glass enclosure, nestled in the original earth, were dried corpses of a Native American mother and a small child. They looked as if some disastrous cave-in took both lives as they lay in a fetal position. They were captured in the layers of dirt forever. At the bottom of the exhibition was a small plaque granting permission for the display. I thought this was a strange way to eulogize the dead, especially those who died so many years ago and under such different circumstances than modern times. I felt a twinge of guilt and thought for a moment I could smell the decay of the past. Suddenly I wished this mother and child could be returned to the ground and let rest. *"I sure hope they don't dig me up some day and put me on display,"* I mumbled as I looked at my watch again and saw it was time for my appointment.

Just as I turned to walk to Sturgen's office, I saw the spunky little man striding down the hallway toward me; with each step rising on his toes in an extra lift like younger athletes walk. He appeared short, thin, and always in a hurry yet unchanged by time. He wore a neat gray suit, solid gray tie to match, high polished gray shoes, nothing that would vaguely detract from his teaching stance. Any onlooker might consider him boring by his clothes, but his abundant energy, displayed a person who really liked life. As he approached me, he shifted his folder of notes to his left hand, extending his right for a typical professorial handshake.

"Hi, Dr. Sellers, right on time I see, Good, Good."

"Dr. Sturgen. It's been awhile. You look unmarred by academia as usual."

"Well, I get by. We've got a great bunch of students this year. Better than ever and sometimes you never know. But this year an older student body is coming and they take education very seriously. I think because they've been out in the world awhile, they have figured

what's valuable in life; at least, that's my opinion."
Sturgen's eyes twinkled. "But I guess you didn't come
all this way to discuss my opinion of the students."

"No, but I did come for your opinion."

"Well, let's go in the office and see what's on your
mind."

We entered a neat office, books and magazines
arranged in precise order for the occupant's own special
system of retrieval. Sturgen motioned for me to sit
in an old church pew, cut short and refinished as a
cushioned love seat, while the old Teacher scooted over
a solid, blonde oak chair with matching padded seat.
Immediately, I presented my special manila envelope,
having the parchment, but in another folder, held back
the interpretation sheet Ruben had given me.

"Professor, I really hope this is not a waste of our
time. I'm not convinced of its authenticity yet, but I
remembered your interest in languages and especially
Aramaic and thought you'd be the most likely person I
knew to view this."

"I have a little time between classes, so we're ok."

"We can talk about the circumstances how I obtained
it and anything else you might advise. My deadline
to check this out was short and I figured you're the
quickest and most reliable way to get an appraisal. I
have full confidence in you and I'll abide by what you
say." I glanced around the office.

"Well, I thank you for your trust." The professor
handled the envelope, carefully removing the ancient
piece and stared. I noticed a slight change in the
professor's breathing as he sucked in and examined the
parchment.

"Sellers, this paper seems genuine and there is

definitely some old Aramaic with intermingled Greek, but I need time to check out the meanings. This grammar doesn't appear to be formal. I don't know if that is good or bad. How much time do we have for me to study this?"

"Uh. . . What's your schedule like through tomorrow?" I asked.

"Well, there's not *that* much here. I could give it a once over tonight and get back with you tomorrow easily enough."

"Ok. Rather than another drive back, I think I'll stay the night, since you can take the time. We can discuss details tomorrow."

"You could stay with me and Millie." Sturgen said.

"I appreciate that but it's too short notice. Maybe another time. I'll just get a motel room and relax."

"Well, ok. I am very interested in this parchment, but you must remember I'm just a layman in Aramaic. I do have a fair library and I'm one of the few around who can translate street language Aramaic. Dr. Bernard at Harvard is the top expert. I have been in correspondence with him for years. We share bibliographies and I suspect our libraries are similar."

"I really do have complete confidence in your ability. Please don't worry about that. Again, the whole thing may be a fluke, but you and I will get to visit and perhaps tomorrow I can treat you to the best lunch in town", I chuckled.

"That's a deal," Sturgen grinned.

The professor reached out to shake and I clasped the older man's hand in both of mine, feeling warmth and appreciation flow through the contact.

■ ■ ■

I left Sturgen's office and walked to my car. Now having free time, I thought about what I could do until tomorrow. I could go shopping, but that activity wasn't one of my favorites. I could go to a bookstore, but everything seemed pale in the light of the parchment find. Then a thought struck me: *Maybe I'll take in a movie after settling into a motel.* After all, I didn't get a chance at many public movies these days. As a pastor, I tended to avoid them because of all the sex, profanity and violence. Generally, I just didn't go to large theaters much in my hometown of Restoration, as I might sit down by one of my church members and then, I wouldn't hear the last of it. I simply followed the lines of least resistance and avoided public movies. Jill and I did enjoy some TV home movies, however. So, for now, I found myself incognito, I felt a little mischievous and willing to indulge myself.

As I drove to the motel, I rethought my meeting with my professor. I felt some guilt since I'd withheld the translation already in my possession. I didn't intend to trick my mentor; I just felt I could use my translation as a check against the one Sturgen produced. It occurred to me a simple way to test my own feelings in the matter. If the different translations conflicted, I would have an answer on what to do next. If they supported one another then I would have some serious thinking to do and some new decisions to make. Simple and no one would be hurt.

For now, I put the whole experience on hold, including putting a damper on my feelings. I was good at that. At least I was until Benny Sapp. Others often accused me of having no feelings, of being able to run on pure reason and objectivity. I felt this one of my strengths. When others might lose emotional control in crisis, grief, or suffering, I could keep calm and become the stabilizing influence. Sometimes I took special note of this ability, but it usually flowed as naturally as breathing, part of my essence.

Certain members of my congregation wanted me to be more passionate or emotional in my sermons. Others however enjoyed my cool logic and rational conclusions about the Almighty. Way down deep, in the private wellspring of my soul, I probably feared strong emotions. Early on in my ministry, I developed cautiousness for any label hinting at the "fanatic" and so developed what I considered solid controls. I feared my stored feelings might gush out upon an unsuspecting society. Although, occasionally, I felt like yelling and screaming out my feelings but I never did. I never let down my guard. I think the energy of those corralled emotions came out in other areas, like my passionate and private sex life. I thanked God every day I was joined with a wife who received me well in all things human.

Soon I arrived at a medium-priced motel, not the best and not the worst. I checked in and at once phoned Jill.

"Hi, hon, how's it going there?" I asked.

"Not too much exciting, how about you?"

"Well, I met with Dr. Sturgen, and because of his time, we decided it might be a good idea for me to stay tonight. Give Sturgen plenty of time to give his views tomorrow."

The silence was deafening. "Hon, you still there?" I asked.

"Yes, nowhere else."

"Please don't be too upset, ok? Sturgen just needs

the time, not be rushed into anything. You know how I think I should pursue this, Jill."

"I suppose so."

"Look, I'll see you tomorrow and we can talk this out. You know it's no good on the phone. Ok?"

"I suppose so." Jill's line went dead.

I looked at my cell phone like it was foreign matter and pushed it in its holder.

I began to rationalize. Surely, this constituted one of those necessary times when we could be apart, like when I fulfilled an out of town speaking engagement. I'm here and I'm committed. I shrugged, feeling I'd deal with things at home later.

Across the room, I spied the complimentary paper left by the management. I picked it up and began to scan the entertainment section. I didn't like to read the papers much; hunger, wars, rapes, murders, energy crisis, child abuse, humanity's inhumanity to each other left me depressed and wondering if there was any hope left for the world. The rest of the news slanted toward advertising, someone trying to sell something. That was ok today. I wanted someone to sell me a good movie, maybe one in which I could lose myself and let negative conditions slide away.

I grinned as my eyes fell upon a film that had some positive social comment, even though it was considered offbeat by many. A small theater had re-released **Field of Dreams**. I liked baseball and Kevin Costner anyway. I'd always wanted to see it on the big screen. After all, perhaps I could get a sermon idea from it. With childlike excitement, I left the motel and headed for the movie. I arrived, bought my ticket, coke and popcorn and settled into the seat like any other participant. Soon, I was immersed in the film, forgetting all else.

■ ■ ■

The next morning, the Texas sun poked through motel curtains like an intruding alarm clock. I sprang awake but felt some back pain from the old motel bed. I don't know why the mattresses are always worn out, it seems. And yet, I was afraid I'd overslept. Quickly I showered, dressed and hurried to the Seminary for my appointment with Dr. Sturgen.

"Shoot", I said out loud as I raced through the parking lot. *"I'm going to be late for sure."* Approaching the professor's office, the door stood already ajar. I gave a timid tap and walked in.

"You're late; Dr. Sellers, but you know what? This morning I don't care. I'm that anxious to talk to you. I could hardly sleep all night." Sturgen beamed. "Where did you **really** get the parchment and where's the rest of it?"

Out of breath, I puffed my cheeks in relief and said, "Like I mentioned, I got it under unusual circumstances from one Ruben Michael. I had never heard of him, have you?"

"No, but then again, there's no reason I should. What kind of a man is he? Can you trust him?"

"I don't know. He called me on my secret land-line. I don't even know how he knew about that. But he said someone had instructed him to give me this parchment and this was only one page. I guess we'll see what he is." Then I related more details about the circumstances under which I'd met Ruben, leaving out my own ambivalent feelings about the man. Professor Sturgen listened intently until I finished with a question:

"Is the material worth our pursuit?"

"I must say in all my years of study", Sturgen responded, "I've never seen anything like this. I have a translation for you and I don't want to be presumptuous, but I would dearly love to translate more if we can have access." Sturgen's voice cracked and sounded dry. "The document seems genuine and is a rare find, but even more than that, do you have any idea the significance of the content? I mean, do you?"

"Well...You seem excited, what does it say?"

I did not want to lie and I didn't want to betray my idea of comparing translations. Sturgen ignored my avoidance and continued.

"This thing could be most significant because, from what I can tell, the content is a point by point recording of an actual house church, flourishing during the first century. At least, it may discuss some of the principles they lived under."

"Ok, so?" I asked.

"Christians, you'll remember, kept their worship practices secret because of many reasons we know. Persecution was only part of the reason, so they met in their homes as a haven. Church historians do not have much detail as to what went on in those meetings or what guidelines they used. This is potent material."

"You mean, like weird potent? I asked.

"No, not weird, I don't think. Not crazy. I mean it would be special to find out their details because those people were the pioneers, spreading the Gospel successfully throughout the then known world. We've never really had this information, at least, not clearly. I'm telling you, this is powerful."

"I hear you, but can you be more specific?" I pointed to the manuscript sheet.

"For example, there are some coded phrases in here and some word about walking through some kingdoms. I need more parchment to get the full picture. How many are there?"

"Uh . . . several pieces," I struggled to soak in all I'd heard. "Let me get this straight. The parchment is an authentic piece from the first century Christians?"

"No question in my mind. We could check with Dr. Bernard if you wish, but I believe it is genuine. Another thing, I would not let many know about these if I were you. I don't know all your involvement yet, but these are very valuable, priceless in fact." Sturgen placed the parchment with his translation on top, back into the folder and handed it to me.

I took the material and nodded yes. "I need to take the material back to its source and get back to you on what's next. I promise you if I'm the one to be involved, you can translate all I get. If I opt out for some reason, I'll put you in touch with Mr. Michael if you like."

"That would be greatly appreciated," said the professor.

"Either way, I'll give you a call in a couple of days to let you know one way or the other. I promised you a lunch. Do you want me to wait around and go today, or shall we do it another time?"

"Let's do it another time. I have a feeling you'll be back soon. You know Jerod, you're holding in your hands an old man's dreams. Take care." Sturgen nodded.

We shook hands again and I felt my old mentor hold

on a little longer than usual. I thought what restraint this old gentleman had, to allow me to leave with what he thought such treasure. I admired those who had such patience when faced with intrigue or mystery.

I hurried to my car and headed for home. Just outside of the city limits, I drove into a small cafe, went inside and sat in a booth by a large picture window. I ordered a cup of coffee with sweet roll and as the waitress left to get what I called my "quick fix", I took out Dr. Sturgen's new translation and laid it beside the one I'd held back that Ruben gave me. I paused to read closely.

The materials matched so well they could have been written by the same person. I expelled a long breath and stared out a window as my mind raced with the traffic flowing past on the major highway.

Chapter 6

I drove back through north Texas toward Oklahoma and thought about my being gone and my short telephone conversation with Jill. Her abruptness on the phone made me wonder if I would face some sort of wrath when I got home. *Would Jill have forgotten the whole thing?* In my mind's eye, I could see Jill scurrying around the living room, rearranging some of her knickknacks she'd already straightened before.

As I drove, I thought back about other homecomings. Jill and I kept a kind of ritual we played out. In the years we'd been together, she'd practiced an important method of communication, a deliberate patience that tended to wait me out, thereby obtaining more details than if she'd pressed as soon as I got home. She simply went ahead with her routine as if nothing out of the ordinary occurred, letting me unwind by my own method. In fifteen minutes or so I would spill some information upon her like a specific point of one of my sermons or even some trivia that came to mind. Then, conversation would flow for what she believed her benefit. The method always worked well.

I remembered Jill telling me one time how she believed men just did not process feelings and thinking, a subtle cultural rule that implied men had to have conversation dragged out of them. She told me men talked with inferences, conclusions, and short answers. She illustrated it by saying, "Jerod, if I ask you, 'how was your day? You'd just say *fine.* But if I wait awhile, let you settle in with coffee or tea, you relax more and process your thinking better, giving details. I think a short waiting period gives you a psychological rest from any tension, allowing you to collect your thoughts." As I drove, I had to smile and feel some comfort as I thought about Jill's ritual.

Finally, after pushing through the three-hour drive, I pulled into the semicircular driveway of our house. I turned off the key in the ignition as I glanced up at the modern brick structure. The rambling ranch style house, built just two years earlier, always caused my heart to beat faster. I remembered the trouble we'd had with some of the congregation who were reluctant to build a three-bedroom house and some who did not want to build at all. I recalled how many of my preacher colleagues believed that any new structure program began the death of one's ministry. I shrugged and remembered how I'd weathered the storm and rode the ship back to calm waters.

Of course, I realized deep down, I really didn't own a home, but I felt this house was Jill's and mine because we'd put so much love and energy into it. I felt good about it. After all, the house finally helped the church in the end by giving the people a project which unified their focus and added a considerable asset to their holdings. In my view, no one could condemn me for that, especially not the Lord.

I got out of the car and walked to the front door.

Jill greeted me at the door. "Hi, sweetheart, I'm glad you're back."

At least, relief washed over me for now because she did not seem upset with my having been gone overnight. I gave her a big hug and brushed her with a kiss.

I stared in her eyes. "Do you mind fixing us some cold tea, I'm parched from the long drive, and boy, do I have something to tell you."

Surprised by my abrupt willingness to talk, she quickly responded with two glasses of cold sweetened tea.

I sat in my favorite recliner, took a long drink of tea and began to relate all that happened, starting with the meeting with Ruben Michael and ending with the comparison of the two translations. Jill listened without interruption, trying to absorb every speedy detail, as well as believe what she heard. Seldom had she been verbally machine-gunned like this.

Jill stifled a giggle. "It really does sound like an old movie plot."

"I know, but just imagine as I did driving home. What if we really did end up with some record of how those early house churches functioned? Remember, they were under secrecy and some persecution. I've always wondered what their secret was, you know, just how they endured and how they spread the Gospel to over eighty percent of the then known world. It would be kind of like having a guidebook you could use right along with the book of Acts."

"That **is** serious," Jill said soberly.

"I've got to get back to Mr. Michael and see if I can get access to **all** the material."

"But what if it's a hoax? You know the old saying, 'if

something looks too good to be true, it usually is.'" Jill said.

"I know, but I've gone this far; I may as well go all the way, don't you think? I feel I should, especially since I have access to Professor Sturgen's ability to translate. Besides, Ruben doesn't know that. Of course, the only thing is, I'm afraid the catch will be some large sum of money. I may have been baited just enough to get me hooked. But, I wonder why me? You and I both know we don't have large money. Maybe he thinks I know someone who does. Besides, he keeps saying someone instructed him to approach me."

"Mr. Michael could have given that material to many others who have more resources than we do, if it's legitimate," Jill injected, "I sure wonder why he chose you too."

"Well, I suppose because I'm so handsome." I beamed. Jill lightly punched me in the arm.

"No, seriously, maybe we should believe the vision thing Michael talked about, even though that all sounds like bull, doesn't it?"

"Uh huh," Jill stared, "but I guess stranger things have happened, just not to us." She jiggled her eyebrows, bugged her eyes, and shot me her professional smile.

I knew that signal only too well...go find out dummy!

Chapter 7

September in Oklahoma was its usual 95 degrees, a cooling trend from the humid 102 of August. Humidity was still high but enough rain showers caused the grass and trees to still burst forth with lush green hues. I found myself driving to Ruben's apartment again, letting the cool dry air from the car air conditioner blow right in my face. I thought how I'd like to give the inventor of car-air a decent reward, something to show how much I appreciated it and really couldn't live without.

Soon, my thoughts shifted to Ruben. How was I going to approach him? I didn't want to appear too eager, at the same time; I didn't want to seem too casual. I decided I'd approach the whole matter as a professional business venture, using fairness but stressing the limitations of financial considerations. Besides whatever Michael was, he was no fool and probably couldn't be outwitted. *"Just deal with him openly,"* I said to the windshield, *"and see what comes of it. The whole thing seems unreal anyway."*

Soon, I knocked on the door of room number ten. The door opened swiftly as if the person on the other side just waited.

"Come in Dr. Sellers and have a seat. I've be expecting you."

I had to admit the old man was unsettling. He wore the same brown suit and tie as before, all old but as neat as if it'd just come from the cleaners. Stiff gray hairs nestled around his ears, down his long sideburns and into his freshly trimmed goatee. I felt it all looked somehow manufactured, like the old guy compared some photo and copied it in every detail. Before I could respond, Ruben posed a question.

"Was your search as profitable as expected?"

My face flushed as if I'd been guilty of something, blinked twice, stammered and said,

"Uh, Ruben let's get right to the point. I'm convinced this page of parchment is, well, special. I don't know if I can deal with you. Quite frankly, I'm not sure I even like all this, but you certainly got my attention. If you're looking for a business proposition then I'm here to try and come to some terms. Surely, you must know, that in the first place, you have something very valuable and secondly, I don't have much money. So, I'm not sure what you want of me."

"I like someone who comes to the point. There's hope for you yet," Ruben smiled, "besides, we don't have to become bosom buddies to transact our business. Right?"

"No, but you always make me feel uncomfortable for some reason." I felt embarrassed again I'd been so honest with this man. *Why'd I do that? I could hold back my true feelings with everyone else.*

"Ok, then, let me tell you what I have in mind. I want you to take all the parchments, study them, and have them translated. I'll give you one week. When you have completed the task, then get back to me."

"And what do you want in return?" I implored.

"Nothing."

"Nothing at all?" I echoed.

"Well, I tell you what. You write me a check for $100 as good faith money for now. That's it."

"But then what will it cost me?" I prodded.

"Come, come Dr. Sellers. Trust me. I have dealt honestly with you. Now, you return the gesture. I assure you, you will be able to handle the transaction. You may even wait to sign your check one week from today, if you like. Then, if you don't care for my arrangements, we'll tear up the check. All you'll be out is time and you may view a full translation of very rare material. On top of that, you have my permission to make copies of the translation yourself."

"Wait a minute, Ruben. How can you treat something as rare as these parchments so casually?"

"Dr. Sellers, I am not treating anything casually. I trust *you.*" Ruben pointed his finger toward my heart.

I felt all my arguments melt like chocolate in hot sun. And yet, the warmth felt good, extending toward this little old man who showed me more trust than any I'd experienced since my early days of ministry, days when I'd felt more the newness of my relationship to God. In those days, I'd run more on blind trust, but with coming years, I'd developed a cautious reliance on my fellow human beings.

Ruben handed me the brown velvet package containing the complete set of parchments.

I looked down at the bundle moving toward me. It came to me as if by slow motion, floating through dense atmosphere. I blinked twice to clear my vision, and then took the package. I wasn't sure what else to do so I reached inside my coat pocket and retrieved my checkbook, quickly writing out the $100. I left it unsigned.

I handed him the check, said my goodbyes and quickly left the apartment.

I drove home in a daze, but from time to time, glanced at the bundle of parchments on the seat next to me. The car bumped up my driveway a little too fast, I got out of the car and hurried through the front door through the living room. I rushed and placed the bundle on the coffee table, then flopped down in a living room chair without a word.

"Well, what happened?" Jill asked, deciding not to wait.

I pointed to the brown velvet package.

She moved closer, took the parcel, and carefully peeked in it. Her eyes got wide, gasping as she beheld the contents.

"Woe, did you get all of them? Jerod! Please answer me!"

I looked at her and smiled. "Pushy, aren't you?"

Jill broke out laughing and flopped down in my lap.

I told her every detail, and then paused for her response.

Jill laid her head back on my shoulder and stared at the ceiling, basking in the shared moment. We both sat there, feeling brief accomplishment. Finally, I sighed and broke the silence.

"I feel I've got to get these to Dr. Sturgen at once. I've made up my mind. I'm going to get a pulpit supply for this Sunday and go back to the Seminary. I'll stay with the professor and give him time enough to do a full translation. I'm in this now, so I'd best go all the way."

"But what about your other duties, the hospital visits

and such?" Jill sat up abruptly. "You know some people won't like your being gone on such short notice."

"I'll get the deacons to cover for me this once. I'll just tell them I have personal business to attend to. It's true, isn't it?"

Jill nodded slowly but with that look that said, 'you've taken me by surprise.' She knew I enjoyed preaching and never missed unless ill. Yet, she also knew my stubbornness. When I'd made up my mind, it just made things worse to argue. In the past, I sometimes learned the hard way by trial and error. Often blinded by some person's control issue, I still would see a thing through to the end, regardless of results. I had a history of willfulness costing me, especially when I'd been stubborn and inaccurate at the same time, but it was my nature of doing things.

Slowly, she rose and laid the parcel back on the coffee table and walked to the bedroom. I watched her go, not sure of her thoughts. Jumbled thoughts poured through my mind, intermingled with mixed feelings. *Why was I not fully including her in this quest? Was it just a guy thing?* I seemed to be living this adventure, only to come back and give her reports. Must I do this alone? And what she'd expressed lately, I knew she must feel left out and **that** was not a feeling she was used to since we'd committed to share life and ministry. I realized certain times occurred when a person had to do things with God on a strictly individual basis, but these latest events did not necessarily seem one of those times. I took a deep breath, just as I heard Jill call from the next room:

"Will one suitcase be enough?

Chapter 8

I heard the line click after the third ring.

"Hello, Dr. Sturgen, this is Jerod Sellers. I hope I'm not disturbing you too much."

"Oh, Dr. Sellers. I've been thinking about you ever since you left. No, I'm just brush cleaning an old bone from some of my Native American Indian artifacts. I think it must be another animal, not human. What's the news?"

"Well, I have in my possession several parchments and I....."

"That's great", Sturgen interrupted. "I have an idea. Why don't you and Jill come on down and stay with me awhile? We've got plenty of room and my wife will love it, someone to dote over since the kids are gone. That way we'll do all the translations. What do you think?"

"That's an offer I can't refuse, but Jill won't be coming this time."

"Well, ok, good. It's Friday and I'll be through classes by 2 o'clock. Do you remember where my house is?

"Is it still the one across from campus?"

"That's right. I'll see you at my front door."

■ ■ ■

The weather held mild and I was back driving to Texas again. Finally, I arrived at Dr. Sturgen's house. I started to go to the front door but started pacing like waiting on a newborn. I looked at my watch. It was 2:15. I glanced up to see him walking down the sidewalk. Grinning he waved and the two of us entered his house, looking forward to a weekend huddled together over the parchments.

I was amused to watch Millie Sturgen wait on us hand and foot, as she seemed truly delighted to have two men in the house again, giving her new purpose from her old routine.

I watched and offered suggestions to certain Greek words, but Prof. Sturgen did his magic with translations. From time to time, we would look at each other, realizing what a good team we were, delighted as small boys with new toys. Both of us ate, drank, and slept those pages Friday through Saturday. I did call Jill at night and chatted to her about our progress. In my mind, she appeared to be ok.

Surprisingly, Sunday crept up on us, so we broke for church services. As soon as church was over, we rushed home; wolfed down luscious Millie made sandwiches and dove into the last sections of the material. Finally, at four Sunday afternoon, exhausted and exhilarated, we completed the work.

"Dr. Sellers, do you realize what we have here?" Sturgen asked excitedly as he scooted back his chair and dropped his pencil in an antique holder.

"Well, I certainly know what you've translated. It's dynamite stuff."

"Yes, but do you remember. There is only one other Christian women writer we know of and she died in 203

AD. She lived in Carthage and was arrested by Emporer Septimus Severus when she was taking a class for Christians for baptism. She wrote a diary of some sort."

"Wow, so this writing could be the first Christian woman writer on record?

"That is correct," Sturgen huffed.

"I think I know what we'd better do. I'd like you to use your copy machine", I suggested, "Make a copy of the translations to keep in your possession."

"Are you sure that's all right?" Sturgen asked.

"Sure. Ruben gave me permission to copy, so, if we don't end up with anything but the copied translations, we'll have something. I'm going to take the originals with me and meet with Mr. Michael again to see what comes next. This way we'll have the content of the parchments. I know it's a little weird, but I almost feel like a scripture writer."

"Yes, I have the same feeling. But I'm a little concerned about that special part I wasn't able to translate."

"Oh . . .yeah . . . the unusual symbols?"

"Yes, I guess Ruben can help, if he wants to. He seems a strange sort, doesn't he? I know this is not some new scripture, more like an exact historical find, but still, I feel like what the writers of the New Testament felt when they were jotting down the inspired word as actual events took place."

"Yeah, me too."

"It really has been a glorious dream for me," Sturgen said misty eyed.

Quickly, Sturgen moved to his desktop copy machine and ran the copies. I gathered the originals, placing them carefully back as they were in their individual wrappings and we awkwardly said our goodbyes. We each felt the regret of leaving the moment, one of those rare events two men share when discovering something new. I hugged Millie and thanked her fervently. She beamed and insisted on my returning soon.

I got back in my car again and started my long drive home. I didn't mind the drive because it gave me time to settle and think. It was too easy for me to get lost in my thoughts while driving so I reminded myself to stay alert. I thought about a long past event. While driving on a back road to the Seminary, one of my pastor buddies was so occupied in thought, he didn't hear an approaching train as he drove through an unmarked railroad crossing. He was killed instantly. *Must not let that happen, ever.*

Then, I began to consider all the events and how quickly things progressed. I thought about the untranslated part of the work that Sturgen couldn't translate. Within a capsule statement of the rules of the first-century house church were some symbols the professor could not interpret. The author of the document, Clarissa, was reporting on the daily activities of the time and stopped to review what she called in the Greek "**Didasko diatheke**." Dr. Sturgen could of course translate the Greek words "*Didasko*", basically meaning things taught and "*diatheke*", meaning an agreement that divides. Put together it meant a teaching agreement among the followers of Christ.

Yet, neither Sturgen nor I could figure out the specific codes within the basic context. That one section had raw cultural Aramaic and Greek language which was interwoven with uniquely drawn symbols. The hint of that section seemed to be a solemn agreement made by each member before they could join this house church.

My curiosity surged as I considered what Ruben might say about it. As I drove, I also considered the whole set of parchments and how I would explain this adventure to Jill. I was truly excited to share everything with Jill and looked forward to home.

My mind did not register my home arrival, but I arrived about seven o'clock p.m., just before late sundown. I rushed to the front door and Jill opened and met me at the door. Animated with conversation and hands flying, she blurted out what happened in my absence.

One of the older church members died and some of the parishioners were upset their pastor wasn't there to take care of the details. Jill decided to work with the funeral home staff who supplied the preaching and officiated while Jill coordinated details for me the best she could. She still wondered if some of the people thought she'd lied about my absence. She reminded me she still felt a twinge of guilt because she hadn't revealed **all** the facts to the members. Although, for years, she'd tried to protect my time by simply leaving out certain details. This way she felt she protected our privacy.

I too felt excited, but not about the events in my absence. I was more concerned about my new discoveries. I stopped her with an upturned hand.

"Jill, never mind about that now. I've got to show you something professor Sturgen translated for me."

"You wait a minute, sweetheart, this is more serious than you think. You know how influential Mrs. Meyers was in our church. She was the kind of person epitomizing

Christianity. I don't know if she ever missed a day of church in her long life. She was like a great-grandmother to nearly everyone who has grown up in the church the last twenty years. You know everyone called her grandma Myers."

"I know, Jill, but I'll deal with all that later. Right now, you've **got** to see this one section of parchment. I want to see if it affects you like it did me. Please be patient with me on this. I've been thinking about it all the way home."

Jill glared and I'm sure felt misunderstood because I didn't seem to communicate on the same wave link as her concerns.

"Are you sure you're not avoiding things or this is not just one of your ideas for the greatest sermon on earth?" Jill spat.

"Easy . . . easy. Come on now; just look at this, will ya?" I pulled out a copy and handed her the section of the translation having the Didasko covenant. Reluctantly, Jill jerked it from me but began to read:

"Again, I, Clarissa, three dekas [30 years, Sturgen's translation] after our Lord ascended back to the Father, remind you of the secret covenant. As our Lord said on many occasion, we become little children to understand and enter the kingdom of God [Teachings on Mount] which begins our pathway of the nine kingdoms. At first, it stayed a mystery to us until the passage of time and the witness of persecution of the apostles and followers of Jeshua. And then the Holy Spirit bore witness to our spirits that innocence has no protection in this world and thus has no reason for excuse. Remorse from sin builds a false protection but loses its excuse. So, Christ became our excuse and we in turn, must partake of his innocence. For us to practice this, we have created a holy bond after the heart of teachings [**At this place in the text, Sturgen couldn't translate symbol drawings of nine steps**] left to us by our Lord. Remember, they are not just hard sayings but livable steps for our daily growth until our Lord comes again. *Maranatha.*"

"We have learned that true innocence has an unbending love. It is the kind of love our Lord showed when he said, 'Father forgive them, for they do not fully perceive what they do'. We have found that this complete love is the greatest releaser of energy in the world. We are to practice loving even our enemies because they do not fully understand what it is that pushes them to do evil.

"We must confess our faults one to another. We must speak the truth in love, never letting a wall of silence separate our community. We are to hold special confidences in our hearts like sacred treasure, for we must not cast our burdens upon those who treat them as dung.

"We will hold truth in the highest order and live daily with clean hearts and minds, always giving clear explanation about the things we hold dear. As we do this, we will move among the people as the *paraklete*, giving comfort and aid to those who have missed the mark of faith.

"We will recognize a mutual respect, holding each accountable for individual actions in this world so that remorse may harbor no reasonable excuse, thus Christ may be elevated to God's supreme gift to the world. Holding each accountable as equals means we commit our resources to help any put back into life where any took away, always supporting one another in the bond of love.

"We will, by our actions, become a presentation to the world of what it means to have the Holy Spirit living in us, remaking us into a new race of people that makes others want to know our Lord. We will hold this pledge in our hearts and walk humbly among the people, never boasting or presuming upon our Lord, but living in this world as best we can, displaying the fruits of the Spirit and doing works of Grace, so that others may come to know the true innocence found in Christ himself."

Jill handed the interpretation back to me.

"Well . . . it's certainly beautiful, but what's all the fuss?"

"Don't you see the implications of this material if people really lived that agreement?" I blurted. "We've known some of these principles, but don't you see if we could translate those unknown steps and symbols about the Sermon on the Mount we might have the blueprint of that first century Christian church. No one's had that before".

I frowned and continued, "I don't know . . . these writings could be the practical guidance we've looked for on how to live a truly Beatitude life, how to really do church. I've still got some time left Michael gave me but I need to get back to him right away. This thing isn't over yet. I know this seems unreasonable to you, hon. but I told Dr. Sturgen I'd see Ruben again and follow up on the untranslated part and find out what's to happen next. Besides, something in me says I should keep pursuing this thing. Ok? I feel I've got to get going."

"You just got home and you're leaving again?" Jill frowned.

"Please hang with me on this, Ok? I don't know, it's just something I must do. You know me." I tried a smile.

Jill crossed her arms over her chest, shook her head. "That's what I'm afraid of, I **do** know you. Why don't I go with you?"

"Not this time. I know you may not understand this, but Ruben is a little strange and I don't want to take a chance and scare him off. I just don't know what he'd think if you came with me. See? Please try to see this, Ok?"

Jill looked at the floor and shook her head slowly. Then she raised her right hand, thumb up like a hitchhiking gesture and pointed toward the door. I scurried out the door before things became more complicated.

Although 7 o'clock in the evening, I sighed gratefully for Oklahoma sun-downs in September which sometimes lasted till 8 or 9 o'clock and later. The evening sky spread its hues of orange and gold across the southwestern corner of the state. I drove straight west and the sun played peek-a-boo with my car sunviser.

I truly was concerned about Jill but I shook that off quickly. For some reason, I felt an urgency to give full concentration to the task ahead. I wanted to arrive at Ruben's apartment before dark. I felt unsure why except I wanted to conduct any final business in the full light of day.

I arrived quickly and soon stood before the familiar apartment number ten. I knocked on the door harder than I meant to, sounding like the poundings on an empty kettle drum. No answer. I pounded again. Still no answer. Automatically, I tried the doorknob and the door swung open easily. Startled, I walked in and surveyed the room. Totally empty. I walked slowly through the bedroom, bath, everywhere, checking all the corners. The apartment stood clean and empty, as if no one had ever been there.

Chapter 9

Trance-like, I drove to the church office on Monday morning. I'd said very little to Jill after Sunday night about Ruben's mysterious disappearance. I convinced her I was too tired and frustrated to deal with things now. She knew from experience not to push too much. If she did, I would clam up a much longer time. I hoped to solve things after another day of thinking what to do about Ruben.

I arrived at the church parking lot, rolling my neck and shoulders, as I turned off the ignition, feeling Ruben's absence in my gut. The skeptical part of me sensed things were moving too smoothly with the translation and all, but I never suspected this turn of events.

Now what am I supposed to do with all the parchments? Had Ruben been a victim of foul play? *Should I call the authorities and report this?* In my deeper self, I realized I liked Ruben Michael, strange as he was. Too, there existed a strong impression to keep all this to myself, not inform anyone, and handle it alone.

I slid out of the car and scurried to my office, gave my secretary a curt nod and went through the door like a man zeroed in on one goal: *find Ruben.*

As I glanced around my office surroundings, I saw very little to relieve my feeling of helplessness. My eyes fell upon my computer, then I glanced over my abundant library, nothing came to mind. Nothing in my earlier dealings prepared me for this—not Seminary, not pastoring, not life. For this moment, I felt adrift, not exactly stumped, but blocked like I'd come to a brick wall, having no way under, around or over.

I took my cell phone out of my carrier and stared at it. Suddenly, I slapped myself in the forehead and reached for the phone book. Quickly, I ran my index finger down the M's...McGraw, Meadows, Michalski but no Michael. Dejected, I let the book flop shut and looked at my hands to see if any answers were there.

I began to think about Ruben, the man. A truth started to remind me that ever since Seminary days, I yearned for someone older, other than my professors, someone spiritual and worldly wiser, a confidant-mentor to whom I could discuss the church, its problems, its need to grow the kind of people who would truly honor God. And since I'd pastored awhile, the church programs were all right as they stood, but I longed to go deeper with God, have a people with me like those first century Christians who fully lived the Christ life. I even felt like Benny Sapp had about needing an honest person. Could Ruben have helped with that?

I didn't want some superstar evangelist or some renowned spiritual guru—just an authentic, down to earth Christian who might serve as a spiritual advisor, someone who was real, openly honest, practical, committed and spiritually healthy. I thought more what Benny Sapp said he wanted . . . someone flesh and blood to feel close to, someone to share everything, someone besides a family member.

Sometimes I considered myself a failure since it was

obvious to me the standard church programs hadn't grown many member's well, especially someone who might fit the role of a personal confidant and guide. I often thought how good it would be to communicate with someone with true God wisdom, like Solomon, just to have a person to suggest ways of leading people to achieve their best potentials.

The last few years, I'd realized sermons were not enough, educational programs came and went, revivals burst upon the congregation for a time, then fizzled like an old roman candle fire-cracker. I hoped for something more scenic, brighter, and more lasting.

At times, I felt a skepticism rise in my soul, not a doubt of God's ability, but a puzzlement of humanity's unwillingness to become selfless, other centered, Christlike. Oh, I saw baby Christians blossom for a while, I recognize the Holy Spirit's work, but then often, personal problems or concerns of this world dampened enthusiasm and people settled into "churchianity" like so many others. Surely the church missed something— some more dynamic principles which would help people grow a vibrant faith. Yes, the Holy Spirit is here, but people seem to forget his power.

In my most discouraged moments, I thought of quitting—just blame it all on burnout, except for one deeply ingrained, searing reason I held on: I truly believed Christ was the only permanent reality. I believed God's plan was the business of remaking people for the better and I had a part in something.

But at this very moment, I truly felt a strange urge to find Ruben. Maybe Michael could be a guide, some spark, or at least, one person in possession of the right God-knowledge to rejuvenate a tired pastor's heart.

Suddenly, I nearly jumped out of my chair. My private, secret land-line rang again.

I hurriedly opened the bottom draw to my desk and picked up the receiver.

"Hi, Doc. How are tricks?" Boomed Ruben Michael.

"Mr. Michael, where have you been? I mean, where are you? What happened? Are you, all right?"

"Fresh and tender as a new born babe or should I say steak?" Ruben laughed, "Anyway, I think it's time for another meet, don't you?"

"Well, yeah. I went to your old place and you weren't there. No one seemed to know about you. At first, I thought something bad might've happened, and then the strangest feeling assured me you were ok and I wasn't supposed to do anything foolish, like go to the police."

"It's a good thing you still can listen to your better self, old boy, or you would have gotten the proverbial egg on your face." Ruben chuckled. "I've simply moved. Come on down to 1500 Locust street, you know that new little motel they just built? I'm in room seven, the perfect number."

"You mean, right now?"

"Time's a wasting. Remember, you **can't** juggle with no hands."

"What?"

"Never mind, come as quick as you can."

"Ruben, what's going on? You drunk or something?"

"Just drunk on life, boy. Come see me quick." The phone went dead as if all sound removed from this earth.

I held the receiver and looked at it like it was a traitor. Blinking several times and feeling foolish, I knew

I **had** to do as Ruben said. Of course, a part of me craved to go anyway, if nothing else, to satisfy this wasn't some hustle. I still wondered if all this disguised emotional effort was like some elaborate rip-off.

I hung up the phone, closed the drawer and grabbed the copy of parchments with translations. Heading through my office door, I passed the secretary, said I'd be gone for a while and left before she could even answer.

Puffy clouds slowly floated overhead, not ones harboring rain, but that circular kind with light gray centers of air and white foam edges, bumping into one another like inflated white balloons. I glanced at them intermittently as I drove, so I wouldn't become one of those clouds by bumping into moving traffic.

Soon, I made my way to Locust Street, wondering why Ruben moved to this new and plush motel, designed with a small Mall and restaurant to cater to the wealthier tourists. As I pulled into the visitors parking zone, I felt anxious and excited, while considering Ruben's actions. I hustled out of the car, clutching the parchments to my chest like a bank deposit sack and walked quickly through the motel lobby, down a short hallway to room seven.

Barely knocking, the door swung open. This time, dressed in an immaculate, brown silk suit, matching artistic tie, alligator shoes, Ruben stood erect and motioned me in. He looked like a wealthy tourist.

I stuttered, "Man, I must admit, Mr. Michael, this is a surprise. This place is great, much better than where you were. I mean, do you ever look prosperous. What'd you do, win the lottery?" I chuckled.

Michael moved to a modern peach colored couch, sat

down and gazed straight ahead. I sat down across from him on a coordinated love seat.

After waiting a minute, I stammered. "You at least must admit, the way you've contacted me has been strange."

I waited for some response from the old man. Michael just kept staring straight ahead. I wondered if the guy was drunk, gone catatonic or was just daydreaming. I thought, *should I just sit still for now?* Minutes seemed to tick by. Then the answer came as if another voice entered my head. *You will never err if you learn to make yourself listen to the silence.* I sputtered, "Did you say something?"

Ruben slowly turned his gaze to me and smiled.

I rapid fired. "Are you sick or something? Do you need time to think? Is something wrong?"

"You have many questions, Dr. Sellers, but those aren't the right ones, are they?"

"Well, I don't know, I suppose not, but I'm not sure what I'm supposed to do next," I answered too curtly, slumping in my seat.

"Why don't we begin with your more exact questions?"

I sat up abruptly. "Ok. For instance, how come you move around so much? Why all the mystery? Are you in trouble? How come one minute you look poor, the next very wealthy?"

Ruben gave me a stare like a disappointed parent. "Wrong questions again. One more strike and you're out!"

I felt my anger surge. I didn't need this, I started to rise then stopped myself.... *Wait a minute,* I thought, *don't lose it now. Settle down.* With concentrated effort, I forced my quick anger down a notch to frustration. Perplexity was better than uncontrolled anger. *Got to think this through. What does Ruben want me to ask? Stick to the point. Aha! . . . the parchments.*

I sat up straighter and cleared my throat, "I was wondering about the gap in the translations, the one with those strange symbols, mentioning something about the nine little kingdoms."

"Bingo. Home run. Touchdown. You won the lottery," Ruben bantered and clapped his hands like an ecstatic teenager.

Wide-eyed, I forced a small grin. "Ok, ok. Why is there no translation for that section? What's the catch?"

Ruben rubbed his bony hands together. "Now you're talking, Doctor. There is a catch, a hook, a crook."

I blinked, wondering what kind of nut I had here. Suddenly, I thought I heard four distinct notes of music, four notes like the beginning of some overture: *ta, da, da, dum.* I looked around this unfamiliar room; the whole atmosphere changed. At that precise moment, I realized I felt warm, receptive, and articulate—like those times in Seminary days when I received rich insight from one of my favorite professors. I glanced back at Ruben, who no longer appeared frivolous and lighthearted, but serious, almost regal.

"There is a condition," Ruben boomed, then softened again, "a heavenly commission if you will, for you to obtain the secret of the nine kingdoms: **You must come to me for specific translation teachings.**"

"I figured you'd be the only one with the translations," I quipped.

"No, No, No. You're not listening close enough. You may be hearing, but you're not hearkening. You must spend at least nine teaching sessions with me to unravel the mystery."

I felt stunned. I expected some gimmick, perhaps a request for money or some deal for me to be a go-between to those who might have great wealth, but teaching sessions? What did this mean? How was I to respond to this corny request?

"Let me get this straight, are you saying you don't know or don't have the complete translations and you want me to help you dig them out?"

"No, I have the specific missing translations," Michael snapped.

"Then, you want me to act like a pupil and just listen to you lecture?"

"Sometimes perhaps, but not exactly. I want you to go on an adventure with me. If I dumped all the information on you all at once, Dr. Sellers, you wouldn't understand it. No one has before."

"You mean there have been others with access to the information? How many?" I puzzled

"Some, but that's beside the point. These are truths for today, right now. No one had them like you will have them. No one can use them like you are supposed to use them. They are intended for you alone as the originator of something magnificent."

I knew there were times when the most unbelievable circumstances fit into the realm of real life instead of some fabled fiction writing or the imagination of the movie writers. This did indeed seem stranger than any make-believe. I felt dizzy, not even sure I heard what I thought I heard. I could think of no way to respond adequately or to back out of the whole enterprise. Finally, I responded with curiosity. "I need to know how many have had access to the information."

"Many have made attempts at the essentials, but

they haven't gotten it right. They made beginnings, but they only produced the unfinished painting. For them, you might as well look at a blank canvass and describe what isn't there and then call it art."

"So, what makes you think I can get it right?" I puzzled.

"Christ's commission guarantees it." Ruben wrinkled up his nose.

"Wait . . . what do you mean 'Christ's commission' guarantees it? I paused but Ruben didn't say anything.

"Ok, just for conversation sake, what is this wonderful knowledge no one knows but you...and soon me?" I continued.

Ruben leaned back, pulled a little Swiss army knife out of his pocket, opened a small blade, and began cleaning his finger nails. Once he finished, he locked eyes with me and spoke softly so I had to lean forward as if hearing a secret.

"Based upon what you know so far, what do you think the subject of the parchments might be?"

My brain spun. "Many themes, I suppose."

Come now, **pupil**, think! What is so lacking in the church today?"

"I don't know just one thing," I protested.

"Yes, you do, take a guess." Ruben rebutted.

I stuck my index finger in my ear and scratched, grimacing on that side of my face. "Genuine Christian living, I guess, as a broad theme. I mean Christians don't live permanent reality every day. Instead, they live pretense and make believe."

"Close enough, oh . . . Dr. . . . Let's call the subject of the missing parchment translations simply: **Kingdom Growth.**"

As he said the words, I felt the truth penetrate my soul. My spirit agreed, bore witness to the truth, my essence vibrated with the old yearning to know God more fully. Ever since my first, fresh spiritual awakening, I ached for new ways to live a genuine Christian life. I thought I knew others who longed to go deeper with God, people I felt a kinship. But I also knew I'd felt unable to become their spiritual guide as I ought. I folded my hands, stared at my wedding ring and sat speechless.

"Yessssss," Ruben purred, "**I will** teach you."

I jerked my head up as if the man read my mind. I stared into Ruben's eyes, trying to see behind the pupils, searching for understanding and wondered what I might trust.

I hesitated but said, "I don't know if you've gained the right to be my mentor. While you are very interesting, I don't know you at all."

"Quite right, but, have I not spoken the truth so far? Where's your faith, man?"

I looked down at my right foot, the one that always went to sleep when I felt contrition. I wiggled my toes inside my shoe. Then I complained, "Look. I don't know what you want...where to begin. I mean, what must I really do to obtain the missing translations?"

"Start with lesson one." Ruben beamed.

"Yeah, sure, but I mean, how do I learn to trust you so quickly? What's going to happen to get me to learn any better than others who tried?"

"We've already begun the method, you see. I shock your lazy sensibilities, get your full attention, then you **really** listen. It's the only way to get you out of the smug rut you're in from just **doing church**."

I considered for a moment. Perhaps that explained Ruben's whole strangeness—a masterful technique to get focused attention. Smart, clever and it works. Sighing with relief, I felt a part of me open, one brick came down from the skeptical wall I'd built over the years. If enough bricks came down, maybe I could see through the wall and learn something new, fresh sunlight breaking through dark areas of the soul. Perhaps it would be worth a try. I could always call a time out, halt, or just leave. I still felt captain of my own ship and the ship wasn't sinking yet, just leaking a little.

"All right. Tell me what you want for lesson one and I'll think about it and try to comply." I commented dryly.

Ruben started bouncing up and down, one time he'd sit, and then he'd stand, several times like a jack in the box. "Whoa there pardner, not so fast" came a perfect John Wayne voice, "there will be no trying. It's all or nothing, the whole herd, the whole boatload, a full net of fishes. Take it or leave it."

"Ok, I get it, no man putting his hand to the plow and looking back...that sort of thing?"

"Yep," Ruben pretended to spit tobacco, "you'll liable to plow a crooked row," he hooked his thumbs inside his belt line and stuck out his chest.

"Can I at least have some time to think about schedules and such? I do have a church to run, you know." I agonized.

Ruben straightened, rose abruptly from the couch and started march stepping back and forth in the room, timed to perfect military cadence, "Ok, you out maneuvered me there son. You go do some church stuff and meet me here tomorrow. Ten o'clock sharp.

Dis....missed!" He performed an exaggerated salute and turned away.

I frowned but slowly stood. "Should I leave the parchments?"

"No", Ruben said over his shoulder. "You keep em close to your heart. Bring em next time."

Hesitantly, I turned and left the room, walking back through the lobby and left the motel, pondering how the strange little man got his points across. I felt a surprising respect for my new-found friend and a clear anticipation for more contact. The only thing was: How in the world would I ever explain things to Jill or anyone for that matter? Should I explain? Anyone would need to see Ruben to believe he really existed.

■ ■ ■

As I drove my car, I knew I didn't want to go to the office nor did I want to go home. I needed a quiet time and place to sort out my feelings and thoughts. Many leaders of churches liked to talk things out with certain persons. I liked to talk to a tree. When feeling some dilemma, often I drove by my favorite park, sat on a wooden bench and looked at an ancient red oak tree. For some reason, I loved that tree, feeling like it held the wisdom of the ages and it never failed as a good listener. Soon, I found myself in front of the old work of nature, staring at the gnarls and turns of one of the larger branches.

For a while, I waited in silence. A young couple walked by holding hands. I waited before talking to the tree, careful not to talk to the tree when others were around.

In the early days, I tended to ignore people, got caught speaking and people stared too much. Their attention and misunderstanding often ruined the moments alone, so I was more careful.

I waited for more complete solitude, and then began to tell the tree every detail of the past hours regarding Michael, fleshing out the story as I would to an attentive child. Sometimes the branches swayed as if to show sympathy, then the tree fell still to show it listened. I didn't rush but when I'd finished my narrative, I walked to the tree, patted it gently and said, "Thanks old friend. Now I think I know what I must do."

I left the way I'd come and drove to my house. Reluctantly, I knew it was time to talk to Jill. As I arrived home and got out of the car, I said out loud, "Surely, I can make her understand, if she'll just listen like the tree."

Chapter 10

Before I was ready to talk to Jill, I sighed and glanced at the outside of my house. Coming home created more discomfort than I'd thought, although I wanted to tell Jill all, the whole idea of Ruben Michael becoming my teacher sounded absurd. I turned the questions over and over in my mind. How will I explain the warm feelings created in me by this strange little man? He's a person who on the surface looks ok but may be a fraud? How will I help Jill understand the time needed to listen to this new-found mentor? Can I keep her from feeling neglected? Can I make her see I feel some strange urge to do this alone?

As I slowly walked into the house, I felt like I'd been doing something wrong and I expected immediate confrontation. However, Jill met me at the door with a smile and a glass of tea. *Maybe things weren't going to be so bad after all*, I thought.

Very soon, I gushed forth with the highlights, leaving out what I considered unimportant details, like some of Ruben's erratic behavior. When I got to the part about interpreting the translation lessons, Jill held up her hand. "He wants you to do what?"

"Come to him for some sort of teaching sessions,

covering the nine kingdom translations. He called it a journey."

"And you don't think that's just a little too weird?" Jill's voice ended on a raised note, like when she wants conversation to stop and her point sink into the listener.

"Well, at first . . . but, I guess he has his reasons, like when he talked about other people not getting the right interpretations or something. Maybe he's made some mistakes and his teaching idea is the only way he knows to keep control over the material."

"So, you want teaching from someone who has made a bunch of mistakes?"

"I don't know, Jill. This is new ground to me too, but I know one thing, I can't just let it go. I really have a deep desire to see this through. It's like a calling. Call me stupid, too trusting, whatever you want, but I've got to go back to get the full load."

Furrowed eyebrows glared at me as Jill jumped up and moved to the kitchen.

The supper leftovers Jill sat out that evening seemed cooler than usual. We sat at the kitchen table to eat. Our conversation about Ruben ended with Jill reluctantly accepting my resolve by changing the subject. She didn't like the result, but she said. "Let's just eat."

After we ate, Jill began clearing away the dirty dishes. I helped for a minute, but the silence stayed painfully strong. I felt I should leave Jill to think through this strange request on her own.

So, I went to our small reading den off the kitchen, sat in my recliner and picked up a book to read. From time to time, I could hear pots and pans banging a little loader than usual. Very soon, I drifted off to sleep as Jill went to the bedroom and picked up her own book to read. She let me alone for about half an hour, then she came to persuade me to go to bed early.

"Um . . . not now, I think I'll read awhile longer, then I'll come. Please don't take this personal. I just want to rest here awhile", I mumbled.

Jill moved away and left me to my own wishes.

■ ■ ■

The next morning at seven o'clock, I still slept in my chair, purring and pooing through my mouth.

Jill shook my arm. I jerked awake. "What...what's wrong?" I gasped.

"Nothing. I've already made coffee. You slept in your chair all night."

I sat up and rubbed my eyes. "Not really. After a short nap, I got wide awake. I kept thinking about Ruben and all. Guess I got what the old timers call 'journey pride' and couldn't go back to sleep."

"Journey what?"

"Journey **pride** . . . you know when you're going to make an exciting trip the next day and you can't sleep the night before for thinking about it. Then, you do fall asleep, but you don't get much."

"Well, it looked like to me you were sleeping pretty well."

"Just resting my eyes for the last few minutes." We both grinned and headed for the kitchen for coffee. We both puttered around the kitchen, making toast and jelly, cereal with banana slices. Finally, Jill asked, "What are you going to do about your Tuesday morning duties at church?"

"I'm going to call my secretary and cancel things because I've got to meet Ruben at 10 o'clock and I've got a feeling I'd better be there early. I'll just wipe the calendar out until after lunch. It'll be ok." I darted a look at Jill thinking *please don't challenge my agenda this morning*.

Jill swallowed hard and shrugged, but I could imagine her blood pressure shot up a few points. With this, I went to shave and shower, remembering to put on some soft cotton pants, a comfortable pullover shirt and tennis shoes. I called my secretary, Betty, and told her I'd be gone. Thank goodness, she was the kind who never questioned my behavior, at least, to my face.

As I started out the front door, I almost forgot the parchment copies and went back to get them. Before I left, I glanced at Jill once more, smiled and gave a little wave. Jill watched me the whole time and looked at me with what I felt was mixed approval.

Tuesday morning found the plush Mall next to Ruben's motel inactive, as I walked to room number seven. I arrived later than I wanted, but my watch showed only nine-thirty and I felt thirty minutes to spare better than nothing. I knocked on the door and to my surprise, it slowly opened. I walked through the little hallway to the living area and looked around. No one greeted me. I glanced up. Neatly stretched across the whole room was a computer-generated banner in red letters addressed to my name: "**Jerod**: **Come to the swimming pool even if early**!" I laughed out loud as I felt like a child on a treasure hunt. I turned and hurried back out the door.

Soon, I walked through the safety gate of the new swimming pool and searched the area for Ruben. The pool looked about twenty feet wide by forty, oval shaped with mosaic blue squares surrounding the edges of the cement deck. The decking spread eight feet wide around the flat ledge, leading to the water entrance. I figured the extra width accommodated more than the usual number of lounge chairs. Clear blue water sloshed around the sides of the pool as if someone swam vigorously in it. But curiously, no one played in the water.

At one end, sitting under an umbrella covered table sat a young couple, eating chips and slurping drinks through candy-striped straws. I thought, *"It sure is early to be eating chips. Who knows? That may be their breakfast."*

At the other extreme end of the pool sat Ruben, dressed in a floral bathing suit and tank top. He wore bright orange sunglasses with a green French beret hat cocked on his head, reclining in a chaise lounge. He looked much like an old tourist of the 1930's, sitting on some cruise ship.

As I approached my acquaintance, I noticed everything about Ruben looked younger than usual. Oh, the basics were there: neat gray hair, goatee and all, but his skin appeared tanned and smooth, more like a man in his prime thirties instead of my guess of sixties. I grinned and started to say something when Ruben waived me to silence and patted another chair beside him, motioning me to sit. Carefully, I lowered myself in the chair and looked out over the pool area to see what Ruben viewed. It was hard to tell since his bizarre sunglasses hid those piercing eyes.

Finally, Ruben spoke: "Just lie back and quiet your mind of all questions. We're going on a great adventure."

I complied the best I could and soon felt amazed

how I could stop the self-talk in my own head, letting relaxation flow over my whole body. I closed my eyes and felt the warm sun against my eyelids like a heated wash cloth.

"Don't go to sleep!" Ruben rebuked.

I jumped, realizing I'd drifted toward sleep.

"I think we will begin lesson one today."

"You mean out here, by the pool?" I anguished.

"Why not? . . . I got your attention, didn't I?"

I groaned. "You've got to be patient with me, Ruben. You always make me feel so stupid, like I just got off the boat, set foot in a new country and don't know the language."

"Good old analogy. There's hope for you yet." Ruben chuckled and beat the arms of his chair with the palms of his hands. Then he jerked off his sunglasses, folded them neatly and pretended to place them in a front shirt pocket that, of course wasn't there. The glasses fell to the cement with a ka-chunk. I just stared at him.

"Did you bring the parchment translations with you?" Ruben mused.

I looked at them in my hand, forgetting they were there. Slowly, I lifted them up to him like some offering.

"No. No. You keep them. Flip to that section where Clarissa talks about the holy bond they agreed upon, you know, the one talking about the little kingdoms."

"Do you mean the untranslated part?"

"You got it, kiddo."

I frowned but handled the parchment carefully, turning to the section after the part I'd let Jill read. I put my finger on the place like a first-grader learning to read.

"Now, why do you suppose that section is

untranslated?" Ruben wiggled his eyebrows up and down.

"I'm not sure. The Greek of each of the nine steps is translated, as you know. The first one is *'Makarioi oi ptwcoi tw pneumati, oti autwn estin h Basileia two ouranwn'*, which I recognize from Matthew 5: 3 has been translated in English to 'blessed are the poor in spirit, for of them is the kingdom of the heavens.' But the symbols that follow each are unrecognizable, at least, they are to me. Hey, as I look at them now, they look like some of the codes the early Christians used to greet each other. There's a fish symbol and loaf of bread and a cross. Could it be the writer Clarissa used those symbols to communicate with other Christians so that the secular religious leaders wouldn't understand? Like not casting the pearls among the swine so to speak?"

"That's one reason. Boy, I knew you had a brain in there somewhere. You are on target," Ruben sighed.

"But, even if I **could** figure out the symbols, they would be so literal, I still wouldn't know the nuances, the cultural and hidden true meanings. I mean, we know a fish symbol stands for more than a fish, like fishers of men which Jesus referred to. But there's more isn't there? How will I ever get the real understanding?"

Michael gave a broad smile. "Now you've come to the true essence of the question why none of this worked too well with others before, and the real reason you have me. I can interpret the hidden meanings of the symbols into language you will understand for today." Ruben folded his arms over his chest like he'd finished some final pronouncement.

"That's a tall order, Ruben. How am I supposed to

believe you are the one who only can do this and has the authority to be correct?"

Ruben unfolded his arms and relaxed them in his lap, his right-hand palm up. He stared intensely straight out at the pool. Suddenly, his dropped sunglasses slowly floated up from the cement decking and gently deposited themselves in his upturned hand.

My lower jaw drooped and I blinked, turned quickly around to see if anyone else saw what I saw. No one paid any attention to us. I jerked back to Ruben. "Wait a minute . . .How did you do that?"

"Do what?" Ruben smiled and started whistling, *mine eyes have seen the glory of the coming of the Lord.*

I began rapid self-talk. *Surely what just happened must have been an illusion, some parlor trick to impress me, well, it worked. I would need to go along with this unusual character despite myself. Besides, even if none of Ruben's teachings meant much in the end, I had to admit this whole business intrigued me.*

"Engaging, isn't it?" Ruben continued, "Dismiss your disbelief for now. We're going to get very serious, now look at the first set of symbols and tell me what you see with your literal interpretation."

I fought with my attention span and concentrated to do as told and viewed the material.

"Well," I struggled, "it looks like a crown, a heart and a palm-up hand, all chain-linked to a theta θ Greek symbol. The way it's drawn, it looks like the hand is uplifted towards the theta and some rays shoot from the theta through the hand into a heart and out from the heart pops this crown. They are drawn with dotted lines so I assume this means process going on, like the lines of a wheel spinning round and round. That's all I can see here, but I don't know how correct that is."

"You have done well, better than most", Ruben responded, "Now go on, what else do you see on the same line."

"Well, there's this cloud or mist floating above three hearts...no wait...they're broken hearts because they have a jagged line through each of them. The hearts are drawn with curved arrows connecting them so they are going around in a circle also. Then there's one big broken heart followed by a smooth, unbroken heart that is line connected to the theta θ symbol. Did I get it right?"

"I must admit, Jerod, you are exceeding my every expectation. Now, go on and interpret the third line and then we'll see what this entire means."

"There's a large heart and inside what looks like a theta symbol θ crowned with a royal crown. Then follows a large crowned heart and inside it is a smaller heart, line- linked to the theta symbol. Man, Ruben.... this is strange but anyway the last three smooth hearts connected by a line to three thetas, all circled and on top sits the large royal crown.

"I don't know what it means but with all the crowns and stuff, I'm sure there's a great deal here about kingdom issues. Those early Christians probably supported a secret belief system since they often feared for their lives. I'm sure Clarissa drew these for them for a special reason. She must have really known her symbols. It seems odd to me that all this got lost over the years, but then, I don't understand a lot going on here, do I?"

"You get more perceptive by the hour," Ruben chuckled.

"Well, tell me what this means then. My curiosity is about to burst!" I agonized.

"Nope, not now. Let's go back to my room. It's getting too hot." Michael sprang up from his chair like a young man and started walking off. I stared at his back that didn't appear hot at all. Then I felt my own sweat running down my inside arms and my legs felt sticky. Here was another puzzle. How come I sweated and Ruben appeared so cool? I moved to follow anyway, thinking more about the symbols.

Back inside the room, Ruben motioned to the banner overhead. "Why don't you take down your little welcome while I change into something more suitable?" He said.

I thought to myself the man couldn't be more comfortable but I went ahead and obeyed, not knowing what else to do. I quickly took down the banner and folded it when Ruben breezed back into the room, wearing clothes very like my soft pants and shirt. The only difference was the color, bright orange and black. I thought he looked like someone getting ready for a football game.

"How do you like my colors? Did you know that this specific orange is not a color found naturally in Nature? It must be manufactured; one of humanity's ingenious achievements. Now sit, and let's talk meanings." Ruben challenged.

I moved to a soft sofa as Ruben sat in a chair opposite, snapping his fingers as if he were searching for just the right beat, either running a melody in his head or looking for the rhythm to set to his words. Again, I sat intrigued.

"Listen very carefully and remember this is just your first lesson as I take on the role of your teacher." He pointed his finger at me, getting my full attention. "Do you recall your scripture pretty well?"

"Well, I don't have it all memorized, but I think I can recognize basic truths, especially from the New Testament, "I responded.

"Do you remember Mark 4 and Matthew 13, when Jesus explained to the disciples why he started teaching in parables? Remember, he had to go out in a boat on the water to get away from the crowd pressing in on him and he started teaching little symbolic stories about the kingdom of heaven. Basically, the disciples asked him why he didn't just speak straight instead of all the clouded mystery. They were concerned that people could not come into the kingdom if they didn't understand him."

I nodded. "Hey, I do remember that one because I often wondered why he answered them as he did, something about they were given the mysteries of the kingdom but those others were not, then something about whoever **has** will receive more and whoever **has not** will have it taken away. Then, I think he launched into a parable about the seeds, sowers and different ground."

"Excellent, oh student of mine. But he said something else before he gave the parable. He quotes Isaiah about many hearing but not hearing and many seeing but not seeing. And that many, many prophets of old and I might say new, would love to know the mysteries of the kingdom."

"Yeah, ok, I'm still not sure all he meant." I stared.

"He meant Jerod, that a certain kind of person will

hear and see and others will not. There's a fascinating statement in Proverbs 25:2-3 and I quote:

It is the glory of God to conceal a thing;
But the glory of kings is to search out a matter.
As the heavens for height and the earth for depth,
So, the heart of kings is unsearchable.

"God conceals himself behind supreme truth and reveals himself through Jesus, but people still misunderstand. The glory of God conceals not because it never wants discovery. It takes what is like the glory of kings to search out the riches."

"But wait," I protested. "I'm no king. If only kings can truly find out the truths, then we're in big trouble."

"Ah....but here is where you missed it," Ruben replied. "The writer did not mean earthly kings On an earthly plane. He meant those people who have an inquisitive king nature, always seeking for the secret of life. So, Jesus was simply saying if you have the right seeking nature, a higher kingly one, the secrets of the kingdom of God will be revealed. The Lord did not intend the use of parables to stop people from seeing, but to help those who could see begin a process for helping those who could not."

I became lost in the words, staring inwardly as it were, and thinking about the concepts. Everything seemed so profoundly simple yet difficult. My throat was dry and the rest of my body felt numb.

I jerked as Ruben boomed at me: **"Now listen up!"**

"The nine kingdom principles are popular as the Be-attitudes and that's all well and good, but the symbols indicate much more meaning than available before. The truth is: *these principles are actually kinds of kingdoms in themselves."* Ruben paused for effect, and then stared at my forehead, right between my eyes. Then he continued, "In the Sermon on the Mount, Jesus began with the **kingdom of Need** . . . What is it? What is it humanity cannot do for itself?"

"You want me to answer?" I asked.

"When I give a long enough pause, I generally want your response."

I thought a minute, feeling like I did as a child in the school play, trying to remember my lines. "I suppose the main thing is humans can't save themselves from themselves."

"Absolutely right . . . hurrah! . . . You win a prize! Now listen. To grow with a Savior, a Messiah, you are told to do something called become 'poor in spirit'. What do you think **that** means? Are you to obliterate self-image? Are you to become a lowly creature and destroy your self-esteem?"

I shifted in my chair, scratched my chin and tried to concentrate all my attention on my newly acquired mentor. "Tell me," I said.

"I will." He continued. "The symbols Clarissa used explain and it has to do with what happened to the human self and personhood. I see I'm about to lose you." Ruben smiled.

"Let me go back a while to the beginning of time," he continued, "Now, listen up! When Adam and Eve rebelled in the garden and humanity lost its innocence, remember, before lostness came into being, there was a time and world without decay. Everything had a single-minded purpose, focused upon the Creator.

The human self could not experience anything like self-awareness because it had no contradictions; it was simply splendid existence, moving along with unity and harmony. You recall, Adam and Eve were beings made in the image of God; that is, their spirits were undiluted and so their personal selves were whole."

I nodded my head in assent, as if I was getting every word.

"When rebellion occurred", Ruben continued, "the individual self got divided into two qualities. One is true Self . . . made in God's image . . . the other a false self, made in self-image alone. I like to call what happened 'schizophilia'—split love. Nice to have a label for the professionals, right?"

I nodded and stared.

"I digress . . .Uh . . . anyway; there is this struggle inside you within the kingdom of Self. The false self always wants what it wants, when it wants it, no matter what. It is always pursuing gratification and fulfillment, trying to persuade itself that every single potential exists in the Self alone. The eyes of the false self are turned inward and continually run on a pleasure principle. It constantly preaches self-renewal and self-improvement. The false self is deluded and blind for it does little without the motivation of getting something in return for its efforts. In the world, it can achieve much and receive much accolade for itself. Are you with me so far?"

I re-crossed my legs and shifted again. "Well, yeah, but what about the symbols?"

"Stay with me Jerod. We'll get to that. They are the house and we're still working on the foundation. Now, **concentrate**. Opposite the false self reflects the authentic self, the true self, the part of self, made in God's image, that wants what God intended. It senses a need outside of self alone and a kind of reality principle influences to turn attention outward, looking for a way to go beyond, to find a lasting potential outside of the self."

"I hate to interrupt, but what do you mean a **reality principle?** I queried.

"It is really that part of you made in the image of God. It is that part of you that wants a permanent reality. One that won't change or trick you. When the true self yearns for more out of life, the Holy Spirit has opportunity to come speak and interpret the Savior Jesus. The false self rejects this continually, trying to convince that nothing else is needed but more earthly resources to enhance a person; and if that can happen, then life can be lived happily ever after. So, the deluded self gears up to get more knowledge, more money, and more power—gratifying the self, thus making life supposedly richer. The false is so strong because it is tied to the very tangible things of earth, things like survival and health and even fairness."

I held up my hand. "Now let me see if I've got this right. Basically, people have two selves, one true and one false. The false always wants what it wants because it's blinded by sin and doesn't know any better. The true wants to seek reliable reality and truth outside of self. So, it tends to look beyond."

"Yes . . . you're getting the essence. See . . . the authentic self struggles to find a way beyond the usual circumstances, sensing that true enrichment must come from outside and from other-centeredness. It wants something bigger. It searches constantly for a channel of expression and it wants a different quality of life than the false. You see, the false self doesn't know it's false. It believes that it is correct and thus a dilemma—a human person cannot save the true self because the false always gets in the way with its limiting inaccuracies and believing it is right."

"At this point," Ruben continued, "a most interesting possibility exists and God provided it. By exposing the Holy Spirit to the true self, the true self can have the power of a plus-quality and say, 'I will conquer the false self by overcoming it, putting it in last place'. Genuine Christian salvation comes when the true self says to the Holy Spirit: *you have permission to crucify the false and place all that is true Self in Christ.* Most don't say it like that. They might just cry out HELP!"

Hurriedly he said, "The process is something like slaying the false self so the true can live free again. Now, Jerod, this is not some psychological aberration of self-punishment, but rather, a giving away of Self to a real person, one who promised He will accept your gift of self if you accept his gift of Son."

Ruben turned his hands palms up in front of him. He raised one up while dropping the other down, like weighing something, finally bringing them to an equal balance. "This then, is the first stage in the walk through the nine kingdom principles to become a be-attituded person: recognizing the kingdom of need, presenting your true self to find your partner, the true king, then facing the first struggles with the false self because it doesn't give up until you die."

"Ok, I think I see", I pronounced. "It explains a lot of things to me, why for instance people chase after the wrong things and even why other religions are formed because they are looking to express the true self and the false throws in its two cents and gets things confused. I can see what you're saying. Is that what Clarissa was saying too?"

"Her symbols speak of the process very well. And you are right about people chasing after things. The selves are always looking beyond. It's what you call creativity or imagination. The difference is in the selves. People will either find truth in truth or they will find what they think is truth in error, but they are continually searching."

"You mean when I'm being creative, I'm exercising one of the selves."

"Something like that. You see, the ability to go beyond yourself with imagination or creative endeavor displays that part of you made in the image of The Creator."

"Fascinating!"

"Yes, isn't it? But there's more. So, you see 'the poor in spirit' of scripture becomes the avenue of renouncing the false self and forgoing the control of your true self or spirit, abdicating mastery to the Holy Spirit who is more able to grow you. Thus, your basic need is designed to give yourself away. When you give your spirit to the living Christ, the Holy Spirit merges with you, resides in you, and you become human-plus. Christ becomes a part of you and you a part of Him. Then begins a partnership with your spirit that starts recreating the Self and affects all you are, even your body." Ruben winked, pointed his finger like shooting a play pistol at my heart.

"You see, Jerod, you begin this journey by starting through the Kingdom of Need—the need to have a

Savior do for you what you cannot accomplish yourself. And what is the major outcome of such a bond? I'm glad you asked......The whole experience creates a quality of life that has the potential to rise above, go beyond pain or pleasure. This quality even teaches you how to use your pain for more productive results. You become a new creation indeed."

"Whoa." I gulped. "I don't know about getting beyond pain or pleasure. I do know that Christians are supposed to be different, but we live in a day when it's hard to tell the difference between the true convert and just a sincere church goer, especially in America. Most people seem to behave pretty much the same out there in the work world, don't you think?"

"Ah......there's the rub, eh what?" Ruben chortled.

"Ok, ok, I see. This whole thing is what I've always wanted too—I mean— a clear set of guidelines from the Sermon on the Mount for everyday Christians to follow. I've got to know, Ruben, will having this material help me separate the real Christian from the false?" My thoughts turned to the recent hospital visit with Benny Sapp and his questions before he died. *Were those doubting questions somehow linked with salvation growth?*

Ruben flinched. "What difference does that make? Who asked you to judge? Do you want to be the bishop of the world and divide people up? I can see you now . . . Ok, people...all you non-Christians and doubting Christians . . . you go to Texas, Louisiana and Arkansas. All you Christians with the answers can have the rest. . . Ha!"

My face reddened, as I squirmed in my seat, like a man about to run away and hide. "I didn't mean **that.** As a pastor, I've always just been concerned that our churches may have people who think they are saved and aren't. Maybe this would be an answer why more people aren't growing spiritually or why some seem burned out with church."

"Jerod, do you think Rev. Sapp's last days had anything to do with a lack of salvation?"

"Well, no. Hey, wait a minute . . . how did you know about Rev. Sapp?" I puzzled and began to squirm more as I wondered if Ruben knew about my own feelings of doubt and tiredness.

"Never mind that now. When you see what it really means to walk through the nine kingdoms, you will have much more to think about than useless questions. Now don't get so upset, your colors are showing, **listen up,** more's coming. You remember the first untranslated symbols —the crown, a heart, a palm-up-hand, chain-linked to a theta θ symbol?"

I sighed deeply and relaxed. "Yeah, I suppose."

"In addition," Ruben continued "there's this cloud floating over three broken hearts which are connected as if going around in a circle, trailed by one large broken heart followed by a smooth, unbroken heart that is line-connected to the theta θ symbol, right?"

"I think that's right."

"So, the crown/heart/hand/theta symbols all stand for the kingdom of need. The three broken hearts stand for body, soul and spirit, signifying you cannot save yourself; the cloud represents the spirit on the move; the large broken heart shows the renouncing of the false self and the smooth heart/theta connection speaks to the experience of accepting the true self partnership with the rebirth of the image of God in you."

"OK, sure...I can see that now you've explained it,

but I surely wouldn't have known without help. What about the last three drawings?" I asked.

Ruben grinned and started patting his knees like playing some drum solo. "Yes, now, the large heart ♥ with crowned theta θ symbol designates the kingdom of God in the hearts of people. The large crowned heart ♥ with the smaller heart ♥, line-linked to the theta θ, stands for people in the heart of the kingdom. This is where it gets really good." Ruben rubbed his hands together and continued.

"The three smooth hearts ♥-♥-♥ line-linked to three thetas θ-θ-θ all circled and on top sits a large royal crown showing the final symbol of the result of the struggle in the kingdom of need. And here is the astounding conclusion: *you may have to stay in the kingdom of need until the kingdom owns you, instead of you just possessing the kingdom.*"

I gawked, feeling stunned, partly numbed. A part of me understood what Ruben said but it seemed so different than I'd heard before. I felt I needed to let things incubate; sink in more so they could pop out more clearly later. I sensed the hidden power here, precious insight coming straight from God if I only had time to digest it. My mind twirled and I felt somewhat confused.

"I know what you're thinking, Ruben boomed. Jerod, you are right. Time will help you, but for now I must go on. For you see, the last part of the scripture reference says 'of them is the kingdom of the heavens'. Some have translated 'theirs is the kingdom of heaven.' This last version has caused considerable misunderstanding because it emphasizes **you** owning heaven, which is true of course, but shortsighted, since heaven is often thought of as a place only. The complete truth is: heaven is alive and reaches out with its own acquisition quality which works at possessing you. Remember, heaven maintains the energy of the Holy Spirit."

I blinked again. "I guess when most of us think or talk about heaven, we do think of it as more of a place. A better place than where we are, for sure."

Ruben sat up straight and pointed to the ceiling. "The instruction in scripture about heaven actually emphasizes experiencing it. It is a place but more like a dynamic position because it is not static. There are no limits of spatial or physical boundaries like some geography, but if any limits exist, they are only set by the person's ability to receive the fullness of the kingdom. Heaven remains a filling up principle as well as a spreading out event."

"Man . . . I think I understand, perhaps vaguely, that the kingdom of heaven is supposed to be within us as well as a place promised. But then, what's all the fuss?" I quipped.

"Yes, but do you understand that owning the kingdom of heaven while it owns you, in reality, contracts with you an unbreakable agreement to receive the full potency of God? He can use you as a channel for anything because you share a special connection with the Son Jesus."

"Well, I thought I understood that."

"What you used to think is incomplete, Jerod, just not enough. I'm emphasizing some of the old stuff so you are ready for the new. Stay with me. We're about done here, so now I make some jumps."

"The kingdom of Christ and heaven are eternal and therefore existed in the past when Jesus started it. All of it is in the present a living reality, remaking the hearts of saved humanity. And it is in the future, as the spiritual existence set forth as eternity with God."

"The poor in spirit keep a unique happiness because Self is in the protection of Christ and the kingdom of heaven will enter the point of every need. Human character and conduct begin to change toward the things that truly glorify God. This, then, is the true beginning for a Christian, one who now has human-plus operating in the daily life, such that, not only do you possess a kingdom not made of this world but it begins to possess you......" Ruben trailed off wistfully and looked down.

"Ok, I think I get it. We must enter the kingdom of need. It's just another way of talking about salvation, isn't it? I admit, a fresh way and more complicated, perhaps, but essentially what I've been preaching for years. So, what's so special about the translations and all?"

"There is a hidden secret within which has caused much trouble and I'm supposed to reveal to you. Many Christians are stuck within the kingdom of need and it's going to be your job to get them out."

"What? What do you mean stuck? My job?" I panicked.

"I finally have your full attention. Good! Enough for today; enough for lesson one. It gets even better. What I want you to do is go for now and call me tomorrow. Let what I have mentioned sink in. Let it soak you through and through. Oh, by the way, I want you to take the next eight days off from church. We cannot have those interruptions. Each day we will take another lesson. There are eight kingdoms left before you can really understand the full teaching Clarissa wrote about."

Suddenly, Ruben sprang from his seat and walked over to an ordinary looking door into a bedroom. Swiftly he opened the door and scurried through, closing the door behind.

Astonished, I stared after my mentor, feeling the frustration of his abrupt action. I waited and soon I was shifting back and forth in my chair, feeling impatient and almost angry. Time passed....3...5 minutes. I looked at my watch. Finally, I went over to the door and knocked. No answer. I opened the door and looked around. No one was there. I called, "Ruben...Ruben?"

No answer. Puzzled, I searched the bedroom, bathroom, and back to the sitting area. Ruben was nowhere to be found. *Not again*, I thought and scratched my head and mumbled, *well, it's a little rude but not much left to do but go home and do like he said*. Finally, I lifted my hands in surrender, glanced quickly around the room once more and walked out of the motel, heading straight for my car.

Chapter 11

As I got out of my car and walked toward my house, I heard the harsh call of a crow...*caw...caw...caw.* According to local myth, old timers said the largest white oak tree in town stood in our front yard. For some reason, it attracted several crows a year. I knew they only stopped here as a resting place, on their way to a tasty meal somewhere.

Suddenly, my mind turned to a time when out in the woods hunting. I'd sat down from a rigorous morning of quail hunting for a brief rest. As I rested, I watched a gigantic oak tree not far from where I sat. I noticed a large dead limb protruding out like a giant landing field. Sure enough, crows began to light on the limb and after a while, 25 or so all settled in a row.

The limb broke right where it attached to the main tree trunk and crows fell like rain. I laughed so hard when I thought I could see their surprised crow faces. It played itself out like a comedy routine—crack—the limb separating from their feet—crow suspended in mid-air—then falling all together, raining black crow. I often thought I'd like to see it again in my front yard but our tree harbored no dead limbs. My church members saw to that. I smiled thinking how Nature's drama was free with entertainment if only people would take time to see. I also could not help but wonder if this entire event with the parchments was some big dead limb I was about to fall from. I shook away the thought.

As I took another step toward the house, the late September wind, laced with hints of a cooler October, blew in my face. I stopped to listen. I really liked this time of year. Stiff brown leaves clacked across the street, sounding like someone walking over a crunchy cereal. I could taste the trace of fall and the notion pleased me. I always felt a fresh anticipation about fall, even though most thought it to be an in-between season; I relished the cooler breezes, the color changes, the time of year for my two favorite holidays, Thanksgiving riding on into Christmas. It presented a time for me to enjoy Nature, get out in the woods, take a fresh breath about life's overall temperament, and evaluate things in general.

Fall always gave me a rest period and I came out refreshed, pumped up and ready for the winter months. Most people molted during winter, displaying symptoms of hibernation. Not me. I felt propelled and tended to motivate others as well.

So, when these first hints of fall passed through my nostrils, my spirit lifted and I needed a lift if I kept any chance to get Jill's understanding of this latest encounter with Ruben. Not that Jill seemed so hard-nosed about the matter so far, but I doubted anyone could fully understand my latest experiences, especially how Ruben made his sunglasses float into his hand.

I entered my house like a man approaching a dragon cave. I didn't like this feeling, dreading what I thought would be confrontation with Jill. She certainly wasn't an ogre like some wives but I felt accountability to my wife, a responsibility to share everything, at least, to help her understand the comings and goings of my life. Jill never nagged in the sense some men categorized their mates. She really didn't push head on, but her gestures, her presence probed a way of asking the most penetrating questions. I often thought because we had no children our bond sometimes felt too close. Her sharpest interest focused always on me. While part of me liked the bond, the friendship, another part of me felt a kind of intrusion into the private realms of my being. I liked the secret parts of my life, just like everyone else, those special little pieces making up the individual self. I wondered if God only should know about those. But Jill wanted in there too; she wanted it all. And when I couldn't give all, I felt like a child and deep down, I held no intention of ever having another mother.

By the time I'd walked into the house, I'd resolved my concern somewhat. Whatever the outcome, I would need to take off the days Ruben suggested. Jill and the church members may not understand, but I rationalized that the benefits of pursuing Ruben's teaching would surely be more important in the long run than any future objections. So, I rushed into the den to talk to Jill and she sat focused intently on a crossword puzzle.

"What's a five-letter word for *buffalo dung*?" Jill blurted as she looked up at me.

"Uh . . . try *chips*." I responded raising my eyebrows.

"Hey . . . that works."

I sat down by her, placing my hand over the puzzle and began to explain my morning. I talked slowly, emphasizing what I thought needed to persuade her going along with taking eight days off from church duties. I ended by saying I needed a break anyway and to think of it as a mini-vacation.

After a long pause Jill finally spat, "**Ah chips**, Jerod."

"Come on, Jill, I've tried to be honest with you about this. It's all new waters for me too. It's not like I'm trying to enter some get rich quick scheme and destroy our budget. Remember, even the check I wrote for $100, I did not sign. I just feel I need this time and experience. I've already learned a great deal. It seems to me the worst that can happen is I spend time with an interesting character and learn something. What's so wrong in that? Anyway, I feel I've got to do it."

"Well, you seem to have made up your mind, why even bother discussing it with me? You go ahead and do what you've got to do and I'll do what I've got to do."

"Wait a minute, Jill, what does **that** mean?"

"I just mean I'm not going to stay around here and answer the phone calls while you're out having your teaching lessons. There's no way I'm going to try to explain to the people what you're doing."

"So, what will you do?" I asked.

"I think I'll go visit my brother and take my own mini-vacation. I'll just treat it like you're on a revival, except I'm the one leaving. You must eat out of the freezer or whatever, take care of yourself. Can you do that?"

I thought about these consequences and didn't like them at first, especially about the eating part, but then I decided I'd not make an issue of things and after all, Jill could still be an individual and do individual things. She didn't always need to stay at home and do everything I expected of her.

"Ok, I can handle that. I'll help you do laundry or

whatever to get us ready to leave in the morning. I've got to meet Ruben again early morning so we might as well leave the house at the same time. Right now, I'd better call the church and tell the secretary my plans of taking off. She can handle the office. I'll announce at church tomorrow at Wednesday night services my plans for absence and get a supply speaker for Sunday; that way, I'll have Thursday on to give Ruben his eight days."

I started to reach for the phone, stopped and leaned over, tenderly kissing Jill on the lips. She stiffened but then relaxed and turned to give me a big hug. The hug lingered. I started to pull away, but she held on tight.

Jill had her own little sports car so the next day, I helped her load her bags. As she pulled away to go to her brother's in Arkansas, I waved vigorously. She didn't even look back, just raised one single wave like the queen of England does. I knew by that gesture that she probably wasn't too pleased with things. I sensed she wondered why I didn't take her with me to see Ruben.

I sighed and let my waving hand slowly drop to one side. I slumped and moved hurriedly to my car, as my thoughts turned to the day and my next meeting with Ruben Michael. I felt too uncomfortable carrying around the original parchments, so I drove by a copy center and made more copies of the untranslated part of the parchments, and then took the originals to my bank safe deposit box.

Soon I arrived at the motel where Ruben lived, only to find a note left at the manager's office, instructing me to meet Ruben in the main visitor's lounge at the Good Sorrow Memorial Hospital. My first thoughts were that Ruben might have become ill, but then I reasoned that a visitor's lounge meant just that: visitors. As I drove to the destination, I wondered how anybody would come up with a name like "Good Sorrow". The only sorrow I knew wasn't good.

Ten minutes later, I pulled into the visitor's parking at the hospital, barely finding a space, slid out of the driver's seat, pushed the automatic car door locks and rushed through the swishing outside door entrance to the hospital. Straight ahead in the lobby glowed a sign of the Gift and Flower Shop. On the left, sitting behind a glass window sat a receptionist dressed in the candy-striped uniform, slowly flipping through a magazine. I started in her direction, then glanced to the right and saw a brightly-lit sign over another doorway that simply said **visitors**, as if people might drop in when they really didn't have any personal business in a hospital.

I headed for the door, walked through, looked around. The place stood empty. I felt some panic. Was I in the wrong place? Then I sighed and sat down. Gazing around the room, I felt an uncontrollable urge, like something pushing me, to pick up a magazine with a large picture of a deer on the front cover. As I flipped opened the first few pages, one of those advertising postcards dropped out and I noticed someone already filled it out in big black letters. I began to read and to my astonishment, it said in bold letters: **Jerod come to the little chapel on the third floor!**

I gawked at the message. *This is too much. Ruben's got to have an accomplice or something who watches every move I make.* I took off my reading glasses, rubbed my eyes, put the card in my pocket, and headed for the third floor. What else could I do?

As I took the elevator to the third floor of the hospital and got off, I noticed the sharp alcohol smell drifting down the hallways—and the chill of the place. Why was it always so cold in hospitals? Oh, yeah, a doctor friend told me one time it was to keep down infections. I wondered if that was true or one of those medical myths, covering the fact most doctors and nurses felt hotter because of running back and forth between patients. Whatever the reason, I never associated that chill with any atmosphere of health. It reminded me too much of funeral homes and death.

I hurried through a narrow chapel doorway, stopped to let my eyes adjust to the subdued, darker lights inside. I looked closely at the hardwood pews for any sign of Ruben. The little chapel had two rows of eight pews, lined to face a simple altar with a stained-glass window as a backdrop. A center aisle headed straight forward to a detailed inlaid glass, life-sized picture of Jesus, standing with his arms outstretched, beckoning for those to approach him gladly. The artist displayed Jesus floating in the air, white puffy clouds in the background, and rays of God's glory shot forth from his whole body. By some secret of artistic genius, the light filtering through made it appear Jesus vibrated with a kind of energy, symbolizing life rather than death; active in people's lives, not passive, but approachable for any who would move toward the light.

The room appeared empty except for a small figure, third pew on the right-hand side. I sensed it was Ruben. His face turned toward the light and for a moment, I stared at my friend's side countenance for a minute. I flinched. His face shown like the same face of Jesus in the stained glass. I blinked owl-like eyes. He never looked up, smiled, and patted the pew, motioning me to come sit by his side. I scooted by him and sat erect, pushing my hands beside me on the pew seat like I was riding a roller coaster. Tension flooded my body.

"I see you made it. You must be ready for lesson two, all bright-eyed and eager today, huh?" Ruben mused.

"Here! You expect to talk in here?" I puzzled.

"Why not? What better place to discover the truths of the kingdom than having our master looking down upon us." Ruben raised one eyebrow and nodded his head toward the picture of Jesus.

"But someone might want to come in here and pray or something. This really isn't a very good classroom you know," I chafed.

"It is so wonderful to count on your predictability when it comes to getting your attention. You inspire me so." Ruben chuckled softly. "But you must not worry about any interruptions. I will take care of everything and **you don't need to whisper,"** Ruben boomed, **"God is not influenced by sound**."

"Must you always make me so uncomfortable? Every time we meet my senses get out of balance from things you do. I don't know when to trust myself."

"*Good. Good. Good.* I'm not going to apologize for your discomfort nor shall I put it like the pop psychologists, your dislodged comfort zone . . . ha. I told you I had to keep you off balance so I can get you to focus properly on your lessons. You think this is child stuff? You are in the big leagues now, so toughen up and listen up, hey, that'd make a good bumper sticker, don't you think?"

"Ok, ok . . . what's the lesson today?" Then I looked at my hands and realized I'd been in such a hurry, I'd forgotten the parchments.

"Oh, no, Ruben . . . I forgot the parchments

translations. I left them in the car. Should I go back and get them?"

Ruben made the motion of withdrawing an imaginary pencil from behind his ear, marking a big x on his palm like it was paper and clucked, "Tsk, Tsk, you get one demerit for today."

I felt stupid and slumped in the pew.

"Man, you've got to quit taking yourself so seriously. Never mind, do you remember what we talked about in our first lesson?" Michael asked.

I sat up straight. "Yes, I do and I was really bothered by what you said about me having to get people unstuck out of the kingdom of need. I have no idea what **that** means, let alone, why it's my job as you said."

"Ah, my boy, I knew you had the makings. Now try to remove your self-centered thoughts . . . remember that in the kingdom of need, whenever the feeling of God's Grace is missing, pride is the cause. Put on your spiritual face, the real one, and focus on what we are about to discuss." Ruben stared holes in me.

I could not help but feel my lack, my self-consciousness, my vanity slide through me like a warm buzzing through my veins. I took a deep breath and gathered all my senses and concentrated by fixing my gaze on Ruben's lips. In my mind, I pictured those lips as a kind of doorway to unsearchable riches. I felt ready to accept whatever came through the doorway.

"Do you remember", Ruben spoke evenly, "our little discussion about some of the symbols Clarissa used in her document?"

"Yeah, that I do recall."

"Good, because I want to clear some things about symbols once and for all so you won't always be wondering and caught up in the hocus-pocus mystery about the biblical signs. I know you feel like everyone else—that if you can just learn the secrets, then you will have something juicier than others. Well, that's too much pride. You are going to discover, through my help some new things and the symbols are important, but not as important as their meaning for you and others you may meet. The applications of those principles become much more significant than any rare parchments."

My mouth opened as if to say something, but nothing came, so I shifted in my seat and focused on my teacher again.

He continued. "Remember, in Clarissa's writings, Christians used things like a loaf of bread, fishes, crowns, crosses—these are pretty universal. A loaf of bread stands for bread of life, God's word. Fishes stand for followers who form communities that move together. Crowns imply a reigning principle. But take for instance the cross. Why do you suppose Christ was crucified on a cross? Why not a triangle or a rectangle?"

I hesitated, and then said, "Well . . . historically, it was what the Roman soldiers used for other crucifixions. I guess it was just handy and certainly effective."

"So, you think it served just convenience, happenstance, historical. Nothing more?"

"I don't think the Roman leaders knew much more, but of course, the modern church has since associated the cross with the height and depth of God's love, the upward vertical slant of the cross stands for our relation to God and the horizontal slant relates people to people, at least, that's the usual interpretation. But I'm sure there's more . . . and you're going to tell me, right?" I smiled and felt I might be giving Ruben back some of his own witty medicine.

He grabbed at his heart like he'd been shot, feigned a fake dying scene, and then said, "Ya got me that time pardner."

I could not hold back a laugh, and then a giggle, then I got so tickled tears formed in my eyes. Finally, I said, "ah...." as I wiped my eyes with the back of my hand. "I guess I needed that to relieve some tension."

"Can't hurt, ole son, and besides, you have a dandy laugh there. Now, seriously, the cross configuration has great significance to show who God really is. Now I'm not talking about Jesus' experience on a cross, I'm talking about the sign of the cross itself. The cross sign is a whole set of languages, getting at the immensity of Spirit God. When you look at a cross, you tend to see two lines intersecting each other that both have beginnings and endings. That's the limit of your two-dimensional sight." Ruben tapped his temple with his index finger.

"But, you need to start thinking larger", he continued. "Imagine the cross with no beginning of lines and no endings because that's more like God who never was created until He became Jesus. The picture changes one's perspective. For instance, if the height of the cross has no end, just how high is it? If the width has no end, how wide is it? They reach out into infinity, forever. So, what does this stand for with God? . . . I'm so glad you asked . . . it stands for the unlimited power of the Spirit God. What do you say to that load, Rev. Dr. Sellers?"

"Well, it is hard to think of infinity for most people. We seem to feel more comfortable having limits, but I consider God to be unlimited creativity. Yet, if I think of the cross having no beginnings or endings to the lines, it boggles my mind picture ability." I shook my head and looked up at the stained glass of Jesus.

"Yes, think of Jesus a moment. How could God, who has no beginning, was never created, become human? Think of our Lord coming through the birth canal of a woman like every natural born human being, born through natural travail of the mother. A special grace was upon the mother, but oh . . . what grace it must have taken God to create himself through lower humanity. God Jehovah, the first unapproachable thought, who never had a beginning, chose to be created in Jesus, to experience all you suffer—an extremely slow way to growth compared to the faster spiritual world method."

"What was in God that He chose this method? Ruben asked. "Some lack? Some need? No! None of it was based on any need. The Incarnation vibrates who God is. He is infinite love. He can **be** no other. He does not just DO love; He is Love. True love is complete with hurt and joy. So, you see, He created a tangible road to travel. He took the vertical line of the cross, from infinity to earth-bound history. That line was His earth connection and He traveled the complete birth canal."

I felt my heart swell and tears came to my eyes. All my senses seemed to merge into a new spiritual understanding which flooded my being. My mind whirled and my body became very still, but my spirit seemed to soar as human pride slid away like a water slide. My spirit felt meshed with the same Holy Spirit, the all-powerful worker who traveled the line of creation with the Savior and with all who claim to be Christian.

Ruben reached and shook my shoulder. "Stay with me now. There's more. However, you must understand the cross before you can ever understand moving from the kingdom of need to the next kingdom, **the kingdom of Sorrow**. For you see, the cross has height, breadth, length, and depth. And they must all be understood in the light of limitlessness. Too many people are stuck in the kingdom of need because they do not look deep enough at Calvary's cross. They hold that event up too much as the one and only event settling everything. And even when they do, they do not realize upon what they see. Because to accept the Crucifixion means to accept eternity's road, infinity's lines of connection." Ruben stared at me and continued.

"Part of your job, Jerod, will be to get people moving again into the next kingdom. So, hear me—just as the height, the vertical line has no beginning or end, so goes the cross dissecting horizontal line, the breadth. If the height stands for the all-powerful Holy Spirit, the breadth or width represents the unlimited broadness of the Holy Spirit, the vast unilateral widening of the Spirit of God, the all-encompassing Love of a True Self. Every time Clarissa uses the cross symbol +in her writings, she means what I'm telling you."

"Wait, wait." I exclaimed. "To try to think of the vertical and horizontal lines having no beginnings and no endings really blows my mind. I can't help but think of them coming together out there somewhere and making big round balls because they finally curve into each other," I said perplexed.

"That's normal human thinking, but remember, God selected a cross, meaning **He** made the lines cross. Nothing made him do that. He wanted to do that. He could have had parallel lines I suppose, or something else, but the lines cross for a reason. At the point the lines cross, signifies God's brokenness, coming into human history and changing it forever. God showed the world what love really is. Think of it—God was going along on a straight, perfect line; He intercepts and breaks that line with another line, Jesus. What is this message to humanity? He is saying, 'you can break my back and I will break your heart.' This stays the arresting truth of the Cross which commands humanity's attention. It is a display of what true love really is. The message is given many times by Jesus, but for the Christian to truly live such a truth and reach a better maturity, you must experience all nine kingdoms of growth."

I blinked, sat still, and felt like a sponge.

"Don't get boggled here, Jerod; just know the lines do cross and accept that their ends are open ended, moving out forever. This is who God is: all in all, all over all, all around all, all through all, all encompassing all." Ruben grinned showing deep set dimples and perfect white teeth.

I grinned back; I couldn't help myself, and then looked around the little chapel to see if anyone entered. No one did. It was as if this peculiar place became our private sanctuary, uninterrupted by anything other than our presence, discussing great theological subjects. I felt amazed again at the fact Michael seemed to control events, environment, and people. I glanced at this little man beside me and wondered if he was a little man after all.

"Now before you get all mystical", Ruben continued, "let's come back to the subject of the cross of God because you must work your mind a little harder to keep thinking in the unlimited terms of God. See . . . if you ask, 'how long is the vertical line of the cross?' . . . the only answer is still that the length of any of the cross lines shows God's everlastingness and the length is always as long as it is right now or when someone discovers it. If you ask, 'how deep is the vertical line?' . . . the only answer says that the depth is all God's wisdom contained in all the Spirit knows. If you ask, 'how broad are the lines of the cross?' . . . the only answer is they are as broad as His Love, for His love extends to all people exactly what it wills for itself."

Ruben flailed his arms around, "So, no matter if you try to ponder the height, the length, the depth, the breadth of the cross, it is God's all-encompassing being. Since God has truly penetrated human history with His all, then where does anyone hide? They don't. No one can really hide."

"Ouch!" I flinched. "That's wonderful and frightening at the same time, and yet, it also adds a lot of sense to ideas, like God always hearing prayer. I mean, if God is really all embracing with His being then He can't help but hear every prayer, thought, yearning, groaning, whatever goes out into the universe in whatever form."

"Well shades of expanding cosmos!" Ruben grinned. "You finally started thinking a little about how vastly bigger God is than usually credited Him. Your brain is stretchable after all . . . so stay as elastic as you can because more is on the way. Let's get this in while I can: **Remember,** *God continually maintains by true essence anything which a human might possess by imported Grace.*"

"What in the world does that mean?" I asked, ignoring the comment about my brain.

"It means most of the Christian world has not understood His Grace essential. It means He always illustrates what He starts. His essence continues so gracious that it means if you died before you finished a prayer or some good work, He would give you full credit when you didn't deserve it, as if you'd finished with flying colors. I like to think of it as God's preventive grace. You don't earn His attention. He has merited your attention by giving His Son. Think of the most gracious person in all history. And that individual will have only a tiny atom of who God is at the point of grace, but that person will be an illustration."

"I may not know all you mean, Ruben, but I do know God has certainly been gracious to me in my life and I can't thank him enough. I'm even feeling a little thankful for you. You have wit and knowledge and I don't know what all and you seem to be willing to share with me. I thank you for that."

"Let's don't get all mushy on me, besides flattery might get you a punch in the nose."

I flinched slightly, feeling Ruben meant every word.

Suddenly, we were interrupted by a noise, a slow wail behind us. I recoiled and looked quickly to the back of the chapel. A young Latino couple came stumbling down the little aisle. The man supported and braced the woman the best he could, trying to keep her from falling. They moved past us, never looked our way, headed for the altar, knelt together and gazed upon the stained-glass picture of Jesus. They crossed themselves as their lips moved feverishly.

"See those two", Michael motioned with his head, "they will know God's graciousness today. Their mother is near death but she will recover."

"Wait a minute," I blustered louder than I meant, then I whispered, "*what do you mean and how do you know that?*"

Ruben reached over and lightly thumped me on the forehead. "This **is** a hospital you know."

Just as suddenly as they came, the two young Latinos got up and shuffled out, paying no attention to any of their surroundings. I looked at Ruben who just shrugged his shoulders.

"Now back to our discussion", he demanded, "Remember I told you that people were stuck in the kingdom of need and that's the first kingdom. So now we must get you into the second kingdom—the kingdom of Sorrow. It is what you know as 'blessed are those who mourn, for they shall be comforted'. Do you remember the part of the parchment translation that deals with mourning?" Ruben asked.

"Ah . . . somewhat, but I have a copy of that part you're talking about in the car. I got too nervous carrying around the originals. They're in my safe deposit box. Of course, you can have them back anytime, the originals I mean." I stuttered.

"No, no, no. You keep them for now. You can have something to refer to about the symbols from time to time so you won't forget. And as I told you before, even the symbols are not as important as their true meaning and we want you to have the true meaning. Run out to your car and get the copies and hurry right back." Ruben crossed his arms, slouched in his seat, and stared straight ahead.

I sat puzzled a minute but then jumped up quickly to do what I was told. I hurried to my car and got the material. Soon, I reentered the chapel, breathing hard and sat down, shoving the translations toward Ruben.

"No . . . No . . . you find the symbols used for the

Greek word **pentheo**, to mourn. Put your finger on the place. What do you see?"

I searched the photocopy of the untranslated part of the parchment. My finger moved to the section he asked about. Finally, I described what I saw.

"There seems to be stick figures of people but with large faces. There are two together facing each other with tears rolling down their cheeks, some larger and smaller figures that might be a family, then what looks like a group of people in a circle, also with tears. Words seem to come out of their mouths toward each other. I suppose this means they're talking to one another, perhaps sharing the Gospel message?"

"You're close, but you don't win the teddy bear! Remember, I told you that people were stuck in the kingdom of need, in the salvation mode and one of the reasons is that's a nice place to be because of the joy of sins forgiven and eternal burdens lifted . . . but . . . you are not supposed to stay there. You are to practice love enough to move into the kingdom of sorrow."

"Sorry for what? Isn't being sorry for your sins enough? Besides, no one likes to mourn. It's too painful", I felt defeated.

"Ah, but, there's where even pastors have missed the point. Clarissa shows the way and knew some things even before the Apostle Paul wrote about them. See, the question is what kind of mourning is this? . . . Again, I'm glad you asked cause I'm gonna tell ya . . . ha."

"This kind of mourning is mourning in general. It includes things like feeling sorrow for the loss of a loved one, sorrow for drastic and negative cultural changes, and grief for Christians in church who show no repentance for the evil in their lives, sorrow for those in the world who do not really understand what sin does to them because of blinding techniques. God's love moves you into these areas because that's where He is. You begin to grieve with Him about the world's hurt and pain. You are to learn how to do confession with love like James said and bear one another's burdens like Paul said."

"Clarissa showed in her symbols people confessing their burdens with other caring persons who help carry the load of troubles. This is what builds true Christian community, a genuine Christ-centered church. When people share their burdens properly, the joy of their salvation is extended, not diminished. Why do you think people, including you, have lost a lot of joy?"

I felt the sting of Ruben's words. It had been a long time since true joy permeated my life. Most days I responded out of duty or habit. I vowed a role to fill and did that quite well, but joy? Oh, sure, I knew happy times in my ministry, but they were so fleeting I'd come to dread those occasions because of the letdown often following. In my mind, the good times came too slowly and passed too quickly, leaving me depressed at least once a month. I always felt something wrong with that scenario, something missing from my spiritual diet.

Slowly now, I began to see the reality of the void. The truth stung me: **I felt no sense of real community**, nor did my church. *Was that what Benny Sapp was wondering about?* Perhaps they were all playing a role just like him. Everyone kept some well-defined role and tended to act it out within their own guidelines of propriety. I saw in my mind's eye how safe that was, how easy a Christianity to stay in the kingdom of salvation as little children.

"Ruben . . . I think I understand what you're saying,

but how do we apply the principles of confessing our faults to each other and burden-bearing? People just can't stand up in a church service and tell all their dirty laundry? It would only promote the sin of gossip." I felt my question feeble but real.

"Methods, methods, methods. You are always wanting the 'how tos' before you understand the 'wherefores'. Right now, I want you to get the principles, the foundation of what I'm saying. We'll build the rest of the house later. Until you understand what real mourning is, what **Sin** instead of sins really is . . . we can't turn you loose on the world with methods that have hurt too much already. I know part of your concern comes from the fear of mourning because you think of the pain. But may I remind you, this is the point where the Holy Spirit can come and be the Comforter. It is a Grace time, one of His opportunities to help you grow because it lets Him in voluntarily. And anytime you let Him in voluntarily, you grow in your other-centeredness . . . ok . . . enough for today. I'll see you tomorrow." Abruptly, Ruben sprang up and strolled out of the little chapel before I could say a word.

My lower jaw snapped shut, as I watched Ruben's back leaving the chapel room. Slowly, I gazed around at the wood benches in the chapel. Highly polished oak shone back at me as if to say, *'we're still alive.'* I could feel the care and love of someone who polished those benches for years. My spirit lifted and I finally felt drawn to leave the room. I left the chapel and began strolling through one of the hospital corridors.

As I walked the hallway, I passed a private room with the door ajar. I looked in and recognized the Latino couple that earlier visited the chapel. Their eyes met mine and I felt compelled to enter the room. I nodded a greeting and walked to stand by the bedside of an older woman. Plastic tubes served to drip her life line in arms and nose. I sensed she was probably the couple's mother.

Gently, I laid my hand on the woman's fevered brow. Hot as the bottom of a skillet, quickly I jerked my hand away, then grasped her wrinkled hand. Suddenly, the woman's eyes popped open and she whispered, "Padre".

"No, no . . . I'm not a priest," I whispered.

The woman's eyelids fluttered and closed. A young voice from behind me said, "Please pray for her."

I hesitated but lowered my head and prayed. *"Heavenly Father . . . I don't know this woman's need but you do. Help her . . . help her family endure what is to come. Let your grace and comfort be felt as real as life itself . . . in your precious Son's name. Amen."*

Awkwardly I turned to face the young couple, shook their hands and hurried out the door. I walked out of the building toward the parking lot, got in my car and drove toward home, thinking mostly about my conversation with Ruben and the events of the day.

Later, I learned from hospital personnel that back in that hospital room, a doctor examined an old Latino woman and turned to a young couple and said, "Good news . . . her fever broke. She's going to be all right."

Chapter 12

I arrived back home, expecting a call from Jill. She'd left no message on my cell. In my mind, she should be settled in at her brother's house, maybe more subdued and relaxed. So, I rushed into the kitchen and went straight to the answering machine to check. No calls. No message from Jill. My first thoughts were for her safety. I wondered if she's had an accident. *No, surely not. Shoot! Do you suppose she's mad at me?* She did appear cool when she left, like she didn't fully appreciate what I was doing with Ruben. I'll call her and make sure.

I decided to call from my cell phone because it was cheaper. I'd left it at home because I did not want any interruptions while dealing with Ruben. In fact, I felt the cell was too convenient for others to catch me and I left it at home most of the time. I tapped in the number to my brother-in-law's house and listened to three rings before pickup.

"Hello."

"Jill....is that you?"

"Yes, Jerod, it's still me."

"What's wrong . . . is something wrong? Why haven't you called?" I queried.

"Oh. . . I just thought I'd let you see how it felt to worry and wait on me for a change." Jill's voice cracked.

"Come on, hon, don't be that way long distance. You know it's too hard to talk on the phone. How's your brother and them?"

"Don't change the subject. They're wondering what's wrong with you." Jill blurted.

"What do you mean, 'what's wrong with me', what did you tell them?"

"Well, I certainly wasn't going to lie and I'm tired of covering up....so I told them the truth."

I groaned. *That's all I need. My whole family thinking I'm nuts.* "Look, Jill, don't you want to just come home early and work this out?"

"Are you still taking the days off to meet with ole Michael?" Jill responded.

"Uh oh, "*what should I say*?" I continued softly, "You know I must follow through with this, Jill . . . once I get started on something. . . what do you want me to say? This has nothing to do with us, I mean, how I feel about you."

"But don't you see . . . it does!" Jill protested.

"I don't get it."

"That's clear," Jill snorted.

"See . . . we're not getting anywhere on the phone. Let's face to face it at home."

"I'll see you at the end of your eight days, Jerod . . . maybe." I heard her bang down the receiver.

I looked at the cell phone in my hand like it personally betrayed me. Touching the off, I pitched it on the counter, shuffled to the living room couch and slouched down. After rerunning the conversation in my head several times, I thought *Ah well, she's a little miffed now, but she'll get over it. It's no big thing. Surely.*

The cell phone rang. I jumped up to retrieve it.

"Jill?"

"No, I'm no Jill or Jack up a hill either...ha...ha. Well, not exactly. It's Ruben. Tomorrow is Thursday. There's a small Carnival on the mall parking lot. Meet me there at nine. I want to show you something. And who knows.... maybe we'll have another lesson."

"Wait, Ruben....at a Carnival?"

"Interesting, huh?" Michael hung up.

Chapter 13

Thursday morning blew in October with the weather hesitating between cool and warm. I liked the in between feeling. I could understand why anyone wanted a carnival this time of year because the weather just begged for attendance.

As I drove into a parking lot, I wore casual clothes, felt like a relaxed person and felt like any other tourist. I parked the car and headed for the main ticket booth.

This time of morning few people were present at the Carnival, but some hearty souls were out meandering among the small booths of concessions and old fashioned midway rides. Men and women, boys and girls could be seen dashing in and out of booths, rides and concession stands. I still admired small towns that let part of school out to go to carnival. It all reminded me of my early youth and made my emotions soften.

A sunbaked, wrinkled-faced older woman sold me my entrance ticket. I told myself I bet she had been with the Carnival all her life and she probably had wonderful stories if a person had time to listen. The ticket turned out to be a shaped-wheel stamp on the back of my hand. For the eight dollars fee and the stamp, I could ride anything in the park. All food, however, cost extra.

Walking through the midway, I looked around for Ruben and finally spotted him over at a booth, throwing baseballs. I snuck slowly up behind him, but before I could speak, he spoke over his shoulder, "Watch this."

Inside the booth, were old-fashioned milk bottles made of wood, painted white and shaped like bowling pins. Three were on bottom, while two stacked on top. Black marks scarred the bottles where baseballs found their mark.

I knew this old game well because as a kid I used to get so frustrated when I couldn't knock down all bottles with the three baseballs allotted. The trick was you had to knock all completely off the platform on which they sat. From the distance you threw, you couldn't tell that the weight of the bottles and the platform being too close to the back wall wouldn't allow most people to wipe them out. You had to hit them just right or one or more would spin and stay on the platform, causing you to lose your dollar. Most contestants tried four or five times, losing four or five dollars in minutes.

The game stayed one of the most lucrative booths in the Carnival, especially when school kids came through, wanting to prove their sportsmanship. Athletic boys wanted to show off their prowess to the girls watching. Occasionally, someone could win, if the person running the booth placed the bottles forward enough, away from the back wall, allowing them to fall more easily through a space between the wall and platform.

Ruben made a windup, just like a pro ball player and let fly. The odd thing though, he threw the ball against the left inside wall of the booth. The ball ricocheted off the side wall, bounced against the back wall like a double pool bank shot, hitting the bottles from the back and knocked them all off the platform toward the front. The attendant stared with his eyes wide and so did I. Ruben laughed as he handed the other two balls left to me and said, "Want to try?"

"Wait a minute," blurted the attendant, "you only get the one because you knocked them all down. That's the rule. Three balls for a dollar...whether you knock them down or not. Now pick your prize and move along. I've got other customers coming."

Evidently, he hadn't intended Ruben to win, I thought.

Ruben pointed to a small, fuzzy black and white Panda bear. The man mumbled what I know wasn't his Sunday school lesson and handed it to Ruben. In turn, Ruben handed the bear to me and we started walking away.

After strolling away from the booth, suddenly, I felt something bump the side of my knee and I looked down at a little boy about four years old, holding onto his mother with one hand and tapping on my knee with the other, then pointing at the Panda. I smiled and looked at Ruben who nodded his head 'yes'. Starting to hand the bear to the boy, I searched the mother's face for permission before I let go of it. She nodded ok and I let go as the child gave off happy little squealing sounds, as he hugged the prized possession.

Michael grabbed my arm and maneuvered me further down the midway. We ambled along, watching people and smelling the familiar odors of popcorn, cotton candy and cheap hot dogs. Then, Ruben stopped and made a hitchhiking gesture, pointing his thumb upward to a medium-sized Ferris wheel behind him. I glanced up at the rotating wheel and frowned. As I turned back to Ruben, I experienced a deep sinking feeling in my stomach.

"You're not expecting us to ride that thing, are you?"

"You got it, oh benevolent one!" Michael jiggled his eyebrows up and down like the comic Jimmy Fallon, imitating the old comic Groucho Marks.

"Wait . . . Ruben, I can't. That thing would make me sick." I could already feel the knot in my lower abdomen. Ever since small childhood, I'd not been able to ride any contraption that went vertically round and round. I could spend hours on a merry-go-round because it moved horizontally, but nothing vertical. I'd not been able to master the sense of falling, even elevators bothered me and I could barely manage escalators only because I felt I could hold on to something solid with the guide rail.

Ruben grabbed my wrist with a super strong vise grip. I flinched. Where did this old man get such strength? Then he guided me to one of the little swinging, bucket seats of the Ferris wheel. Ruben twisted my wrist toward the attendant, allowing him to view my ink stamp. He showed his and then, both of us squeezed in a seat and Michael fastened the safety bar before I could offer another complaint. I grabbed the bar with both hands and sat frozen.

"Try to relax because I want to show you something and I know this is one of the ways to help you see our next lesson." Ruben patted me on the shoulder. "It's ok to hold tight to the bar but relax the rest of your body, take some deep breaths." I found myself doing exactly as Ruben suggested and took a deep breath.

Soon the Ferris wheel gave a jerk and started moving up and around. And of course, we were turning backwards. I felt every muscle stiffen in my neck, shoulders and arms. My stomach rolled. The wheel made one complete round as I gulped short bursts of air and stared straight ahead to fight off nausea, my knuckles looked like white rocks as I gripped the bar.

"Why are you doing this to me, Ruben? I think I'm going to puke." I turned paler as the Ferris wheel moved slowly up again, suddenly, we got right to the top and the wheel stopped. The little bucket rocked back and forth, bile rose in my throat and I almost lost it.

"Hang on," Ruben said, "We'll just sit up here a minute and look out over the Carnival grounds. Look away from your hands, Jerod. Look out toward the rest of the area. Fix your eyes on one object out there and stabilize your vision. Your stomach will settle. Now relax your whole body. . . That's it. . . Now, get the umbrella perspective up here. Glance away from all the movement, people, and things. Focus on a tree out there beyond."

"Feel your body." Ruben said. "You can trust it up here. I'm with you. Think of it as no more than sitting in a large chair. You put faith in an unknown chair when you sit in it. Trust this too. Yield to the new perspective and position. Don't feel so powerless. Even though you feel gravity has changed on you, you still have power because you are still you. Give yourself to the lack of gravity, knowing you still have the power to change this condition. Choose **not** to use this power, but submit yourself to this uncertainty. Give your fear away. Release the thing that traps you."

"Easy for you to say." I moaned. But then suddenly, there was a pop, like a rubber band being stretched and let go quickly, deep down inside me and I literally started to relax. I glanced around the country side, then looked at people below, watching their ant-like movements, seeing everything from above was indeed a different perspective for me. I'd never really looked from this vantage point, but slowly I became fascinated by the view.

I let go of the bar, sat back more in my seat and smiled, feeling more in control than in a long time. The sky around me drifted in puffy little white clouds, a cool breeze brushed my face. As I gave myself over to this event, something like contentment harbored in my soul. I turned to look at Ruben.

"I don't know how you have this changing effect on people, but I really do appreciate this experience. I never would have believed my feeling comfortable up here in a thousand years. It's quite lovely up here and not so bad once I gave into it— like you said."

Gleefully, Ruben clapped his hands together and with a jerk, the wheel started moving in the opposite direction, frontwards. Quickly, I grabbed the bar, grinned at my friend and slowly let go, showing I could ride with no hands. Then I thought: Did He start this thing going again? *Nah . . . just a coincidence. No matter, I'm beginning to like it.*

As soon as the wheel made two more full rounds, it stopped at the bottom landing and the attendant unhooked our bar and we walked away. I stuffed my hands down in my pockets, then walked like a man who'd just conquered my major fear, head and shoulders thrown back and chin thrust forward. I glanced over at Ruben who was shaking his head, no, but gave a sly little grin in my direction. Michael began to weave in and out among some other people nearby and stopped in front of a hot dog vendor. I kept pace with him. He ordered two hot dogs with everything, cold drinks, paid the man and led me to a small bench area to sit down.

"Boy, I never would have thought I could ride one

of those things, let alone eat something afterwards and the truth is I'm starved. This is a good idea you had." I took a bite of the oozing hot dog and all but smacked my lips. Ruben gobbled his down, drank a long time from his drink, threw his trash in a can nearby and spoke in all one movement.

"While you finish your refreshment, let's talk about lesson three."

I started to put down my food and drink and in my mind, tried to shift my thoughts to the seriousness of the parchment symbols.

"No... No ... Don't worry about the parchment symbols now. Finish your food and just try to focus some of your attention on us and block out your surroundings."

I looked startled again. *Could this guy read minds*?

"You know", Ruben continued, "the first century Christians had a lot of distractions too. Their lives were not so simple. They spent most of their time trying to find shelter and food, just for survival in any given day, so they had to learn to stay focused or they didn't live, especially when they had to juggle daily living with the persecution which fell upon them . . . Anyway, I think you are ready to discuss and enter the third kingdom. Do you remember what is commonly known as the third beatitude?"

I surveyed Ruben's face, but kept slowly chewing my food. Then, I took a drink, swallowed and said, "Yeah . . . uh . . . blessed are the meek, for they shall inherit the earth."

"Good show! This is probably one of the most misunderstood principles in all scripture. What do you think it means?"

I looked up at the white, puffy clouds, swallowed hard, and then turned to my friend.

"I think most scholars connect it with the idea of 'turning the other cheek' or operating daily with a quality of kindness, but I've often wondered about that. You have all these sayings today about when good people do nothing the bad take over. There really doesn't seem much place for meekness today because you turn the other cheek and most will take undue advantage of that."

"I didn't ask what others thought. I want to know what **you** think."

"Well . . . as a Christian, I know we are to be kind to each other but I think we should take up for our rights too. You must in this world, don't you think?"

"There", Ruben said, "I think you gave the usual interpretation even though there are still some who think meekness suggests a wimp like condition, a kind of passiveness when it comes to tough ethical issues. 'Blessed are the meek' doesn't mean happy are the uninvolved, for they will be untouched by the hurts of this world."

"Yeah . . . I agree with that . . . so what does meek mean in context?" I asked.

Just about then, two boys about 12 years old, jostled each other, pushed and shoved and ran behind and bumped into me, knocked some of my drink into my lap. Wet liquid leaked onto my pants leg.

Aggravated, I jumped up, frantically brushing at the wet spot. I glared daggers at the boys. Scowling I hollered, "Hey . . . watch it you guys! What do you think you're doing? You could hurt somebody. Where are your parents? Why aren't you in school?" The boys skittered away, looking a little frightened, but one yelled back, "It's school day at Carnival. Where you been old man?"

Ruben smiled. "What are you feeling right now?"

"What do you mean, 'what am I feeling', I'm upset I guess."

"You want to give those boys justice, don't you? Because you feel you have the right and the power."

"I don't know that I think of it that way, but, yeah . . . I want to correct them, and I suppose, put them in their place because they wronged me." I pronounced.

"Good. We can use this about meekness . . . See, true meekness is just the opposite of what you felt. You felt wronged and mistreated by the action and behavior of those boys. You automatically wanted to retaliate . . . set things right, at least what **you** think is right. Your culture has taught you to at once take up for your rights without thinking. It's as automatic as a knee jerk. And yet, Jesus proposed just the opposite. He gave you meekness, a result of the kingdom poor in spirit and kingdom of mourners. These two linked together issue you into the kingdom of meekness . . . it is a **kingdom of yielding**."

"You mean I'm supposed to give up every cause of justice?"

"I didn't say that . . . calm yourself and listen. Get a hold of your reason and step back and look at what I'm saying. I said your **habit** tends to respond with your own kind of justice. It is packed with strong emotion and hard to let go. Jesus calls for Christians to show a different behavior. A person who is saved and keeps a compassion for a lost world must not be threatened by every injustice you may think you see. In fact, true meekness in a person actually means you do have the power to retaliate but you decide to respond a different way."

"I'm not sure I get what you mean?" I protested.

"Meekness contains a willingness to be renounced in spirit **combined with** compassion of service for others. The meek are those who want nothing from this world now, but are willing to share everything because Christ is remaking them into a new species of humans, beings that can show the world a different kind of love."

"Does this mean I'm supposed to forget about my rights?" I queried.

"Your questions are just what the world asks. The truly meek individual can and will waive privileges, not because of weakness, but because of Christ's strength. The greatest example is still Jesus on the cross. Remember, the warrior angels were waiting on the rim of heaven. If Jesus would have said for them to come, they would have come then to avenge Him. But He chose to show what real meekness is, what real love is."

Ruben paused, then continued. "Remember, in our discussion about the cross, I told you that part of the cross meant God was saying 'you may break my back but I will break your heart'. Part of God can waive His right and let others behave in ways they thought right even when wrong. Like the Roman soldier who kept doing his part in the crucifixion, following orders. But then, by watching Jesus' suffering love he finally had to admit that 'surely this was the Son of God'. See . . . Sometimes, you may have to give way to others, not wanting your own way, so you can help others."

"Are you saying even when they're wrong? That's a tough concept in our selfish world." I argued.

"Yes . . . you also must accept that true understanding of God's way is not always the same as consent of another's behavior. For you to understand with meekness is not the same as consenting to some bad behavior. It's as hard as your overcoming the Ferris wheel. Think about it. Until you yielded to my words, the experience, and the bucket we sat in, you were immobilized. The kingdom of meekness resembles that event. You are to yield to the principle, even practice it, until it becomes as much a part of you as the old habit of retaliation. Every chance you get may be an opportunity to rest in the strength of Christ, not having to exert power over anyone. When you can behave humbly, in difficult situations, it gets people's attention. Then when they ask how you can do that, you can tell them and show them Christ in His fullness."

"You mean you took me through all that misery on the Ferris wheel to show me meekness?" I pleaded.

"I had to get you to let go of your old self control. Sometimes it takes a dramatic experience to shake you free from things that trap you. Most people are like that. They want to set up life for total control, so much so some Christians even have a sickness—control addicts. It's a sad state when all the while, Christ gives principles of freedom. Permanent truth sets you free. See . . . how can faith mean much when you place everything in control by simply buying it or organizing it? To be truly meek means you risk some things for Christ, having the faith active enough to know God will take care of things properly. You are also to let someone else become great as you serve them."

"I see what you're saying, but in our modern culture, it's pretty hard to do things like let someone else get positive credit for something you've earned. Is that part of what you're talking about?" I quizzed again.

"That is exactly one place to practice the kingdom

of meekness so to break the habit of always striving for your own interests. Even small cases like letting others get the compliments so they can have greatness, instead of striving for those short- lived ego boosters that are supposed to add something to your worthwhileness. If you are already worthwhile in Christ, you don't need the artificial." Ruben entreated.

This statement stung because I knew how much I often craved **any** compliment from my congregation about my sermons or any other service I might perform. Part of me needed the feedback that said I did a good job. Often, I wondered if something was basically wrong with me for wanting compliments. Ruben's ideas explained very clearly the unrest I felt. I thought: *I'm not truly meek.* And yet, deep down I knew I wanted to be all that Christ wanted, no matter the cost.

"Don't you see, Jerod, why the meek principle must rule and why it will inherit the earth?

"I don't guess I do . . . not entirely."

"Because the people who are truly putting the interests of others above their own are good stewards of what they have and the main thing is . . . you can trust them. You won't have to worry about them being too selfish . . . so . . . they can be trusted to inherit the earth." Ruben started pointing at various people approaching the Carnival booths.

"I never thought of it that way but it makes a lot of sense", I muttered.

"Right you are, now . . . let's walk." Ruben jumped up, grabbing my shirt sleeve, tugging me like you would a child who might try to run away.

We hadn't walked very far and what appeared to be a drunken man staggered into our path. Ruben stepped quickly to one side but I responded more slowly. The man bumped head on into me, nearly knocking me down. Roughly, I grabbed the man.

"Hey . . . watch it," I snarled, "you ought to be ashamed." Then I stopped abruptly, glanced over at Ruben and back to the man. "Uh . . . sorry sir, I guess I didn't see where I was going."

The man looked at me with hazy eyes, grinned and staggered on his way.

"Boy, that's one of the hardest things I've ever done", I sighed.

"I know, but you can see now why most must practice with every little experience they can; otherwise, you form the habit of **reacting** instead of **yielding**." Ruben tapped his index finger to his head like some school teacher teaching young children.

"So . . . does this mean I must give in to everybody?"

"Boy, it's sort of all or nothing with you, isn't it? You must remember, you still have the power to respond with what you think is justice, but you are giving the Holy Spirit more opportunity when you don't feel you must use that power all the time . . . whether with words or action. You give the Holy Spirit a chance to filter your actions more by not automatically responding with your cultural sense of correctness. All the little things **do** matter, Jerod. Why do you think Jesus talked about the small effort of giving a cup of water in His name? Or, the scripture talks about caring for even the little sparrows. How you respond to people with words or deeds can affect the kingdom tremendously. Remember, Christ is the all in all. That means God is in control of the accumulative effect of everything, so, everything you do is part of the accumulation."

"Do you really mean to say that everything I do is important to God?" I suggested.

"Everything you **are** is important to God. Your 'doingness' should come out of your 'beingness'. Unfortunately, this world has it backwards. Too many people are defined by what they do or don't do. For instance, some stranger may see you and ask another who you are. The answer will be, 'oh...he's the pastor of Restoration Church . . . see . . . telling what you do. God is more concerned who you really are in relation to Him. If your authentic self, your true essence is on target, your behavior will follow likewise. In this money conscious America, people are conditioned from childhood that they must grow up, get a good job, make good money and become somebody. This is a backwards philosophy. You are somebody when you're born, especially when born of God."

We walked slowly toward the exit gate. I took a deep breath, smelling the mustiness of the Carnival mingled with the odor of food. With great conscious effort, I blocked out my surroundings, and slowly began to daydream, considering all that happened. I did feel refreshed, not tired at all, wondering why I didn't feel more exhausted. Delighted in the renewed experience, I marveled in my spirit at this strange little man, so full of wisdom and knowledge.

I entered one of those longer day-dream states for several minutes, mentally chewing on fact and experiences of the last few days. Finally, becoming aware of my surroundings again, I turned to ask some questions about Ruben's educational background.

I viewed blank air. Startled, I looked around thinking I might have wandered off course from Ruben. My companion vanished again. I looked right and left, among the people leaving the area. I rushed to the parking lot, thinking Ruben might have walked on ahead. Nothing. There was no question. Michael had the uncanny ability to disappear in the most obvious circumstances.

I made my way to the car and started a slow drive home. At least, I didn't feel so perplexed as usual. Maybe Ruben's disappearances were becoming the norm and perhaps, I grew more used to his comings and goings, remembering what the man said about shaking my perspective to get my attention. It certainly worked so I didn't feel so childlike anymore, at least not this time. Maybe I'm learning some meekness, I thought, as I drove unconsciously down the road. Soon, I pulled into my driveway and entered my house. I hurried to the answering machine to check messages. The red light blinked. I pushed the play button, hoping it was Jill.

The voice blasted unmistakably. "**Meet me at the public library** tomorrow at ten. The adventure continues. Don't be late!" Ruben laughed and coughed so hard, the speaker phone risked being blown. Quickly, I switched off the answering machine.

I groaned when I thought about another agonizing, slow night of waiting, another night of what the old timers called extended journey pride and no phone call from Jill. I reached for my cell and tapped in her number. Her voice mail chimed. So, I texted: "Miss u. Love u much. Call when u can. Have good nite"

Chapter 14

Friday morning, I dressed and shuffled into the kitchen, opened the freezer, took out two frozen doughnuts, pitched them into the microwave and hit the thaw button. My automatic coffee maker wheezed its last perk and soon I sat watching the News, munching doughnuts and sipping hot coffee. My mind didn't focus much on the events of television; I simply needed the noise since Jill was gone. I thought about her absence and began talking to myself. *Should I call her or just let her cool down awhile? Maybe it would be best to let things be for now. I can't do what she wants anyway.* I can't stop seeing Ruben.

A big part of me wondered what would happen if I took Jill with me to see Ruben at this stage. He may not like it and quit talking even to me. He might just disappear altogether. Several of these thoughts convinced me I'd better not involve her at this point. I figured surely, she would understand once I explain when it's over. She's probably pouting a little, but maybe having a good time at her brother's anyway. *Yeah, I'll just let things be*, I sighed.

I looked at my watch. Time before my ten o'clock appointment at the library with Michael, so I pulled out the copy of the parchment and began to gaze at the symbols. I looked at the loaf of bread. As far as I knew, the next section to be covered must be "blessed are they which do hunger and thirst after righteousness, for they shall be filled." I moved over and stood in front of my bookcase, surveying my section of several Bible translations. I always made sure I stocked my personal library with any new translation printed and I had one of the best collections of any minister in town. Soon, I gathered some other standard translations and began noting the different word usage. One version said, "For they shall be satisfied." I thought what an uplifting and wonderful thing it would be to be satisfied.

Then, I peered closer at the un-translated symbols on the parchment. That first century Christian writer, Clarissa, had drawn what looked like a king washing some people's feet. I remembered my discussion with Ruben yesterday about yielding, especially about letting others be great instead of taking credit yourself or letting others have the right to be wrong. But now, what I saw was a connected set of bread loaves and what looked like a person pouring well water into three cups. Obviously, these related to hunger and thirst, but what did they really mean?

Of course, anyone who truly wanted the knowledge of God should hunger and thirst after Him. But what did the chain link from the king to bread mean? Was it just symbolic metaphor to confuse non-Christians? I knew the first century Christians used codes to baffle their enemies, but did Clarissa and others do so good a job masking the truths meant for everyone?

My heart raced as I thought about Ruben Having the answers and being willing to share them. I hurriedly closed the Bibles, placing them back on the shelf. I placed the parchment copies back in the folder. I scrambled out the door, heading for the public library, wondering what Ruben had for today.

After circling the block twice, looking for a parking spot, I pulled up in front of the library, smiling to myself. I wished the library really was this busy with people wanting books, but the truth was, the building sat next door to a wholesale clothing store whose shoppers took most of the parking spaces. I mumbled, *People were always more interested in bargain clothes than bargain books.*

I hurried through two large glass doors and looked around for Ruben. I spotted him sitting over at a large oak table, leafing through the periodicals. Ruben looked like a wealthy senior citizen, dressed in a purple jogging suit, complete with purple running shoes.

"Good morning, Mr. Michael. You look like you're ready to run the course." I joked.

"It's the color of royalty, you know." Quickly, Ruben pushed back his chair, stood in a pose that looked like the weight lifters do and started walking back and forth, stopping to make little gestures of his muscles, like a male model. I grinned and started to sit down.

"Not here. Let's move over to the book reading section." Ruben nudged me playfully.

The center of this large library formed an egg-shaped room. A person entering took three steps down and found himself in a sitting area. The ceiling and roof structure displayed unusual see-through Plexiglas so the outside light glowed through softly. The walls were padded with sound absorbing carpet. Earth-tone colored chairs and couches scattered around for easy access. Abundant lighting flooded the area.

Some practical thinking library committee must have won out on this idea. Better to try to contain the readers and talkers than to overly enforce the rule of silence. It worked amazingly well. Even the children appeared to behave themselves in this environment maybe because of the unique atmosphere.

We stepped down into the quiet area and sat on a soft, cushy love seat. Across the room, a woman softly finger-read to her small child. On another couch, an older man and woman sat reading intently. Across from them, a gray-haired woman sat and hurriedly flipped through a magazine. Even with these occupants, the room looked spacious and airy.

"This is more like it," Ruben intoned, rubbing his hands together and stared up at the transparent ceiling. My eyes trailed Ruben's to see where he looked.

"Kind of makes you think of a cathedral, don't it, pardner?" Ruben stared back at me.

"In a way, I suppose."

"Relax; man . . . Why do you imagine the real reason libraries came into existence?" Ruben asked.

I peered at my friend. "Well . . . I guess . . . I suppose it might have been a poor man's way of getting to experience books, since early in publishing, the average man couldn't afford to buy them. On the other hand, I don't suppose the poor could have been the ones to get libraries started. But, I guess I don't know the exact reason. Do you?"

"Of course, . . . they were started because of humanity's hunger and thirst for knowledge." Ruben made a playful gesture of spoon feeding himself.

"Well, yeah, but I thought you meant what was the specific reason."

"Don't you think it's strange with all the Christians in the world, there does not exist a system like free Christian book libraries for the public?"

"Well . . . there is, sort of. Our church has a library and so do many others." I shot back.

"Ah . . . but how many outside your church membership use or even feel they can use your library, like the public ones? If you did a survey of all churches that had libraries, I imagine none would have the community at large checking out books on a regular basis. Why do you trust that is?"

"I never thought of it that way, but you're right I'm sure. I guess most churches have experienced losing books so they feel they can only trust their own membership."

"*Perhaps there's a deeper reason,*" Ruben whispered so low I strained to hear him.

"*What is it?* I whispered back and glanced over at the other people in the room to see if something happened to cause the whispering. All the other people looked up from their reading and stared at Michael. He just grinned and spoke back in a natural voice.

"See . . . everyone hungers after knowledge." As soon as Ruben spoke, all the other heads in the room quickly looked down in unison and resumed reading again. "It all depends on how things are presented."

"Yeah, well, there is certainly a difference in hungering after gossip." I retorted.

"Yes, but don't you see. When we spoke to each other in our natural voices, no one paid much attention, but when I lowered my voice, it got attention. There exists so much noise in the world many have learned to turn off true listening until some dramatic change occurs to get their attention."

"But I don't see what you're getting at?"

"Why do you think those people over there are **really** browsing through printed material, searching, searching, searching?" Michael licked his thumb, quickly turning imaginary pages of a book.

Then he continued, "They have a built-in hunger for knowledge. They aren't just bored, but if you asked them, they probably would tell you they're doing it to have something to do or because they like it. But this is just a result of the deeper yearning. They forget they are made with an appetite to learn. But it's gotten off track. The noise of the world became the 'hungering and thirsting after knowledge'. People switched off the true yearning by searching after world knowledge only. And yet, the Bible says to hunger and thirst after righteousness or God. This is my point about the libraries also. Your world does not have true Christian libraries because it has lost its hunger and thirst after God . . . if it ever had such." Ruben beamed.

"What do you mean **my** world?"

"Your Church world. It has become too insulated and missed the point. It has turned in upon itself. Like the old preacher said 'saved, sanctified and satisfied'. Part of your task is to start a revolution and shake them out of ease."

"What . . . wait . . . did you say revolution?" I looked horrified. "Oh . . . do you mean . . . uh, do you mean something like start a system of Christian libraries?"

"Not especially . . . but that wouldn't be a bad idea. No, keep in mind we are thinking about the revolutionary ideas Jesus started with his teaching on the mount and we are ready for lesson four."

"Oh", I blinked.

"I suppose you looked at Clarissa's symbols?" Ruben stared.

"Yes, but I only understood some obvious about the king washing feet and the cups of water. . . I mean, how they must relate to the fourth beatitude of hungering, thirsting."

"Good show, let's stay with the obvious awhile. Remember I told you that all the principles of the Sermon, the nine, can be linked together? I want you to understand this linking a little more. The truth is they are also linked together by threes and as three get hooked up properly, they can build a foundation for those that come after."

"I'm not sure I follow", I puzzled.

"Let me put it to you this way. The first kingdom of need was the renounced in spirit, gaining heaven. The second kingdom sorrow of mourners gains Holy Spirit comfort. The third kingdom of yieldingness was meekness, gaining the earth. These three form a link, a foundation for the beginning of the next three kingdom principles. What would you guess is the link with need, sorrow, and yielding?"

I thought a minute, then blurted, "Hey, they all must do with the individual's response to the power of God . . . I think."

"Sometimes you do amaze me with right thinking, but then, you must've had divine help with that answer. You are correct. They are stages of a person's inner self journey with God. These are like the child stages of growth— crawling, walking, and talking. Everyone must go through them to reach any kind of maturity. They are all kingdom cycles, meaning you may have to do some of one before you move on to the next cycle."

"How does one know when a cycle is completed?" I asked.

"It's not unlike what happens with a child. How does a child know to move from crawling to walking? Some of it is a natural progression, the child just senses it's time to try something else and makes the move to stand up."

"Do you mean a Christian's growth is all natural?" I asked.

"No, but the supernatural Holy Spirit tries to make it natural. But first there is a choice, awareness, a decision— whatever you want to call it. Natural growth must come from the person's need to join a partnership with the Holy Spirit. Then you can choose the next kingdom and practice there until the principle becomes imbedded so it becomes a part of your automatic response. Then, you can respond with God's principle more times than you do the negative opposite."

"Huh?" I responded wide-eyed.

Ruben reached over and tapped me over my heart. "The particular kingdom principle, like compassionate sorrow, becomes a natural part of your subconscious emotional makeup, just like ambition or love is. Those qualities are always down underneath your awareness, wanting to express themselves when given a chance. Because they are down deep, people can easily forget them, get out of practice. It takes some event, some reminder to wake them up. The Holy Spirit uses all kinds of things to wake up people . . . even you."

"Ouch . . . but I think I see . . . like you can actually practice and learn to respond with meekness more times than you respond with self ambition. Does a person get perfectly natural in every cycle before moving on to the next?" I questioned.

"There is none perfect but one. You don't just move through the principles one right after another. I mean, you might, but with a given occasion, you might jump say from some mourning to our lesson today, hunger and thirst. See, you would have skipped a little kingdom of meekness. But, that's ok. I'm just suggesting that if you can move through the nine kingdoms, three at a time, you will find a chain link that helps build a better habit."

"But what if I get stuck, say, in hunger and thirst? I asked.

"Then, you might go back and practice more meekness. The truth is you will slip sometime. But if the good habit has developed like the chain-link, you will know it the second you do and with God's help, make the necessary adjustment. Even though at times you may feel alone, you are never alone. The Holy Spirit, remember, stays a built-in sensor, registering when you stray, if you are paying attention. The truly growing person works hard at paying attention."

I shifted in my seat and turned more facing Ruben. "Ok, but I'm thinking now about people who seem stuck in the poor in spirit, salvation experience . . . you know, they haven't grown much in twenty years. You would probably say they were spinning around in the kingdom of need. How come they stayed locked in that cycle and never moved on?"

Michael quickly began to grab invisible containers and mix them together like pouring flour and sugar together for a cake. "There may be as many reasons as why certain children don't mature through their stages properly, like parents doing too much **for** the child and children feeling pleasure to stay the way things are. Sometimes churches make it too easy for their members by avoiding certain challenges to risk. Jesus introduced a peculiar quality with his kingdom principle . . . commanding people to move through cycles of distinction. You are to go a different way than the world goes."

"Yeah, I can see that. Like instead of always dishing out human justice, we're to work at serving up mercy. So, people can get stuck in any of the cycles if they're not careful?" I inquired.

"You got it Einstein. Go to the head of the class," Michael chuckled.

I felt my face turn flush, although I knew Ruben teased me, yet I still was never quite ready for those zinger remarks.

"See that woman over there, flipping through a magazine?" Ruben pointed. "She comes here and does that nearly every day. Why do you suppose she does that?" Ruben kept nodding his head in her direction like his head was stuck in a head jerk.

"How do you know that?" I probed.

"Trust me, I know. You see she's stuck in a rut. The truth is even small unwillingness to take little risks can slow down one's growth for full living. She has given in to the familiar and thinks she's secure. Yet, her life has become dull and she feels useless and unloved. She needs a little push, a nudge toward new challenges that can enrich her life, so she searches things like magazines. Come on. Let's stroll around the library." Ruben sprang up like an athlete, grabbing my arm, almost jerking me up from the seat.

He weaved in and out of the stacks of books like a person hunting for a lost treasure. He clasped his hands behind his back and bent and bobbed between rows like a chicken looking for a hidden worm. Section after section, he glanced and touched the books. I followed feeling childlike and lost. Soon, we came to the section of paperback mysteries. Ruben pointed to a man browsing.

"He's stuck on mysteries", Ruben whispered and kept walking.

I glanced at the well-dressed man who looked to be about fifty years old. *"So, what if he is"*, I whispered a little perturbed.

"Do you know why people read mysteries like eating candy?"

"I'm sure you're going to tell me", I said a little too surly.

"Don't be huffy, ole son, you're still learning here. People like mysteries because they're safe. It is one of the few fiction categories that still can show a clear moral. The good guys are usually good and the bad guys are usually bad. You'd be surprised how many Christians like to read even murder mysteries and yet you'd think because you're against killing, you wouldn't like to read a murder mystery. But you do because you can trust the clear-cut moral. When the bad guy murderer gets caught and if the book is any good, he or she always does, the law is fulfilled of 'thou shalt not kill'. See . . . it's black or white, neat."

"So, what does this do with the fourth lesson you were going to talk about?" I exclaimed.

"Oh, pardon, I guess I was still trying to impress upon you that people are hungry and they will fill that hunger in the wrong places, but they are going to fill it.

They will search for truth in error if they aren't searching for truth in truth."

Ruben started maneuvering his way back to the sitting lounge by darting in and out of the library stacks. I felt reprimanded but obediently trailed along, the best I could, without appearing too childlike.

Finally arriving at the sitting room, no sooner had we sat back down in the step-down room, the man from the mystery section came in behind us and sat across in plain sight. I felt somehow Ruben must have willed the man to come in just as a reminder to me who the teacher still was and who was in control. I had better not forget that.

"You've got to cut me some slack, Ruben. Sometimes I get impatient, and well, this is all still rearranging my world. I do see a lot of what you're telling me and though I don't know how you got so wise, my spirit is with you and I want to learn all I can. You just need to give me more time sometimes to assimilate. Everything seems to go so fast."

"We don't have time to waste, Jerod. You only have the eight days remember?"

"What's going to happen then?" I asked alarmed.

Ruben stared sternly at me. I couldn't help but shudder as an electrical shock traveled from back of my neck down my spine to the back of my heels. Then Michael softly giggled and wiggled his fingers at me like a magician waving a wand. "Wouldn't you like to know in advance?"

I shook off the feeling. "Well, of course I would like to know the future."

"Can't do that. You owe me the full eight days."

I shivered again and looked at my feet.

He continued. "You are so used to filling the cravings of hunger and thirst that they have lost their dynamic in your culture. You get hungry you eat. You get thirsty you drink. Not much trouble when you live in a world with a fast food place on every corner. But in Jesus' time, most days centered on getting enough food to survive the day, the hunger and thirst desire stayed foremost in people's mind because of the physical inconveniences to find food. Hunger and thirst are still the strongest of needs. You just don't concern yourself about thinking of them until your body signals you."

Suddenly, I felt my stomach growl. I grinned at Ruben.

Michael just continued. "So, Jesus used what showed priority of the moment, hunger and thirst, to set up his next set of building blocks in his teaching, to show the **Kingdom of Appetite**. And so, our Savior proposes a higher level of desire. Instead of an appetite for the basics of this world, you are to have an appetite for righteousness, following the things of God. In other words, seek truth, so much that if you were to fail at this on a given day, you would have spiritual hunger pains and a growling for spiritual thirst."

Ruben faked drinking from a glass and patted his stomach. "The seeking should become so natural, you would go through withdrawal symptoms in your spirit if you missed a single day of searching after God. And just as there are different food groups for the body, there are different food groups for the spirit, falling under the righteous category. Part of your search is to discover those groups for the spirit and partake in healthy ways. Too many Christians have the wrong spiritual diet. They do not have a balanced intake."

"What are those food groups for the spirit?" I asked.

"Have you ever wondered why the Scripture uses food references so much for the spiritual? Why the Apostle Paul wrote so much about the body, comparing it to the church? Why the parables often use food, especially fruits or plants, as vehicles to teach some truth? And by the way, Jesus used the parabolic teaching method more than any. Parables have hidden messages . . . the kind of thing you like."

"So, what are the spiritual food groups?" I repeated.

"For now, just think of the fruit of the Spirit in Galatians 5, you know things like love, joy, patience. Don't get off track here. I want you to be sure to get the principle of the kingdom of appetite not just rules. You mustn't skip anything. This is the whole point. You must take each step of the kingdoms one at a time. Jumping around can cause confusion in the Christian world. People have tried to avoid the growth factors. For instance, individuals have been taught they are to hunger and thirst after God but they have not grown enough in yieldedness or submission. They try to jump from the kingdom of Sorrow to Appetite, skipping the Yield realm and it doesn't work; they're in such a hurry . . . No . . . Don't try to avoid the growth or try to make these stages too easy. Let them happen one at a time, at the pace God chooses for you. Ok?"

"I'm trying, Ruben, but my head is spinning with questions. I see much of what you're saying relates to issues I've thought about for years and I've had to live with the non-answers."

"But isn't that a good definition of what faith is, Jerod . . . the ability to live with the non-answers?"

"Yes, it is . . . but I'm saying, you seem to have some

explanations of things I've wondered about over the years. That's all I meant."

"Well, oh student of mine, I know you mean well, but sometimes you don't know your own selfhood or what it is you mean. Right?"

"I suppose you're correct. I was just trying to say, I don't think I have the wrong motives when I may think what you consider a stupid question."

"I will never question your motives Jerod, only your values." Michael wiggled both his ears and then his eyebrows up and down.

I sighed and slowly nodded yes.

"Now to continue, the kingdom of appetite starts the beginning building block for the second set of three expressions for Christian growth. The hunger and thirst are the two energies which push you toward something. Just as certain engines thrust a space vehicle toward outer space, the hunger and thirst thrust you toward what?"

"The scripture says righteousness." I answered.

"Correct-e-Mundo! Ah . . . but what kind of righteousness?"

"God's kind, I suppose."

"Yes and no . . . for you see . . . it's not what you call imputed righteousness, the kind given to you by the Grace of God, what God did in Christ, although that's involved. It's more of an overall effect of righteousness which covers a method of growth happening in humans. Now listen up very closely. I want you to see the course of action very clearly."

"I'll try. I think I'm following so far." I admitted.

Just then a ray of sunlight filtered through the clear plastic ceiling, sending a perfect circular beam surrounding us, as if on a cue from above, someone turned on a bright spotlight. The event was so dramatic; I looked around to see if anyone else noticed. I blinked at the others in the room for they seemed to be frozen in time. Then I glanced back at Ruben who continued as if nothing happened.

"Here's how the practice goes . . . on a given occasion, you feel **not right** with God. This discovery causes some distress in your inner being and strips away stubbornness, and then the Holy Spirit shows you've missed the point about one of God's guidelines. Then comes this longing after the things of God, to know His ways better. He shows you that right doing is really what you hunger for so you leap at it and find it fits your need. This action creates more hunger for right doing in Jesus. As a forgiven and pardoned person in Christ, you now want to be right in conduct, language and thought. So, I'm really talking here about a kind of integrity, a road that starts you onto certain values."

"Is this how we get our value system worked out about the self?" I asked.

"Not only do you value the true self . . . that's the first three beatitudes, but then you value seeing other people finding true selfhood. So, you yearn for others to experience what appears right and free. This right is not only a sense of moral right, but right in the sense of accuracy, being more correct about living the God kind of life. Remember, you are made in the image of God and even though you sinned, missed the mark, got off track and back on again, the right life for Christians continues one which searches after God. After all, God in Christ is the permanent reality."

"So . . . my young friend . . . this correctness, this

right, this Godly person, hungers and thirsts after a kind of righteousness that includes other people as well as self. See, the journey has changed. Before, it was an inner pilgrimage only . . . now . . . it's an inner **and** outer journey"

"That explains why Christians become other centered, but why do many seem to remain selfish?" I asked perplexed.

"One reason is like I said before. They are stuck in one of the first three kingdoms, usually number one. Of course, there are blockers of growth in each kingdom, challenges which need overcoming," Ruben drew an imaginary sword again and started play fighting." Just like the need to fight off a mythical dragon. The false self throws up a dragon and stays active, throwing up obstacles, barriers which slow down or stop growth. Jesus mentions several disrupters in Matthew 6 through 7:6."

"That makes sense. So, our part is to have appetite after God by yielding, then God gives us the spiritual energy to fight the dragon, but we still must do battle and most are stuck because why? They don't want to do battle?" I queried.

"It's hard to do unselfish prayer when you're surprised or frightened, isn't it? That's because you still try to overcome discomfort with some pleasure principle. It doesn't work with fighting dragons, when you try to mix this world's pleasure principle with the kingdom principles and this leads you to **avoid** the real struggles needed for growth. Most tend to want to run when facing a dragon or upcoming pain. The real challenge is to remain faithful in things like prayer, even when you hurt."

Suddenly, Michael pantomimed eating, tasting and

slurping from a plate of food, then he jerked his head up like feeling some emergency, grabbed and made a movement like drawing a sword, shrugged his shoulders, changed his mind, slid the sword back in its scabbard and started eating again, smacking after every bite.

"Ok . . . I get it . . . avoidance huh . . . I guess that's it. I know people in my church avoid all kinds of things. What is avoidance anyway? Is it a lack of courage? Is it fear?" I commented out-loud.

Ruben hesitated, tapping his chin with an index finger. . . "It's a spin-off of blaming. If you can blame someone or something else, then it's not your fault and you can avoid the truth. Avoidance is just the opposite of truth. It's another way people have of trapping themselves. Trapped people are not free people. And remember why Jesus said one reason he came?"

"Yeah . . . to set the captives free. Hey, Ruben . . . that'll make a good sermon."

"Don't lose it boy. You'll have plenty of thought food for sermons later."

"Oh, right chief", I saluted.

Ruben grinned and continued. "So here is the final point: those of you who yearn for right thinking and right doing, flavored with a seeking desire to know God more intimately, will . . . I repeat **will** . . . be filled with a God kind of contentment. And yet, at the end of this journey, there is a huge dragon to block your way. Many have ended growth here because they have misinterpreted the contentment. The dragon appears beautifully disguised and plants a misrepresented self-righteousness in the road. Many have fallen for it."

"By the way", Ruben continued, "another part of your job will be to strip away the deceit, uproot the error and shed true light for others to see how truly ugly this dragon is."

"Whoa . . . what are some other dragons that get in the way? I puzzled.

"Well, that is another lesson beckoning for later. I think it's a good idea you go now and get you some lunch. While you eat, think clearly about what we've covered. Let it sink in slowly like a warm hot bath. Then meet me in the park at two o'clock. See ya."

Ruben shoved me up off the couch and pointed me toward the door. I glanced to see if others in the room were looking at us. No one noticed. Pleading with my eyes for more information, I turned back to face Ruben. My mentor started drawing an imaginary sword again, jabbing it toward me, and pointing toward the exit. Finally, I gave in. It was time to go whether I liked it or not. I shuffled out of the reading room toward the library exit, jamming my hands in my pockets and thought, *at least Ruben didn't disappear on me this time.*

Chapter 15

The sun reflected off a chrome bumper from a high-back pickup truck and struck me in the eyes as I drove home. I thought about some hundred miles to the west, any traveler moving through the Wichita Mountains of Oklahoma could look at the sky and not distinguish between the clouds and the tips of those balding mountain tops. The dark gray of the mountains matched the dark gray clouds which could spill moisture quickly, causing small water ponds to rise an inch or so and dry grass to gasp at the cool drink. The deluge might be welcomed by all, except perhaps the Texans, who always thought the downpour passing through their dry country should stay there and not travel on into the southwestern border of another state. But today in Restoration, Oklahoma, I didn't mind the sun because the sky turned bright blue with only intermittent puffy white clouds.

Finally, I pulled into my driveway, jumped from the car, rushed into my kitchen and slung together a sliced turkey sandwich, all the while thinking about Ruben's discussion of hunger and thirst. In my mind, no question about it, these were still extremely strong cravings, even in a modern world of plenty. I bolted down the last bite of sandwich and finished off the last of my drink.

Then it hit me: I should give Jill another call. On the kitchen wall phone, I punched in the number. The line to my brothers-in-law rang once, then twice, five times, no answer. Alarm washed over me, but then I calmed, thinking perhaps they'd just gone out for a long lunch. I hung up, crumpled my napkin and drink can, then opened a cabinet door under the sink and threw the paper in one trash container and the can in another for recycling. Both were filled to overflowing and my new pile of trash hit the discarded pile of kitchen refuge and clunked to the floor. *Oh man, I must empty those sometime.* I don't know why these things always get so full so fast. Seems like I empty them every other day. Jill will be more upset with me if I leave the house messed too much. I'd better take care of it now.

I fumbled the full plastic bags out of their containers, jerked the ties together, feeling irritated. I don't know why I hate taking out trash so much. It isn't like I had to do it growing up. I didn't do it at all. *Hey, maybe that's it.* I never had to as a kid and now, it always feels like an interruption.

I lifted the bags and headed out the back door, storing the aluminum can bag in the recycle bin and taking the trash to the alley garbage containers. While I wrestled with the lid and tossed in the trash bag, I wondered what was going on in Arkansas.

I would not know until later that at her brother's house in Arkansas, Jill had let the phone ring twice when I called and quickly hung up and thought: *Not this time. I don't like playing games but I'm not going to be the one who apologizes first.* Anguish would cross her face, but she held her resolve. She would argue with herself and conclude that I must wait. She would rub her forehead, take a deep breath and walk back to the living room to visit with her sister-in-law. There they would quickly view their newly purchased items from the mall.

In the meantime, I hurried back from my trash ministry into the house and stopped abruptly. *Was that the phone?* I listened intently. Nothing. I passed it off and moved to the kitchen sink, glancing at the phone machine. No light blinking. I picked up my cell and saw no missed messages.

I stared a minute out the kitchen window at a red bird perched on one of our trees. Then, I washed my hands, dried them on a hanging dish towel and ambled into the den, easing down into my favorite recliner.

Time enough to rest before my next meeting with Michael, I thought. I looked at my watch. One o'clock . . . an hour to rest. My eyes fluttered closed, my breathing slowed. Soon a pooing sound sputtered from my lips as my body sank to unconsciousness. Thirty minutes later, I woke with a jerk, feeling I'd overslept, looked at my watch. Hastily I went into the bathroom, used it, washed my hands and face, brushed my teeth and scurried out the house to my meeting in the park.

As I drove, it occurred to me that Ruben hadn't given specific instructions **where** in the park to meet, so I drove into the north entrance and slowly eased around the circular road that traversed the whole park. Gazing left and right, I searched the surroundings. It was not a large park and not too many people were there. One older man was walking a white poodle, neatly wearing a pink ribbon around its neck. What appeared to be a Native American family picnicked at a park table.

I kept driving and looking and suddenly realized I came close to where I visited my favorite red-oak tree. I gaped as I approached the area, for scattered close to the base of the giant tree were two sleeping bags and paraphernalia of the homeless. I spotted Ruben, apparently talking to two men. Still dressed in his purple running outfit, he had something in his hand, passing it over to the men.

I parked the car, got out and walked closer to see what was happening. As I approached, I saw what Michael had been giving the men were new pairs of socks, neatly wrapped in clear plastic containers. I stood with my hands on my hips watching closely. Soon, the men scurried to gather their belongings, which weren't many, and shuffled over about thirty yards away and sat down on the ground. They began to take off their battered shoes and put on their newly found wealth.

Ruben turned to me, "You know, the poor are always with you."

"Yes, I know. It's one of the issues that disturbs me most. And sometimes these aren't just the poor, but mentally dysfunctional individuals who used to be able to get hospital care. Our system has let them down." I anguished.

"You are right there . . . but those two aren't mentally impaired, they are capable men who are out of work and can't find any because they're in their fifties. They have no families left who have faith in them, no usual support systems. No one wants to hire them because of their age and what employers think are risks. Of course, the companies won't say that. Those men have rich experience but keep getting told they're over qualified."

"Yeah . . . they're so qualified they end up in the park, like beggars." I spat.

"Why do you suppose church people aren't helping more?" Ruben asked.

"Man, you sure know how to hurt a guy. I've been after my church members for years to help more with this issue, but about all they do is have this benevolent fund. And it's so strict and watched by a committee that very little help gets out there. They are so afraid someone will rip them off and I understand that. But my goodness, they've gotten scared of their own shadows. I gave up on that issue a long time ago. No use trying to whip a dead horse to run faster."

Michael motioned me to follow him to the bench by my tree. He sat down and patted the space next to him. I slouched down and looked up at the tree branches.

"Your society and church have truly reaped what they've sown." Ruben remarked.

"I've often felt that myself, but what do you mean exactly?"

"More and more, a lack of love lives in your world, even in your church. Oh, love is dished out to those who respond back with love—like kind to like kind. If people look acceptable, dress properly, smell right—they get love in church. But church people have lost their ability to handle diversity in a loving manner. What would happen in your church if someone stood up some service and admitted openly to some sin . . . say stealing, and asked the church's help and forgiveness?"

"Well I would like to think some would respond truly in love, but I must admit, many would be horrified and shun the person. They may not be rude, but their opinion of that person would change dramatically to a negative view."

Ruben razed his brows and pointed his thumb like a hitchhiker directly at the red oak tree. "And yet doesn't the scripture clearly teach Christians are to **confess** their faults to each other in love?"

I flinched at the gesture but knew in my heart what Ruben meant by it. I, myself, had only been able to confess to an oak tree, let alone some person. I puzzled how Ruben was aware of this fact. No one should know, not even Jill.

"I know the book of James . . . I think it's 5:16 . . . talks about confessing for healing" I stammered.

"Would you want to venture a guess why people are not living a clear mandate of the scriptures? Why they seem to ignore this truth?" Ruben queried.

"I think I can give several reasons, like being afraid of image or thinking their sins are only between God and them or not really having a place in the church service to have confidential confession . . . but I don't know which answer you want." I speculated.

"All those reasons may be facts but they are just the symptoms of something much deeper. There is a reason and it's as deep as any tap root of that great old oak."

"If you want me to think symbolically, then I would say it has to do with something about a root process. Let's see . . . roots feed the tree . . . so Christians must not be getting the right food." I beamed.

"You are getting better and you are mostly right. Think about the next beatitude we need to consider. What is it?"

"Oh yeah, blessed are the merciful for they shall . . .

Uh . . . they shall . . . get back mercy, something like that. I can't recall the last part right now."

"A true confession . . . refreshing . . . *for they shall obtain mercy.*" Michael answered mildly. "And this suggests the realm of the next kingdom."

"Hey, I think every Christian knows we are supposed to be kind, gentle hearted. We've heard those words in Sunday school since we were children."

"Yes, but don't you consider it strange that most put on their kind faces and gentle spirits just on Sunday. Then, through the week, they take on the same aggressive behavior as non-Christians? Christian business men are just as ruthless in business. Mothers yell and treat their children like pets instead of little people. Fathers treat their wives and children like interlopers. Then on Sunday, everyone wraps themselves in fine clothed packages and present themselves at church like they have lived in a kindly manner all week. Isn't this sham and pretense perplexing to you?"

"Sure, as a pastor, I've certainly been bothered by that. I feel like my sermons often don't get anywhere, but occasionally, I see someone really grow and I feel like it's all been worth it. I suspect the little bit of hope keeps me going."

"But what do you think would happen if you had **the right word . . .** such power in words to move many more into living authentic lives?"

"Hey, Ruben . . . you give me the formula and we'll bottle and sell it." I laughed.

"I am giving you the formula . . . if you're listening. Remember, what you think of as formula is really a progression, steps linked to each other to help you become something based on beingness and not just doingness."

"Ok, ok. Can't I joke a little too . . . Uh . . . right? Ok, this morning at the library you said something about coming to a big dragon to fight after traveling through the first four kingdoms. Did you want to tell me what that meant or did you want me to guess? I mean, when you said it, I admit, my heart flopped some. It sounded scary."

"Well, well . . . I'm glad to see you **are** learning to listen some. Yes, I said the dragon exists as misrepresented self-righteousness. For you see, after you travel through the kingdoms of need, compassion, yieldedness—you come to the realm of appetite, the first of the next trilogy of kingdoms. When you work your way through appetite and truly receive the correct flavor of righteousness, the dragon appears to tempt you into self-righteousness. This happens because you do feel some contentment about being correct and on God's side. The hidden dragon of false self comes in to capture that feeling of contentment and make it its own. Instead of God contentment, it becomes self-contentment, a misdirected self-righteousness."

"So, it's like what happens to people's attitude when they want to give out their kind of justice at any cost—like the Pharisees in the New Testament." I exclaimed.

"Exactly right and no one is immune to the dragon, simple church members or church leaders. Leaders are even more prone because they are in positions of authority. Pride gets in the way. You can see the need for the kingdom of kindness. Mercy becomes the leveler of the human justice dragon."

"All right! I think I get it. This is where the idea of

'*do unto others*' really fits. It's not the idea of returning like action with like action . . . it's returning mercy for justice."

"It's returning mercy for what others **think** is justice. That's very insightful, Jerod. I think you're catching onto some things. See, God's justice can be His mercy and His mercy is also sometimes His justice. He can do this with no contradictions."

A soft breeze swirled from the north and rustled rich brown leaves of the old oak. Some leaves let loose their hold and fell. Others clung for life. Autumn air stroked the atmosphere like a cool wash cloth on a fevered brow. I looked up to register the feeling and sound. I thought I heard a faint, shivering sigh come directly from the tree.

Ruben broke through my reverie. "Do you remember the symbol of a king, pouring out water? Kings don't usually serve, but this kind does. These stand for **the kingdom of kindness** and offers a journey to give away aspects of yourself, like consideration. Your sword is God's love and you're to cut away that false self that wants only what it wants. It wants a fake contentment based on pleasure, control and no-risk living. To evidence love in action means to practice giving away self, and mercy is the bridge for true righteousness of God. For you see, mercy embraces a peculiar quality; that is, if you really want to have mercy you must give it away too."

I reached inside my jacket pocket and pulled out the photocopy of the parchment and pointed to some symbol drawings. "Then that's what Clarissa's symbols meant, the king pouring water, the people harvesting grain, putting into containers and looks to be passing it out among many others. All this represents *mercy*?"

"From antiquity, food always represented the self just as water stands for the life blood. The basics in life are continually linked with the deeper principles God put into motion. Understand them and you will see God's strategy for human kind. It is indeed a fascinating, cosmic event."

"Let me see if I've got this straight. It's like the reaping and sowing business. If you give away mercy, that's sowing . . . then you reap mercy, that's harvesting back what you gave away? Which one of God's principles is that?" I asked.

"That is the resurrection principle." Ruben responded. "Think about how often earth, seed, planting and harvesting are mentioned in scripture, trying to show death and life go together. Something must die for something to live and sometimes it's someone. Sowing and reaping, dying and living, burying and rising . . . the Bible is full of it. And if you apply that to the self, the self should die for real self to truly live. This is not a literal death. Christ did that for you, although, there are still true martyrs in the world. But most learn to conquer personal dragons by giving aspects of self away. A better way to say this is to give away that false self so that you have the true self made in God's image return to you. See . . . a reap what you sow benefit."

"And doing mercy will accomplish all you mentioned?" I asked.

"I said it was a bridge, only one, but it is one of the most important and therefore, one of the most difficult to perform. The reason it's so hard is about the time you truly practice kindness for a week, the seeming harmless little dragon called **'I think I've got it'** sneaks onto the bridge to block your way, then growth stops.

This little fellow gives a sense of false accomplishment with disguised happiness of 'now I've got it made.' In your this-world struggles, it's so tempting to feel you've solved one set of problems, at least, so you can go on to something else. But there really exists no such truth as 'having it made', although if you give yourself away properly, you can experience God's joy such that the nature of your struggles can change to become less of a temptation for you. You see, the real temptation becomes that moment when you put off or quit the journey."

"Are you telling me that every time I can be kind to someone, I'm actually giving a part of myself away and **that's** mercy?" I recounted.

"That is right, oh scholar deluxe . . . But the real test becomes feeling kind and acting kind toward those who aren't dishing out kindness to you. Your tendency is going to be to give them back justice for their injustice. Fight your enemies . . . they deserve it. That's what you'll think. And even if you do succeed and return kindness to people who are being unkind, they may get madder at you and pour on the steam. That's another real test, to see if they can push one of your anger buttons. If you succumb and switch on an anger switch, they cause you to join them in false action. You become 'blessed are the judgmental' instead of merciful.'"

"But Ruben, you know I can lose my temper. How do I ever get to where certain issues don't cause a knee-jerk anger reaction in me? I don't see how I can win this one." I baffled.

"You learned anger over your lifetime. You can learn peace. You must exercise conscious commitment to peace. It begins with choice and belief. With effort, trade anger for the better emotion of peace. You truly must learn that peace can give you more energy than anger . . . because it does you know."

"But didn't Jesus himself get angry at the money changers in the Temple and when he saw the strong misusing the weak?" I countered.

"Yes, in a way, but Jesus could get angry without malice. His was something else than worldly anger. His was true righteousness in motion, a kind of anger not based on fear but love. He was sadder by their misunderstanding. He corrected them because he loved them, not to put them straight with judgment. Remember, His judgment is always flavored with His mercy. There are times it becomes necessary to put things right, but it must always come out of God's love or it will turn into the wrong self-righteousness. When you can love God properly, perhaps then, you can get angry and not sin, but until then, you must practice a lot of peace through mercy."

"What do you mean, 'get angry and not sin'. I thought many psychologists encouraged people to get their anger out, rather than let it smolder underneath."

"That's only a half truth. Most humans cannot get angry without the added emotion of hate. And if you start to hate, then you want to destroy. And if you can destroy, you will. Even when people are not able to destroy, they will work until they get into position. It's often called revenge. For you see, anger and hate can smolder for years in the subconscious and explode out into the open with terrible destruction."

"So, I'm supposed to go about doing mercy no matter what."

"Do not miss the point, Jerod. We are talking about

the kingdom of kindness. Mercy does not stand alone, remember, it is linked to the kingdom of appetite, true right living. This means if you do too much righteousness . . . that false dragon without mercy, then you become the Pharisee judge. If you do too much mercy, without proper right doing, you become a person who is restrained by a sense of false morality or responsibility and become too sentimental to help anyone. Righteousness and mercy must walk hand in hand. Stay with the link now . . . this is the fifth kingdom all chained together. If you have moved through the first four properly, you will understand the fifth kingdom of kindness much better."

"Let me see if I've got the connections that Clarissa meant with her symbols which you say no one has gotten before now," I suggested.

"The kingdoms of need, sorrow, yieldedness, appetite and kindness are strung together like a chain. The first three are the foundation of a person's inner self travels. The second three, of which we've just done two, appetite and kindness, are the transformation of a person from the inside to outside, working to get other centered. And still all these are hooked together somehow. Is this right?"

"Right on target", Michael held both thumbs up. "Now, answer me this, student of mine, why are Christians not growing properly?"

"Oh, man, that's a broad one . . . Ok . . . they have broken the chain of growth."

"Yes, but that's too general. That is the principle but give me more."

"Well if I can use your analogies, maybe they broke a sword or they got fooled by a dragon in one of the kingdoms, got stuck and don't know they're stuck. Or they feel trapped and don't know how to get out. Hey, maybe they achieved some kingdom and are feeling too comfortable in there to leave. Or . . . or . . . hey I can think of a lot of reasons. Which one is more correct?"

"Perhaps all are correct, Jerod, that is why you are needed."

My pulse increased. "But it sounds too overwhelming, too many variables. How can one man . . . Uh, how can **I** make a difference? It seems too complicated."

"Don't be fooled by the dragon, complication. You have the equipment to deal with it otherwise I wouldn't be here talking to you."

Suddenly, Ruben jumped up and shadow boxed an imaginary enemy for a couple of rounds, then he slowly drew an invisible sword from an invisible scabbard and started battling an invisible enemy. He sheathed his sword, puffed out his chest, abruptly sat down, and brushed his hands together as if to show 'it is finished'.

A strong autumn wind blew through the park, scattering leaves, pieces of paper and other human debris like candy wrappers. The old oak creaked and moaned as if to say it was still capable to do battle against any force. I felt the season in my soul and knew there were times ahead to challenge all I was and all I was ever going to be. I shivered and gazed across the walkway to a little park pond. Domestic ducks and geese floated lazily around its banks, darting their beaks in the water, hopeful of forgotten food.

Suddenly, my imagination clicked in and I envisioned myself standing upon the little stone bridge that arched its way over the duck pond. My body was dressed as the knights of old, my hand held a jeweled gleaming sword.

Fiercely facing me was an enormous dragon that kept changing into a disguised, beautiful princess of the court. I saw myself hesitate, whether to strike or not, and in my spirit, I shuddered, "*what if I fail too, what if I'm not up to the challenge, what if I can't mature as God wants?*"

I shook myself from daydreaming and looked around for Ruben, who unknown to me moved some distance away behind another park bench, talking to another homeless. I rose from my bench and walked over just as Ruben handed a woman a pair of socks.

"Give her something," Michael exclaimed.

I searched my pockets for loose change . . . None. The woman's stench invaded my nostrils and I repelled, but I reached in my back pocket and pulled out my billfold. All I had was a twenty-dollar bill. I took it out and handed it to the woman, feeling awkward. She snatched it, said *thank you, big spender* in her foul breath and shuffled across the grass, headed for the two homeless men seen earlier. Gall crept up my throat. I swallowed hard before it became anger.

"Why must they be so aggravating?" I gushed.

"Oh, maybe it's because they're so well fed and adjusted to their standard of living," Ruben chortled.

"You know what I mean."

"You mean, you think they like forcing charity from people, going around dirty and uncomfortable. Do you think that's what Jesus meant when he said the poor would always be with you?"

"No, I just meant many of them are often ungrateful when you do help them in some way." I responded.

"They are angry, Jerod, some have good cause, others do not, but they are still hurting and they have turned to anger because to them, that's the only energy to help them survive. You will not find many homeless who are at peace with themselves, except maybe the mentally deranged, and they don't even know **who** they are."

"I can understand that." I mumbled.

"But what you don't realize is many of the homeless were angry before, even when they were successful by world standards. Their anger finally led them down a road of self destruction. There are even Christians among them. They're not all heathens, you know."

"Ow, really? I've always wondered. Are there many Christians among them?" I asked.

"Many more than people realize."

"Say . . . Ruben . . . what kingdom did they get stuck in?"

"Many did not make it out of the kingdom of sorrow. They grieved too much for themselves, instead of others. They would not let the Holy Spirit comfort them about what seemed the injustices done them and so could not move into the kingdom of yieldedness. People who stay self preoccupied will always be disappointed sooner or later. Then, disappointment leads to disapproval. Disapproval flows right into judgment. And it's not far from there to anger. The dragon anger can easily stop those who stay self-centered. One of your big tasks, in future, will be helping others get other centered."

"You keep reminding me about anger. You must think I have a real problem with it?" I anguished.

"You do not have it like some. At least, you can move onto other kingdoms, but you may find anger to become one of your larger temptations, and remember, anger is just disguised fear. But, we don't need to go into that now. You must admit, you need more practice in the kingdom of kindness. I know you think you are often too tired and you often have good intentions, but you must learn to do mercy as a second nature; otherwise, some smaller dragons will blind you and block your way."

Ruben started walking down the pathway toward the parking lot.

I caught up beside him. "What kingdom am I stuck in?"

"That's not open for discussion now."

"Well . . . what do you think my tendency of anger is based on?"

"Now you want me to be your free therapist?"

"No, no. I was just wondering . . ." I trailed off.

"I will say this. Your easy irritation stems from wanting to please too many people. The cost of being misunderstood appears too great for you. But you see, this deals with a later kingdom. We're not there yet. But we will be." Ruben's eyes twinkled.

Soon, we arrived at my car. I unlocked the doors and Ruben slid into the passenger seat.

I started the engine and turned to Michael." Where are we going?"

"Drive me to the corner of Broadway and Main. Let me out there and you go on home. Enough for this evening. I'll call you in the morning." Ruben smiled from ear to ear.

I arrived at Broadway and Main and opened the car door to let Michael out. An outside tingling hot air whooshed through the open door, releasing the comfort of my air conditioning. Hurriedly, I reached across and shut the door, then settled back in my seat and watched Ruben walk down the sidewalk, whistling.

A cloud laced sun began to sink as I watched Ruben

get smaller and smaller. I slowly drove away and looked through my large rear-view mirror at him as he just seemed to disappear down the street. For a moment, he was there, then gone.

Chapter 16

Friday evening when I returned home from the park, my light blinked steadily on the answering machine. I still refused to carry my cell phone because I didn't want any interruption with my time with Ruben. I had to depend on my machine. Quickly I pressed the message button, hoping to receive a call from Jill.

A radio type voice boomed: "Hey, pastor, I missed you on Thursday night visitation." Gary Butler, a church deacon clucked on the line. Butler thought himself one of the more solid pillars of the church and he did have a following. He and wife, Doris, married late in life, having turned thirty, and started having children right away.

Gary was a successful insurance salesman, gave money generously to the church budget and stayed active in most of the church programs. The problem with Butler was his imagination wouldn't let him fear anything and he often went overboard on issues. Some considered him a kind person and others believed him to be tough as a night in jail. Whatever Gary was, he kept an ever-present personality in the life of any pastor and could not be ignored. *And here I'd ignored him*, I thought. Well, it's too late now, I'm glad I was gone when he called. I'll just deal with him later. I can't let him know what's going on with Ruben.

The machine beeped and another message: "Rev. Dr. Sellers," Ruben's voice intoned. "Meet me at the Day Care Center, the one which also cares for the blind children, tomorrow morning at nine. Don't be late."

The machine beeped its last beep and shut off. No other messages. I still wondered about Jill. I wondered what in the world Ruben wanted at that Day Care, an unusual place with mixed reputation. Rapid-fire self-talk broke through my mind. I still wondered what was going on with Jill. But too much was happening right now. I just felt I should let that issue ride for now. Then I thought I ought to make a courtesy call to Dr. Sturgen in Ft. Worth, Texas. I felt I'd left the man in the dark long enough.

I punched in the required number of the old professor's home and soon related to the scholar some of what happened, leaving out the weirder parts. I continued to make light of the parchments, not wanting to stir up the professor unduly. I let him know that apparently, they were genuine enough and the investigation for further translation progressed but it was taking longer than expected. And certainly, I would keep him informed of the progress, but please have patience as it might take some time longer. And no, the good professor would not be forgotten in the matter. Further information would follow in future.

The next morning, I drove and parked at one of the few spaces in front of the Good Hope Day Care Center. The 1950's brown brick building, surrounded by a chain-link fence, sat on a corner of one of the heavy traffic intersections on the east side of Restoration's 20,000 population.

In the not too distant past, the town struggled with the concept of small public schools. The education board obtained a tough-minded school superintendent who got some smaller schools to merge. This building had been one of those schools abandoned. The grounds had swings, see-saws, monkey bars and merry-go-rounds. The old brick structure rested in a barren dirt playground, constructed in a distant past which did not consider those play items dangerous.

The building became an ideal location to convert to a day care. Bought and paid for by a private group, they'd turned the building into a combination day care and temporary home for abused mothers and children. Part of the structure also converted into small bedrooms for battered women. These wounded souls found a temporary haven from violent lives while the authorities tried dealing with legal issues.

Another unusual program developed as a spin-off of abused children, centered on blind children. For myriad reasons, the community spawned physically abused kids who suffered different degrees of blindness. Of the five staff and five volunteers of Good Hope, one staff member happened to be a person with enough formal education to work with these children and the program flourished. The courts seemed especially slow in what to do with some of the children and there were about ten still staying at the center. These blind children ranged from 10 months to five years of age. On various occasions, all the staff pitched in to help with these children, as their sad innocence compelled the workers to do no less.

Part of the controversy surrounding the Good Hope program came from certain community citizens who were uneasy about such people being housed smack dab in the middle of their residential houses and properties. Too many police cars and ambulances were heard and seen at the place at different hours of the day. All kinds of rumors spread as to the types of women who often stayed there. However, several working mothers with average incomes still used the normal day care part of the program because the cost stayed affordable.

Year after year, Good Hope managed to stay financially afloat, due to a handful of benevolent Christians, but other active Christians, some of my church members, were the very ones who complained about the place. I supported the program the best I could, but I usually stayed clear of any controversy except for an occasional phone call or referral. Somewhat bewildered, I could not imagine why Ruben wanted to meet here. I guessed it to be another one of those odd developments on the part of my mentor.

I got out of my car and walked up old concrete stairs to enter massively constructed combination metal and glass doors. Childhood memories flooded me as I remembered past entryways from my own school days. I was reminded of the huge door I went through for years, a monolith brass-trimmed giant that was hard to open for youth as small as I was.

I heaved open the door and moved to a reception desk, sitting directly in the hallway. No one could enter the main building without first passing this desk. A 50ish, well-groomed woman greeted me brightly.

"Good morning. May I help you?"

I smiled back. "Yes . . . I'm looking for . . . Uh . . .

Mr. Ruben Michael. You may not know him by name, but he's a thin, gray haired older man."

"Oh, quite right. He's down the hall, first room on your right. Just look through the small glass window on the door. Knock gently and go on in. And your name is . . .?"

"I'm doctor Sellers."

"Are you medical or religious?"

"Uh . . . religious."

"What organization?" she continued.

"First Church."

She wrote my name in a book. "Thank you, sir. Please go on down."

I strolled down the hall, gazing at the freshly painted plaster walls and well-kept hard wood floors. I glanced at the ceiling and surroundings and could tell at once the place gleamed vintage old but stayed well kept. I arrived at the designated door, peered through the little glass window and tapped to enter.

As I entered the room something about its design struck me as unusual. Surveying the space, I became aware everything in it appeared round, even the walls. I looked closely at the furniture, three round baby beds lined one section of the walls and small rounded tables with rounded chairs were scattered about. There was not a sharp object or corner angle in the entire area. Someone designed a place if you bumped into anything you would slide right on by without harm. I knew at once this must be the room for the blind children I'd heard about. Sure enough, inside small children mingled, all involved in various activities.

Ruben sat on the floor, crossed legged, playing patty-cake with two small children. He would alternate patting palms with the two in perfect timing. I stood entranced, seeing how well the blind kids kept the exact rhythm. They seemed to know how to reach Ruben's hands based on some instinct and tilting their heads to catch any sound.

Suddenly, something rapped around my leg, clamping so tight the hairs on my shin were pulled. "Ouch!" Annoyed I jerked and looked more closely to the floor. Holding onto my leg, like a monkey shimmying up a tree, clamped a little girl about five years old. Two bleached brown eyes stared up at me, *"Are you my Daddy come to take me home?"* She asked.

My heart melted and I stood frozen, unable to speak.

Soon, one of the workers rushed over and smiled, unclasped the little girl from my leg.

"Now . . . Julie . . . let's don't bother the nice visitor," the worker said as she whisked the little girl over to one of the tables.

I watched with moisture burning eyes, and then turned just as Ruben took me by the arm and led me back out the door. Outside in the hallway, he spoke.

"Not everyone can stay in there very long. It's too painful."

"Man . . . you know Ruben; I don't have any children and when that little girl asked me if I was her Daddy . . . something in me about said yes. I wanted to take her home, present her to my wife and say, 'guess what, we now are parents'".

"That might not be such a bad idea."

"Goodness, I never felt that way before. What is the story on her parents?"

"Julie is the product of abuse, like the others. Both parents were alcoholics. One night in their stupor, the father became irritated at her, slapped her down. The girl hit her head on the edge of a coffee table, resulting in brain damage, affecting the eyes. She will never see again. Interestingly, she is a happy little thing and still loves her Daddy very much. She just tells everybody: It was, as she pronounces it . . . an *ack-ser-dent*."

"The courts and agencies are still struggling what to do about her," Ruben continued. "I think they're trying to get the grandparents involved, but they don't seem to be in much better shape. The judges tend to get extended families responsible when they can. It's truly a sad case, as so many, and again, like I said, I think many stay away from these kinds of problems because the injustice of it all stays too hurtful. Most people tend to feel for one of the kids and they end up wanting to take them **all** home."

"Yeah . . . I know what you mean . . . why did you want to meet here anyway?" I asked.

"Oh, the ole 'why' question again. Come on. Let's go look at some more of this building. Ruben moved down the hallway, peeking into various windows. Curiously I followed. Soon, Michael pointed through one of the little glass windows.

"That's one of the regular day care rooms. Notice how well- mannered they are."

I peered through and shook my head yes.

"Let's go out back to the playground. Follow me!" Ruben commanded with a spring in his step. We walked through a back door, down concrete stairs with old iron railings to the outdoors and sat on one of the merry-go-rounds. Since it wasn't a recess time, we found ourselves totally alone.

I glanced around the yard, noting the worn paths

where the children made indelible tracks upon the ground. I closed my eyes a moment and felt I could see the children at play, smell their freshness, and draw from their innocence and energy. In my heart of hearts, I knew all children were not only the future in motion but reminders of hope. But sometimes the world needed reminding of that hope. It was too easy to forget.

I looked down to see the two-inch groove, dug out in the dirt all around the merry-go-round I sat upon. I almost felt like a child again myself. I took a deep breath and with it, for some unknown reason, began feeling a dose of hope rising in my chest.

"It's a good day to be alive, isn't it Ruben?"

"More than you know, my boy. More than you know", Ruben seemed gloomy.

I felt alarmed.

"Don't get excited", Ruben shot back, "I'm referring to me, not you."

I tilted my head and stared in the old man's eyes. A feeling of void passed through my whole system.

"You're not going to disappear on me again, are you?" I pleaded. "It's so frustrating when you do that."

"You still don't get it, do you? My presence with you is in direct proportion to your attention span. When your endurance creeps away, I melt away also. Only if I start to lose your focused concentration again, do I lose my power with you, but so far lately, you're doing much better."

"I'm not even going to try to understand all that, but I think it's one of the first compliments you've given me." I puffed out my chest.

"Hey, don't let the ole dragon **conceit** creep in and get in our way." Ruben wiggled his ears and made a sword stabbing motion in the air. "It's time to consider the sixth lesson—the_**kingdom of Cleanness**. What is your definition of purity, Rev. Sellers?"

I moaned at the word **reverend,** clasping my hands together, resting them in my lap. I pondered a few seconds, then said, "I suppose it means undiluted or unmixed."

Suddenly, Michael jumped off quickly and started pushing and spinning me on the merry-go-round. I raised my feet and held on tight, feeling I might spin off any minute, as I went around and round. Nausea started creeping through my stomach. I tried to focus my attention on the center of the wheel to avoid my discomfort. Soon, I slowed, and then Ruben reached out, grabbed a bar and abruptly stopped the spinning, snapping my head.

"I had to get your attention again . . . get the old brain cells realigned. You gave me a formal dictionary meaning, eh boy? No, I mean what is the concept of purity in the scripture, you know, *blessed are the pure in heart*?"

I swallowed back the lump in my throat and stuttered, "Probably something I have no idea, but you're going to tell me." I sounded a little miffed.

"Whoa there, don't get pouty on me." Michael reached out and tickled me in the ribs. I squirmed, not able to hold back a grin. Nausea flowed away as quickly as it came.

"All right, all right . . . I suppose . . . since it says the pure in heart business, it probably has something to do with God's righteousness working in a person to cause that individual to become clean. Whatever clean means." I responded.

"Much better. But, keep in mind though, this is a kingdom, so I want you to think of it not only as a state of being but a place for growth to move along with action. Of course, we are talking about a **kingdom of cleanness**, but it is a realm of cleanness linked to forgiveness, not undiluted righteousness."

"For instance, Ruben placed his index finger to his temple, "think of those children back in the building, they have their scars but kept innocent because they are protected in their souls until they can choose what they will do with life's hurts. As a Christian adult, your innocence is protected by Jesus but you have scars too. Or, another way to look at it, God's cleanness is like your healthy skin with no blemish. The purity of forgiveness appears like your skin with scars on it. But don't take that analogy too far."

"So, you're saying, our cleansing always has some healing connected with it?" I quipped.

"Speak for yourself, boy. **Your** cleansing will have healing with it. It can come no other way. The battles you fight with your personal dragons will leave wounds. They need be healed. Some take more time than others. Instantaneous healing of the spirit stays rare because most types of forgiveness must work their own medicine. Much depends on what you've discovered through the earlier kingdoms. Remember the other kingdoms sometimes link together."

"**The kingdoms of need/sorrow/yieldedness**," Ruben boomed, "provide the inner self-strength. Then comes appetite, kindness . . . and now cleanness to complete the Christian's inside-out journey. But you won't get the right kind of cleanness if you're lacking in the other travels."

"What kind of cleanness are we talking about here?" I pleaded.

"It's the kind of cleanness the Psalmist asked for when he prayed for a clean heart, a wholeness to be able to see the things of God. You can't have complete righteousness in this dimension but you can become clean enough to avoid letting the smog from the dragon's breath block out the light of God."

"Doesn't the Christian need to get rid of the bad things in life, though, before God can trust him or her with much truth?" I quizzed.

"This kind of cleanness isn't a matter of emptying the self alone or just getting rid of the bad things, as you put it. If any self emptying happens, it is done to replace those things with hunger/thirst, right doing and mercy/kindness. The concept does not promote any idea if you can get rid of all the bad, then you will automatically be good. But rather, the proper amount of kindness and hunger/thirst after God will lead to a purity of heart which isn't blinded so much by the things of this world. Remember . . . this is your inside/out journey and it comes after your inner-Self skirmishes which help to turn your eyes outward upon a hurting world." Ruben answered.

"So that's what it means . . . 'blessed are the pure in heart for they shall see God.' Is that what the parchment symbol meant when it showed a full heart without a crack in it?"

"You got it. It means for you to **really** see God becomes a filling up course of action, not an emptying one. The fullness of the other kingdom adventures pushes out what shouldn't be there, rather than you having to push them out. Having fought your way through the dragons in the kingdoms of need, sorrow, yieldedness, appetite, kindness, then toward cleanness . . . you have done enough to allow your spiritual eyes to see who God really is and what he's doing in this world. You will experience what I like to call the great 'Aha', a clearer sense of wonder and insight. And now because you can really **see . . .** your ability to worship, will be enhanced many fold."

Just then, several traffic sounds broke through my attention. Various cars discharged their obnoxious smells and sounds, just outside the fenced school yard. I stared at them for a moment and thought how busy everyone was, always in a hurry to what? To hurry up and get to the next destination, only to stop and wait. Hurry up and stop. Hurry up and stop. That's the way most people live, even Christians. How would I ever get people's real attention for this message of knowledge?

I looked back at Ruben. "This sounds almost too difficult. I don't know if I can keep it all straight. I don't know if I have enough of what it takes. If I didn't know better, it sounds like people must **work** their way through the kingdoms to earn their way into heaven."

Michael wiggled his ears and flared his nostrils several times. "Ah, but these adventures are not 'works of work' but works of grace. Grace has already started the salvation progression. Often when you feel lack of God's Grace, pride has blocked your path. You need to trust the grace given you so your work attempts become normal growth as your partnership with God. The Holy Spirit will remind you, nudge you in the right direction . . . if you listen."

"And by the way, Jerod, the old **'work your way to heaven'** dragon is in the last part of kingdom four, appetite. She's a doozy and many get stuck there. People misinterpret their right doing and turn their moral living into some justification for judging others. For you see, the dragon pride wants you to think she's one big issue to conquer and once you have her defeated she's no longer around. But the truth is she's a bunch of little, subtle beasts that disguise themselves and can slip into any kingdom at any given time. She sends her fire and darts at you, aimed at your weak spots. You can't help but be wounded by her from time to time, but you can heal and move on. But she may never be fully defeated in this life so, at times, you must move on wounded . . . however, that's a kingdom we haven't covered yet."

"Hey . . . wait a minute . . . why is the dragon pride labeled a she?" I retorted.

"Ah . . . you caught that, did you? It's as old as Eve herself. Of the two beings God made, she's the only one clever enough and she can duplicate by having children. Remember, Adam was content after he was given a mate like the other animals had. So, he was satisfied to stay at home in one section of the Garden of Eden. All the while, Eve was of a different nature. See, Adam was made from dead dirt . . . a nothing. Eve was made from Adam, living tissue, so she was a something, already a work in progress. Because of this development of her nature, the female does networking differently than the male. She can come up with more ideas. Adam had one conclusion, focused mostly on the Garden. Eve went out prospecting and found the Evil One. That wasn't bad, but she went one step too far and promoted pride when she wanted to be as the gods."

"You're saying we should blame Eve for all the trouble with pride," I mused.

"No, certainly not! Although Eve has been blamed for causing the first sin. But the subtle truth is **Adam sinned first**."

"What?" I said shocked.

"Oh . . . you're gonna love this," Ruben grinned, "See, there was Adam in the Garden of plenty, even walking and talking with God. He had protection, all the food he needed, companionship with the animals and God. He had intelligence; after all, he named all the animals. He had everything. But one day he noticed the animals all in twos. He pouted yet he had it all. However, that wasn't enough. The dragon Discontent crept in. The irony was, having all that God could give, wasn't enough. This kind of discontent became the first sin. It's a kind of greed, wanting more when having everything isn't satisfying. It's a kind of theft because Adam's discontent robbed God of his full attention. Too, it's a kind of pride, saying there's got to be more than even God."

"Goodness . . . a lot of people won't accept my telling them Adam sinned first . . . but, it sure makes sense."

"Jerod, don't get too sidetracked. All that's history. That's not what matters now. It's of no importance at this moment." Ruben bore into my eyes with a hypnotic stare. "Do you recall what I said earlier about the kingdoms linked in three's?"

"Uh . . . yeah." I stuttered.

"So? Where are we?" Ruben demanded.

I jumped. "Oh, well . . . let's see . . . we're talking about the sixth lesson, so we're at the end of the second set of three kingdoms appetite, kindness, cleanness."

"Good." Ruben snorted. "I cannot over emphasize the importance of the connections because this is the factor many have missed in the past interpretations. People did not have access to the Parchments with Clarissa's symbols and their true meanings like you have. The true picture goes something like this: You've traveled your way through need, sorrow, and yieldedness to tone up your basic selfhood. These led to the next three adventures and then, because you've hungered/thirsted after righteousness [kingdom of appetite] and combined it with mercy [kingdom of kindness] you can come to a purer and undivided heart [kingdom of cleanness]. This connecting and meshing, this passion for hungering and compassion for humanity leads to an unclouded heart."

Ruben continued, "You will be able to see the law of God but also be able to show mercy, not only to yourself but others. Jerod . . . you will be able to see God in the lives of ordinary people, struggling with their private dragons. It is indeed an awesome sight but one you have been called to do."

Ruben stared and continued. "Understand, however, there are three more kingdoms left and you are to travel all of them with me so you can share these with the universe. The whole cosmos will rejoice with you through your adventures, as you conquer and journey through each realm, leaving your mark for the Son of God."

"When you say things like that . . . like universe and cosmos . . . I can't help but shake in my socks, Ruben. The earth is too huge, my gracious, this town is big enough, let alone the universe. I'm only one small person feeling pretty overwhelmed right now."

"Ah, but it's not God who made you feel small just now, it's an overwhelming false humility. That's a result of the disguised dragon fear. The correct question is how big Jehovah is anyway?" Michael flared his nostrils three times, jiggled his eyebrows three times, and pointed to the skies three exaggerating motions.

"Ok, ok. I'm just human." I flushed.

"How well I know, my friend, but that's the joy and the sadness of it all . . . Don't you know, son . . . Even all the angels are in love with those captured by time?"

I stared at this strange little man and my heart sank. I felt the forbidden lump rise in my throat, choking back possible tears. My ears started to ring like a steady chorus of crickets, then a soft pop seemed to calm all and my whole body bathed in a wave of peace, flowing like rays from Ruben himself. I felt chills run through my shoulder blades and sensed I shared the presence of someone very special.

Suddenly, the most amazing feeling and thought swept over my entire being: *Right this very minute, I truly feel loved.*

Chapter 17

Michael grabbed me by the arm and pulled me up from the merry-go-round. Alarmed, I stumbled in the dirt.

"Let's go get one of those famous Super King hamburgers with French fries and malt." Ruben announced.

We made our way, back through the Day Care Center, nodding to the woman at the receptionist desk, saying nothing. Soon, we got into the car and drove across town to the drive-up hamburger place. On the way, I stopped at a drive-up bank and retrieved some cash since I didn't know who would end up paying for our burgers. I thought *drive through bank, drive through food, I guess we'll have drive through churches before long.*

Finally, we reached the eating place and as I pulled in, I noticed each drive-up space sported its own king figure, all decked out in colorful attire. I drove into position, rolled down my window and talked to a large, majestically adorned plastic King, whose speaker system lay squarely in a large black belt buckle connected around an ample waist.

"**Can I take your order**", blared the belt buckle.

"We want two burgers in a basket with everything

and two chocolate malts." I yelled into the speaker. Then I turned to Ruben.

"I hope that's all right with you?"

"Boy . . . you read my mind." Michael bobbed his head toward the King figure. "Nice theme for our kingdom discussions, huh?"

Soon the food arrived by a young woman on roller skates, delivering the tray of goodies. I paid the ticket along with a generous tip and felt she earned it for just not falling from those skates. I thought, *Boy, this place never got out of the fifties, but it's kind of nice.*

We started munching on the succulent meal. Ruben gobbled his down like a man who hadn't eaten in days. Slurping through his straw the last of the malt, he burped and said, "Nothing like a greasy burger the size of a saucer to get the juices flowing. Let's drive. Go down Main Street to Dave's Music Emporium. Sounds are calling us onward."

I folded half my burger back into the sack, sat my drink in a beverage holder, and then hurriedly backed out of the space. As we drove away from the driveway, Ruben leaned out the window and gave an exaggerated salute to the king. From my rearview mirror, I blinked as I thought I saw the king slightly nod back.

Dave's Music Emporium spread across the top of an old red brick building on Main Street. Built in the early nineteen hundreds, it sprouted a new cosmetic face lift. Earlier in the year, the downtown businesses met and planned a way to help save downtown from losing business to the developing strip malls. They hit upon the strategy to redo the front of the buildings in a country kitchen style.

Extended shingled-wood overhangs served as

awnings when you entered any doorway. Antique lettered signs announced individual businesses. Bright reds, blues, whites adorned the fronts looking much like clean candy houses. Many of the once abandoned spaces were now holding antiques, uniques, and junk. Some specialized in home-made crafts of the early pioneer days and these markets intermingled with the regular retail business stores. People from all economic stations in life came from miles around to stroll through the shops, especially those with garage sale, swap meet, find- a-bargain mentality.

One of their biggest problems was parking, so the town fathers created public spaces behind the stores where anyone could park free. There was no parking on Main. This left Main Street five blocks of wide street with no parking and open sidewalks for walking. For those five blocks, the city planners landscaped the outdoors with healthy trees and shrubs, interspersed with sitting benches. Outside vendors sold ice cream, hot dogs and bagels. People could bring their families, eat a snack and stroll the well cleaned boulevard like something out of the movies. The people loved it and business boomed.

I pulled into the back driveway by a bright red sign announcing **public parking**, easily found a space and we got out of the car. We walked across the alley toward the back door of the Music Emporium. Anyone who didn't want to go through the front entrance on the boulevard could enter back doors, covered with simpler but neat canopies. It was easy access for those who didn't want to negotiate the crowds on Main Street. As we opened the door, a lively rock-music piece bombarded our senses. Ruben snapped his fingers to the beat of the music. I thought, at least, this is better than some music I don't understand.

Entering the back door, we meandered through counters of harmonicas, snare drum sticks with accessories, guitar picks and strings, reed instrument paraphernalia, sheet music and other incidental equipment. Toward the front were rows of guitars, evidently a popular item, and across the aisle stood brass instruments surrounded by electrical equipment and sets of snare drums. Anyone could tell the store arrangement showed well-loved attention. Someone here truly loved music and all associated with it.

Michael strolled among the items, humming softly. I glanced around at the various items, marveling at the precise layout of everything. The aisles seemed designed to let any shopper stroll through the maze of this musical fantasy land. The atmosphere of the place combined with the music swept through me, giving me serenity and feeling of belonging. I watched Ruben and felt how good to spend time, even waste time, with a friend, especially in such pleasant surroundings.

Ruben looked up and motioned for me to join him where he stood. He nodded toward one corner in front of a rack of sheet music. I moved over quickly, expecting anything.

"Look at all these symbols, squiggly little lines on paper that get transformed into beauty. These little lines can make you laugh, cry, pat a foot, dance a jig, cover your ears, change your mood, make a touchdown, turn to God . . . the list is unlimited. It doesn't matter what your nationality, what your language, who you are. Music burrows through the senses and lands right at the heart of your soul. Have you ever wondered why music is one of the few things in life that can do all that?"

"Well . . . I'm not a musician so I've never thought too philosophically about it. I just know I like it." I responded.

"Think about it now, oh slothful one." Ruben imitated playing a trumpet, then a guitar, then a set of drums. It was as if his imitations fit in exactly with the music playing through the store loud speakers.

"Ok . . . Ok . . . I guess I would must say it's a universal language."

"See . . . you can think philosophically. But I want to know **how come** it's a universal language."

"What do you mean, 'how come'? Isn't being a universal power enough to penetrate anyone's senses? If it's universal then it fits everyone. In other words, there are no blockers to keep it out. I've never heard of anyone who didn't like some music unless it physically hurt their ears or something."

"That's pretty good . . . but that's what I want you to tell me. How come everyone seems to like this one thing?"

"The only answer I can fall back on is for some reason God wanted at least one issue all the races could agree on." I frowned and waited.

"You're getting close but I'm going to let you in on a little secret" Ruben leaned over as if to whisper in my ear. . . "Music is the original energy for the Creation."

"What?" I sputtered.

"I didn't stutter . . . Music energy created the universe and all in it."

"Are you telling me that you think God **sung** the world into existence?"

"I don't think, **I know,** and yes . . . something like that."

"Wait a second . . . how do you know?" I retorted.

"That's another discussion. Don't get off track. Is it so displeasing to you to think God may have sung the universe into place?"

"Well, no, I suppose not."

"Then, go with it for now. You see, it makes sense when you realize music is one of the true constant energies, like naming. Everyone needs a name or designation. You remember in the scripture the verse in Revelation that says when you enter heaven; you'll have a new name?"

"Yeah . . . along with a new heavenly body, we're supposed to get a new name." I remarked.

"Well, I have another secret for you: You'll get a new song too."

"Wow . . . Ruben, that's exciting, especially for me, who sure can't sing very well in this dimension."

"There's a very good reason music contains the power it does."

"Yeah . . . what?" I stammered.

"The hint of the creative power rests in the book of Genesis when it says after God created everything, it was good. What that really means suggests the whole universe and world vibrated peace and harmony. Everything rippled in balance. Nothing was left undone. Music is the result of the ripple and continues the wave channel bringing peace."

"But . . . Ruben. Some music we know isn't very peaceful."

"God's true music is peaceful. In the human realm,

this energy can become twisted like so many other things."

"You know, Ruben, this makes a kind of sense because when I'm out in the woods enjoying Nature, I often think I can hear the different sounds of birds, wind, tree noises combine into a symphony, like there's music produced by Nature. And it's usually those times I'm most at peace with things. I've often laughed and thought I could actually hear the stars or planets sing also."

"You probably did hear them, in your spirit. And sometimes they groan the music. See, they wait also for the end time."

"Man, I can sure see the need for peace. Our world needs a dose of that every other second."

"Yes, Jerod. The cosmos would crumble if music were removed because it's so linked with the beauty God gave to help offset all the ugliness in the world. One of the main purposes of art generates a balance against ugliness. And those who can put the right symbols together or the right notes have a sacred responsibility to keep going for the betterment of humanity."

"But what about us who can't do musical notes or art work either, for that matter?"

"Ah . . . I like it when you ask the right questions. You are to discover other symbols and use them for peace. You are to become art and beauty in yourself . . . which leads me to tell you about the last set of three kingdoms. The first of these is blessed are the peacemakers . . . the **kingdom of Harmony**."

Just then, three teenage boys jostled their way past where we were standing. They goosed, punched and picked at each other in friendly play. They began to reach around Ruben for some of the sheet music found on the rack. The peaceful atmosphere melted with this interruption. I felt annoyed and wondered what Ruben would do.

"Boys . . . boys . . . have you seen this particular piece. It's great." Ruben reached and grabbed a sheet of music and handed it to one of the boys. At first the boys looked bewildered, then smiled and took the music, glancing at the title and notes.

Ruben turned and patted me on the back. "Let's move back out to the car. We can talk there."

Soon we were seated in the vehicle and Michael began staring out the side window, making me uncomfortable with the silence.

"Ok . . . so . . . what about the kingdom of harmony?" I finally asked.

"Ah . . . yes . . . the peacemakers. Sometimes you must use a loving encounter, just like I did with those boys. But that's getting ahead of myself. You see the first six beatitudes, linked in sets of threes, describe the journeys of the inner-self and the inside/out struggle. To complete the nine beatituded stages of growth, the last three become the most challenging of all because they equip you with how to deal with the world at large."

Michael pointed to his temple. "In the past, many scholars would have you believe the lessons given by Jesus on the mount were just high-sounding principles, ideas that were new and revolutionary but mostly unlivable, except certain specially called people might live them out. They were not viewed for everyone because they appeared impractical and too hard for living in the real world. So, through the years, the result of this thinking caused Christians to ignore these vital issues as practical. People just tend to take one of the guides at a time and try to live them. Like they might try mercy for a while."

"I'm not sure I know what you mean. Haven't there been a lot of sermons and books on the Sermon on the Mount? The subject appears to me one of the most talked about." I questioned.

"Yes . . . I don't mean the subjects have been hidden away somewhere. They've been tried individually as living principles or misinterpreted, but people never acquired the whole picture. But I do mean the true interpretation of them gets missed in your modern culture. For instance, your modern culture pretty much promotes the idea that 'might makes right', the ones with the most health, most money, most popular, most power get the privileges. It's always the idea if a person has more, then that equals quality."

"Some in the Christian community," Ruben continued, "have tried to use the Sermon's principles to combat the 'more stuff' philosophy by saying Jesus meant you to have less . . . and **that** was supposed to offset selfishness. This missed the whole point. True harmony promotes the God given ability to learn a **holy indifference** to the '*more or less*' issues. See, you really can't give anything away if you value it too much for yourself, whether that's valuing the 'more' or the 'less'. Unfortunately, there really are those who value their poverty too much as well as their prosperity."

"Are you saying there are people who like being poor?"

"They don't necessarily like the results of being poor, but they hold onto an attitude that poorness itself, becomes true humility. Doesn't that seem ironic when

God is so rich? Sometimes circumstances may make you poor and bring with it a humbling result. But, the point of the true revolutionary idea of Jesus' teachings is God doesn't want you poor or rich. He wants you to be content, at peace, having both the ability to receive or give away so you can honor Him. That condition can be called the *holy indifference*, and it's actually found when you travel through this seventh kingdom of harmony."

"Ok . . . but what about those boys back in the music store? You said something about doing a loving encounter." I pointed through the windshield toward the music store.

"Sometimes when people are obnoxious and rude, they are being poor. Often, they don't know they're holding onto poorness, but rudeness comes from being haughty and that's the *'might makes right'* disguise. See, those teens don't have the kind of peace Jesus offered. Sure, I suppose I could have fussed at them, lectured them on manners . . . like you probably wanted to do, but I chose a small loving encounter instead. It's part of what peace making is all about."

"Huumm." I murmured.

"So, you see, the last three kingdom principles do not leave you looking up to heaven with glorious high-sounding phrases, but actually turn your eyes toward people. Jesus makes this a significant point. He wants you looking at each other, dealing with each other on the same level. Last time, we talked about the 'pure in heart' and you saw it was not some rigid rule of living but a method of filling up life with God, instead of trying to empty life of the bad things? You can do the 'pure in heart' because earlier you found it laced with mercy. Your next challenge moves you from purity to peacemaking."

"How do you go from purity to peacemaking?" I still questioned.

"Well, I'm glad you asked. Jesus is saying the purifying progress opens you to God's clear word and instruction . . . and clearly, Godly words start with willingness to perform loving encounters. The purifying force turns you toward a loving assertiveness which motivates you to become a reconciler."

"A what?" I stammered.

"One who can bring harmony, get people back in tune. The love of God motivates you to become one who distributes peace by reconciliation. This kind of peace will not let you sit back and wait for things to happen, but rather, you are to become aggressive with your love. You can take the initiative, step in and settle differences. There are many issues and people in the world who disturb peace. They are the disrupters. Of course, the final disrupter is death. But before that end, many people use emotions like worry and intimidation to upset the peace of God. It becomes your job to actively assert love and help reconcile the differences between individuals."

"But how am I to do this? I can't just take the initiative and step into people's lives without their asking me to?" I objected.

"If you are doing what another said long ago: *practice thinking on what is true, what is honorable, what is right, what is pure, what is lovable, what is excellent in Christ,* if you continually make yourself aware of these, the Holy Spirit will bring those into your path for you to do loving encounters. You won't have to go looking for them.

They will cross your path as naturally as the spring rains. Besides, you are traveling through the kingdoms and along the way; you will be challenged by strife and contention. You have the heart. You just need to learn all God has for you. So . . . Boy . . . sharpen your sword. There are new dragons out there."

"There you go again, scaring me. I flinch every time you talk of fighting."

"Well, of course, no one likes confrontation, except those so full of hate and anger they don't know what's controlling them. But you will do loving confrontation and that's a whole different motivation. Confrontation couched in the love of God becomes exciting and enriching. Heaven watches those adventures with awe."

I tilted my head toward my mentor and nodded yes. Questions swirled through my brain like electricity jumping between computer chips. A part of me wanted to ask all the questions at once and have them answered, but another part of me knew such vast information was too overwhelming. With Michael, I felt I should always fine-tune the questions, really get to the point. My mind began to sift through the maze and finally I inquired.

"Ruben, you mentioned having a holy indifference and then now, you're saying I should do loving confrontation. How can I be indifferent and confront at the same time?"

"Hey, now you're thinking. See, the holy indifference isn't aimed at people, but rather at your circumstances, depending on whether you are in possession of the 'more' philosophy or the 'less' in this world. Remember, holy indifference is a bridge for your inside/out growth. Loving encounters happen with people relationships. You need to learn creative fighting."

"There you go again; using what seems to be a

contradiction in terms. What is creative fighting? I thought I was supposed to have peace." I looked exasperated as I stared at my friend.

"The Word says you will be a *peacemaker*. Sometimes that may mean you get right in the middle of a fight. Another way of saying scripture is: *blessed is the person who can step between diversity and offer peace.* See . . . it takes confrontation with love to perform the verse properly. For example, you may find yourself literally stepping between a husband and wife who are fighting."

"Wow, how did you know that? Just the other day, I had a couple in my office for counseling and I had to get up out of my chair and stand between them because I thought they were going to hit each other. I've never seen anyone so mad before. I really didn't know what else to do, but just stand between them. It was scary."

"Yes, the Spirit of the Word will help you step between people who are having clashes and more. The Spirit helps you weep with those who weep and share joy with those who have joy. So, creative fighting stays your challenge to distribute harmony. You don't fight with the idea of one side winning; you fight so all can win with peace. Sometimes, you really must turn on the creative juices and become active, at other times, you're to wait on a person's readiness. Timing is extremely important to carry out true balance in people's lives. Understanding God's timing clearly shows one of the benefits of creative fighting."

"Ok, but what about things we feel we ought to take up for? You know, like maybe a civil rights issue or some moral concern." I peered at my mentor.

"You must be extremely careful you do not fight a battle for selfish reasons. Remember, offering Christian understanding is not the same as giving consent. Jesus understood a person's sin, but did not consent to specific behavior." Ruben said.

"On the surface, many concerns appear other-centered but are motivated by something selfish. For instance, a person may fight, let's say, for minority housing, but underneath that individual may have something to gain financially with the outcome. The minute you get self-centered, you lose your holy indifference, your contentment, your own peace. Certainly, there are issues that need to be discussed by Christians, but the simple measurement stays a matter of harmony. If it is not within your power to bring God's peace to the situation, you may be fighting the wrong fight."

"But some people's definition of harmony can certainly vary from mine?" I blurted.

"Yes, but remember. Jesus gave examples, like he never said or did anything to offend a little child. True harmony promotes a kind of innocence because it levels the playing field."

"I think I see what you mean." I trailed off.

"Another point to remember: **people are not just at odds with each other, but they are also at enmity with God.**" Ruben shouted like an old-time preacher.

"The stark reality is most persons who do not know God are either mad at Him or afraid of Him." Ruben announced. "To them God remains some awesome righteous principle who will send lightning bolts of anger at them like the pictures of Zeus. Or, He is some mean father who will take away all their pleasures, their life, a child, anything to make them suffer. One of your wonderful opportunities as peacemaker is to let harmony flow through you so much you will develop a Christlike winsomeness. This unique winsome quality will attract people and they will begin to ask you to define the power and they will hunger for it. At this point the Holy Spirit will come and do the divine work. This winning quality will be so attractive it will help people fall in love with Christ through you. Because, you see, it's a picture of what Grace really is. God's grace shining through in the form of peace is so relaxing to stressed people and so appealing that it turns on their love mechanisms. For us who watch, it's a magnificent sight to behold."

"What do you mean *those of us who watch*?" I queried.

"Never mind. Stay with our discussion . . . now the rest of the verse says the peacemakers will be called the sons of God. This really means children of God, both male and female."

"You don't mean we must become peacemakers before we can have the salvation experience?"

"No. No", Michael injected. "The scripture is not giving that definition. You already have the position of child of God when you accepted Jesus as Savior. **Other people** will call you children of God when they see the quality of peacemaking in you. It's a reference like when someone says, 'like father, like son; like mother, like daughter.' So, in the distribution of harmony, you will be complimented by others calling you children of God. Truly heaven delights when one of you gets called a true child of the king. When you help reconcile someone to God, all of heaven rejoices"

"Man, there's a lot here, but I think I know what you're saying but could you explain more what you mean by reconciliation?" I wondered.

"**Everything** becomes reconciled in Christ. He **is** the

harmony, the peace, the balance. You see God's creative music placed everything in balance. For instance, every physical reality has a spiritual equal. Heaven is looped with earth by the same principles. Let me illustrate. As we still sit here in the car, put your hands on that steering wheel. Feel its reality."

I reached and did as I was told. "Ok . . . I feel it."

"That steering mechanism will not exist a thousand years from now, but the idea, the unseen spiritual principle behind the physical result will still exist somewhere. Heaven and earth keep this looping effect and in the beginning of time, all was in harmony. Not until Sin, the sour note, the separating principle entered earth, was there possibility for any interrupters. Jesus' sacrifice destroyed the disturbers and created a bridge for a return to a balance."

"Can I let go of the steering now?" I asked.

"Of course, as I was saying, reconciliation by a peacemaker is simply a process of allowing the Holy Spirit to do the work of reestablishing an original harmony. One of the reasons so many people are confused about life is they have too many disrupters, blockers which continually break away any balance they might obtain. A simple thing like worry can become a huge blocker."

"Jerod . . ." Ruben stared at me, "a most exciting part of your pilgrimage allows you seeing the blockers banished, individuals aligning themselves with their new natures, and seeing lives become new songs for the Lord. Right now, you have little idea the privilege you have, but you will in time. You are a vital part of what the scripture declares. I like to put it this way: Blessed are you who bring harmony to a fragmented person, for you will be labeled a true follower of Christ."

"Man, Ruben. I don't know where you get all this stuff, but in my deepest spirit, I know what you're saying is true. You just leave me speechless sometimes. I must let it all soak in for a while."

"If you are becoming a sponge . . . and letting it soak in as you say . . . then I'm getting through to you. *O happy day*!" Ruben chuckled.

I felt embarrassed and gazed out the car window across the parking lot. So much happened and so much said made me feel overwhelmed, not overcome by frustration but saturated by a sense of joy. A sudden rush of all my senses moved me and I felt surrounded by a protective, unseen bubble of energy. I felt like I floated alone in the universe, but not truly alone.

Slowly, a sense of deep pleasure washed over me, knowing I belonged to an active part of the divine kingdom, and my lack of full understanding did not seem to matter. I trusted more in the future power of the Holy Spirit to interpret meanings when the time proved right. I could feel my old earth-bound nature shifting toward the better part of me that aligned with the Holy Spirit. Finally, I shook myself from my reverie, sighed deeply and turned to look at Michael.

Ruben quietly started closing the door behind him, for he'd already gotten out of the car unnoticed.

"Wait . . . where are you going?" I pleaded. "I need to talk to you about tomorrow. You know it's Sunday and I don't need to be seen around town since I've taken off from church. It might not be good for my image. Ha. Ha. . . Uh . . . so what are we going to do? You're not going to display me around town in a humility exercise, are you? Where can we go, sort of quiet like?"

Ruben smiled, turned and kept walking away from the car.

I fumbled with the door handle, hurrying out the door on my side. By the time I moved around the other side to catch my friend, Michael was nowhere in sight.

Chapter 18

A big part of me felt criminal, like doing something wrong. I remembered once in high school, skipping classes with some other boys to go shoot billiards at a downtown pool hall. In those days, in my small town, for youth to shoot pool and skip school was highly illegal.

For a while, we thought we got away with it, but then we'd been caught by a local truant officer and taken to the police station. The officer pretended to run us through the finger printing system, showed us the jail cells. It all became very real to us then. Unknown to us naive boys, it stayed the method the officer used to put the 'fear of God' into students so they wouldn't skip again. It worked well on me.

So, here I was on Sunday morning, feeling much like a high school student again, disloyal fugitive, hiding out in my own house. It was one thing to miss services when gone out of town on some speaking engagement. But to miss services so close to home became a gut wrenching, uneasy feeling to say the least.

Since early morning I'd paced the floor, wondering what Ruben's next strategy would be. Even though I'd put my car in the garage, I could feel the judgment of some of my church members who might have passed my house, guessing what might be going on. Why was Michael making me squirm like this? I contemplated. Did the man derive some pleasure out of making me nervous? On the other hand, Ruben never did anything without a good reason. I wish he would tell me beforehand, instead of the weird surprises.

I went to the kitchen for more coffee. I'd already drunk two cups but kept it up like I might not get any more. Suddenly, the doorbell rang. Not answering would deepen my childish guilt. Answering might mean dealing with negative confrontation.

I crept to the living room window blinds and peeked out a corner. Peeking back at me, tongue sticking out one side of his mouth and crossed eyed with a cornball expression viewed Ruben. I jumped back and hurried to open the front door. I reached out, grabbed Ruben's arm, dragged him into the room, and glanced up and down the street, then eased the door shut like I didn't want to disturb someone's sleep.

"Whatsa matter? Spies around? Are we incognito today?" Ruben jibed and giggled as he walked straight to the kitchen and poured himself a cup of coffee.

I followed him into the kitchen. "Why in the world didn't you let me know what was on for today? You know I have a church to run and how the people won't understand this at all? I should be in the pulpit at church instead of hiding out in my own home feeling like a fugitive." I anguished.

With coffee in hand, Ruben moved to the living room and sat down on the couch, looking every bit right at home, like he'd been here before. I joined him by sitting in a recliner, angled to the right of my visitor.

"Loyalty is a wonderful quality," Michael commented, "But sometimes placed in the wrong place."

"What do you mean by that?"

"Where is your church, Jerod?"

"The corner of Broadway . . . wait . . . you know that."

"No . . . **Where** is your church, the members, really?"

"I still don't know what you're asking. Some are down on Broadway, some are at home I'm sure, and some are scattered where we don't even know where they are."

"Right! . . . the church resides where the people are, right?"

"Yes."

"So, is it possible you could be at church right here in your own home?"

"Yes, but I strongly believe in the idea of 'forsake not the assembling of yourselves together' business. Sounds like you're giving me the same excuse others have given me why they won't come to be a part of our congregation. They say they can worship at home better than down on Broadway . . . I just don't buy it."

Ruben formed his hands into a steeple. "I understand . . . and Christians should congregate, but you mustn't think the building is the only place people may have a worship experience."

"I didn't mean that." I objected.

"You do see, though, if you're not careful, you can put undue pressure on yourself and others, like false guilt, thinking you may not experience God except in a structured environment. Come on . . . you, the Holy Spirit and I can be a congregation this morning."

"Well, yeah, but how do most Christians know where

to draw the line? Home is much more comfortable, with the T.V. and all. I suspect most would just stay home if I propagated the idea of church being wherever people are." I puzzled.

"Not if individuals were truly traveling the kingdoms with you. It would turn around and people would **want** to congregate whenever and wherever possible. You wouldn't beg them to come. They'd view the church gathering as more of a filling up station because they'd want to share with everyone the good news what happened during the week. The atmosphere would become more of an excitement of gathering, an opportunity to share how God became honored through the week, how it really makes a difference people know Jesus."

"You mean like have more personal testimonies in the morning service?"

"That's just one method of sharing. The excitement would change some of your methods. Remember, Clarissa and the first century church didn't have big buildings to meet in. The method of interacting with each other took place in small groups. You already have small groups now . . . called Sunday school, but it's what you **do** in those groups that could change for the better. And by the way, nothing says in the Bible they must be **only** one hour in length. If people are genuinely being fed and experiencing growth, blocks of time do not become a problem."

"I've known of other churches changing their structure for certain Bible studies, but our church doesn't seem to be interested in much change." I reflected.

"Nor you either. That's what I mean by tacking your loyalty to the wrong place. You too are stuck in some of your loyalties and those may not be bad in themselves, but can sure stop certain growth . . . So . . . now we come to the eighth lesson and kingdom. I like to call it the **Kingdom of Loyalty**. Get out the copy of the parchment and look at Clarissa's symbols. Tell me what you see."

With no hesitation, I obeyed and spoke. "Well, first, there is 'blessed are those who are persecuted for righteousness sake, for theirs is the kingdom of heaven', then there's a stick figure with short cropped hair, probably a man, drawn with lines coming out of his mouth, like he's shouting. But the strange thing is he's pointing toward three crosses +++. Is he yelling at the crosses? I don't get it."

"Not many have because of the extreme difficulty inherent in this kingdom. Most had rather skip this struggle. Of all the letdowns Jesus experienced, which do you think hurt Him the most?"

"I've always thought of His hurts as being equal."

"Wise man . . . but if you had to imagine one hurt above others, which would you pick? Would it be Peter's denial? The betrayal of Judas? The temptations? The misguided religious leaders? Would it be His actual death? What do you think?"

"Ruben, don't you think that's a very subjective question? I mean wouldn't you think each of us would answer what we, ourselves, felt the most pain about? For instance, if I were a champion for children's rights and fighting child abuse, wouldn't I probably say that Jesus' main hurt was when He saw adults misusing and mistreating children?"

"That's an excellent point. You must throw a switch

on Sundays and turn on your better thinking. Aha. Aha. Aha."

Suddenly, Michael reached over, picked up a magazine, tore out a sheet, folded it into a dunce cap and placed it on his head, grinning like a happy-face cartoon.

Suddenly, the front door rattled. Someone jiggled the lock, and then the door swung open with a swish and in walked Jill, bag in one hand and keys in another. Dressed in blue jeans and casual shirt, she looked at the two of us sitting in the living room. But she stared at the grinning old man, sitting placidly with a dunce cap on his head.

"Oh . . . I'm sorry . . . am I interrupting something?" Jill quizzed.

I jumped up and hurried to my wife, hugging her tightly.

"I'm so glad to see you sweetheart. Let me take your bag." I turned to Ruben. "Would you excuse us a minute?"

I grabbed the bag and Jill by the arm and ushered her into the bedroom with one quick motion.

"I was wondering about you." I spoke softly.

"Yeah . . . I can see you were." Jill retorted.

"Look . . . could we talk later . . . I want you to meet Mr. Michael and listen to him awhile, just for now, ok?"

Jill stared her icy look.

"By the way, you smell great . . . and look good too." I smiled.

"Oh Jerod, I look a mess and I sure didn't know we would have company."

"Come on, Jill . . . trust me. Ruben isn't company,

once you get to know him. Just look at him. He's at home wherever he is."

Jill stepped over to look in the dresser mirror, fluffed her long hair, pulled at the corner of her shirt-sleeves and turned back to face me.

"All right. I'll go in there, but you've got to remember I've had a long drive from my brother's and I'm not in the best of moods now. I'll be civil, but I can't be the perfect, entertaining pastor's wife. You take your chances with me now. Understand?"

I motioned 'after you' with my right hand and we walked back into the living room. Ruben stayed on the couch, but the dunce hat was gone and he looked the dignified gentleman.

"Ruben, I want you to meet my wife, Jill."

He rose and took her hand gently in both of his, gave a princely bow and moved her to a seat like a well-trained usher. I could tell, Jill felt impressed by his manners. Neither of us could help but sense the warmth radiating from the man.

Michael returned to his seat and asked: "Shall we continue?"

I directed my attention to Jill. "Yes please . . . Ruben was talking about the beatitude, 'blessed are the persecuted' and what it meant."

"First, I asked the question . . . Jerod do you remember what it was?"

"Uh . . . I think . . . what I thought hurt Jesus the most."

"And your answer is . . .?"

I rubbed the bridge of my nose. "Well, like I said, I would just guess, but I suppose it would be the one thing each of us feels the most hurt about, like death or some suffering. There's always one issue that gets to us more than others."

"And what would yours be, Jerod?"

I glanced at Jill and lowered my head. "The thing that gets me most is when you feel misunderstood and someone lets you down, especially a loved one."

"In a sense, you have just put your finger on the real pain of Jesus." Ruben responded. "Think with me a minute about the Cross experience. At first, people followed Jesus. Then, step by step, before the Crucifixion, people started misunderstanding Him. The Pharisees thought he blasphemed. The Sadducees were materialists and believed in only physical answers for everything. The Roman leaders misunderstood His purpose about power. The public demanded to set free a thief rather than Jesus. By the time of Golgotha, the disciples, including his mother, did not understand him. And all these were bad enough, but there came more. Did you ever wonder why Jesus cried out on the Cross: *Eli, Eli, lama sabachthani . . . my God, my God, why have you forsaken me?"*

"Yes, I've always wondered about the theology of that question." I pondered.

"It's not just theology. One of the most significant events in all history happened with that declaration. The very essence of Jesus repulsed by the thought of having to experience any separation from the Father, anything like a spiritual death. That's one of the reasons He literally took from Psalm 22 and prayed on the Cross. He knew He was going to die physically, ever since the Garden of Gethsemane. He just did not want to die spiritually, which means utter separation from God the Father.

"What do you mean die spiritually? How could He do that?" I felt a confusing theological dilemma coming on.

Ruben continued, "Jesus was already praying for resurrection. Jesus felt the true loneliness of what sin does to the human heart. As fully human, he felt misunderstood by everybody, even the absence of His father. Jesus didn't feel the victim kind of misunderstanding, but a genuine condition of being the only person choosing a way He alone thought right. To know you are right and have no one understand your point of view, not even God, caused a colossal dilemma. This predicament is exactly what Sin does. It creates a void through separation, a non-connectedness, lostness."

Ruben glanced at Jill and continued. "To be human in its completeness, Jesus had to experience the same thing you do and yet not sin. He had to go through something He did not deserve. Since Jesus could not sin, He had to experience the result of sin like a spiritual death. And so, God the Father withdrew His sense of presence from His Son. Up until then, the Father's presence had always been with Jesus no matter what. But on the cross, Jesus stayed completely alone to show the real love of God. The Father voluntarily disconnected . . . and by the way . . . that's more of a risk than you can image."

"What do you mean . . . disconnect . . . a risk?" I stammered.

"I'm not sure you can understand all now, but basically the unity between God the Father, the Son, and Holy Spirit remains so complete and perfect that its complete connectedness holds the whole universe, all that is permanent reality, together." Ruben circled the room with his right arm like a rodeo cowboy twirling a rope and continued.

"When God the Father disconnected, He took a chance as it were and placed the whole creation upon the shoulders of the Son to bear all alone. Jesus became vulnerable to all the negative forces and He could have chosen to give in to that loneliness and the universe could have been changed, even lost forever. But He didn't give in. In fact, He withstood more than anyone realizes. He showed the whole cosmos what God's love authentically can do. It can suffer its own negative creation pains and still come out loving."

I sat speechless as Ruben continued.

"Jesus as much as said, *'I'll show what real love is. Although no one is with me. I will die and live for the God that ought to be.'* And then, He gave up the spirit because divine closure occurred. True love exists in believing and living what remains right even though you may be misunderstood by those who are supposed to understand and be on your side."

Suddenly, Jill chimed in, "That sounds like everyone must be a martyr."

Ruben turned in her direction. "Ah . . . but you see, true love of God has the ability to keep on loving without those negative feelings of pride. God's love is laced with mercy and judgment in harmonious cooperation in such a way the result is an ability to go beyond petty feelings and stand firm, even if it means death. Anyone can die properly, if they have first learned how to live properly. Living and dying are all part of the same creative energy, that is, the resurrection principle in Nature and what Jesus showed literally so well. The whole cross experiment displayed a confirmation of what

God already did in creation, except He needed to take part in it more precisely through His Son. The Cross was to the resurrection as good soil is to the healthy plant."

I felt elated and stunned at the same time. For a moment, I couldn't speak. Then I said, "That's incredible and it makes sense of something else. It explains why every human must face the Cross alone. Alone, we must accept Jesus or reject. No one can do that for us. Does that also mean, there are other specific things we must do by ourselves?" I glanced at my wife. Jill looked down at her hands.

"Right on, but what were you thinking of specifically?" Michael blurted.

"Well, ok . . . like making our individual ways through the kingdoms you've talked about. Not even a husband and wife can walk those together, can they?"

"A husband and wife can walk the kingdoms together **only** in cooperating with each other's differences in their various paces. They must be tolerant of individual growth. Individuals are so different they must move through the kingdoms individually. The real challenge of the husband and wife relationship becomes that occasion when one gets ahead of the other in growth. The one ahead must not become smug or feel superior to the other. If that happens, an over-under relationship occurs, only to develop discord and hurt feelings. Two different species, male and female, must learn to be patient with each other and allow God's timing to work in the individual lives. However, on occasion, a specific couple might move through the kingdoms at the same pace. But that is rare indeed."

Jill's head jerked up and she stared gravely at me. I caught her look and felt I should change the subject.

"Ruben . . . what about Clarissa's symbols . . . you know, the man and three crosses?"

"Ah, yes, the Kingdom of Loyalty. The symbols show the challenges in this journey. When you speak or when you behave, you will confront three kinds of crosses."

"You mean I must bear three different kinds of crosses?" I questioned.

"Don't think so literally here. Remember these are signs and symbols. No, it means you will confront three different kinds of people in their different responses to you. One cross stands for the non-believer, the person who outright rejects any true Christian value system. He or she may have some of the Christian values that have spilled over from church into culture, like the idea of 'you shall not murder', but they do not have the Spirit of Truth in them and so cannot understand you completely."

"So, these are what I call lost people, those that need salvation." I agreed.

"Yes, they are the ones who must enter the kingdom of Need, the very beginning of the growth journey."

"What does loyalty do with them?" I inquired.

"Because they do not have full accessible truth from the Holy Spirit, they tend to live half-truths and confuse the issues of this world. You can become trapped in those issues and find yourself caught in moral dilemmas. For example, a person spouting half truths about, let's say, a teenager having an unwanted pregnancy, can command a following on both sides of the issue. Then Christians start fighting about part truths. If you chose involvement in an issue like this, you will be persecuted no matter which side you're on. With such emotional issues, people can become cruel scoffers of your Christian values. These scoffers bombard you with outright painful opposition. The real challenge will be to stay loyal to the kingdom principles among those who will not understand you."

"I can see that." I murmured. "It is especially hard for me to deal with emotional individuals who appear to have no ability to accept the truth when it's right in front of them. Then they often turn on you with personal attack. That's a tough one."

"Yes, but there's one even tougher in the second cross." Ruben's eyes darted at Jill.

"Ok . . . so what's the second cross stand for?" I asked.

"The second cross represents those who are believers, but just barely. Remember, we talked about Christians being stuck in the kingdom of need?"

"Yeah . . . those are ones who haven't grown much since a salvation experience, although they may have been saved twenty years or something." I agreed again.

"Yes, they know the saving and forgiving love of Christ, but they have not acted upon it for others as much as they have cherished it for themselves. These people will appear to support your values and make you think they are on your side for a while. But the minute you propose a mature growth quality based on the kingdom principles, they begin to balk. And in time, they will break your heart with what seems to be their unbelief. But it is not they have unbelieving hearts, but rather they have hearts of unbelief. There's a great difference."

"What do you mean?" I glanced at my wife, then back to Michael.

"People with unbelieving hearts are persons who refuse to accept Jesus as a real person in every part of life. Some openly reject, but most use a subtler way of belief. They believe in the idea of goodness. To them, God is a principle of goodness only, like gravity—out there in the atmosphere somewhere. In other words, God appears more of a law and not a person, not too concerned with what they think to be real human events. And to them, this belief gets set in motion and applies to everyone. It is very non-personal and a follower simply goes along with it or goes against it with the corresponding results."

"Can you give a Bible example of what you're talking about? I'm not sure I understand. What is a specific picture of an unbelieving heart?" I grilled.

"Some of the Jews of the early Christian era gave an intellectual assent to the Messiahship of Jesus only. They were warned of this because of their unbelieving hearts; that is, their hearts were solely and entirely controlled by unbelief. In other words, there was no faith in them—only an adherence to law. These persons were not saved in your terms."

"You mean like some of the Pharisees and Sadducees, the religious leaders of their day."

"Right, or like some of your leaders today. Their hearts, which by the way really means—emotions, minds and wills—had no room for more mature faith because they thought they'd figured out everything by all their laws and rituals which were supposed to honor the main law of goodness. The result was a legalism that trapped people into false security and half-truths. Clarissa and her group met in houses to avoid these evil people as much as possible or they'd become exposed to frightening retribution on the part of those religious leaders."

Ruben extended his hands out like he was begging. "Jesus himself did not persuade many of them because of their unbelief. Jerod . . . these kinds of people are around you today. They are the ones that will misunderstand you and are still under the first cross we mentioned. But remember, earlier I was talking about Clarissa's second cross symbol. These have hearts of unbelief."

"Oh yeah . . . so what is the distinction?" I asked.

"People who harbor hearts of unbelief can be Christian believers, but residing within is the tendency to turn back to a former life of non-belief. Let's say, for example, you have grown in the kingdom principles and are suggesting to these people they should respond to an unjust situation with the quality of mercy. It could be something like speaking against war when the idea of war seems righteous. Their tendency will be to revert to justice only—the law—instead of offering mercy. They will return to their old worldly ways of solving problems instead of Jesus' teachings on the Mount. This can happen with any of the nine kingdoms and their growth stages. At the point of reverting back shows the point where people get stuck. Again, part of your job is to encourage Christians along their kingdom paths so they won't get bogged down."

"Who does this fit in the Bible?" I prompted.

"Believe it or not . . . the apostle Peter displays this heart of unbelief during his betrayal period. Even when Peter cut off the ear of that Roman soldier, he reverted to his old self, dealing with a problem more on what he thought justified violence. The kingdom growth principles do not propose justified violence as a necessarily first response. For instance, in the kingdom of God, you are to use love to turn away violence or sometimes to absorb it. You use peace to turn away anger. Even the disciple Thomas had a subtle form of this disbelief when he refused to believe some things about Jesus until he touched the scars. See . . . you are to use faith to cast out this unbelief. This kind of unbelief lies in wait among the old nature and becomes active when you feed it."

I reflected. "So, the second cross symbol stands for sort of weak believers who will misunderstand me, give me difficulty because they haven't grown enough. And I'm to endure their bombardments with loyalty to Jesus' teachings. Won't this appear haughty or pompous on my part? You know, like the Pharisees attitude of *'I'm better than you because I do more than you'?"*

"Not if you have experienced genuine growth so the Holy Spirit in you shows the result of Christlikeness. Remember, you're not doing this on your own. Besides, true growth will radiate who you are in Christ, not just what you do. Demonstrating loyalty to Christ will only help others to consider their own resolve about Christian living."

I looked at my wife again. Jill sat still, but I could tell, her mind spun ferociously. I could sense many questions traveling her nerve paths, but still, she appeared to thaw toward Ruben and for some unknown reason, seemed to feel a part of the discussions. Finally, after a pause in the conversation she spoke.

"Mr. Michael, I was just thinking . . . Uh . . . do you mind if I make an observation?"

Ruben turned to me. "Do you mind her commenting?"

"Heavens No. I'd welcome her input. She has great analytical skill." I quipped happily.

"Well, I have many questions" Jill responded, "but

I was just considering the three crosses you were discussing and I wondered where Clarissa got the idea of those symbols in her writings and I started networking in my mind and my thoughts returned to Golgotha, that bald hill where three other crosses stood."

"Yes?" Ruben returned.

"Is it possible the three crosses on Golgotha which held two thieves and Jesus actually represent the three kinds of people any Christian must deal with?"

"Why don't you elaborate on that, hon." I added.

Jill sat up straight and continued. "I mean . . . there hung one person scoffing at Jesus, trying to get Him to come down and save them from their troubles. He could be the first you mentioned, people who are the nonbelievers. Then there displayed one thief who barely had a chance to believe anything but Jesus said he would receive paradise. He would be the second kind of person, one that knows Christ but hasn't grown very much. Then there was Jesus Himself, who I suppose could represent the more mature Christian."

I stared admiringly at my wife, threw back my shoulders and rested my gaze upon Ruben, as if to say 'how do you like them apples'. Michael shifted in his seat and spoke.

"That's not a bad analogy as long as you stop right there. You are to be commended because you have good symbolic skills. However, the example breaks down at the point of the third cross. Yes, it could stand for mature Christians because Jesus is there, but Clarissa was trying to warn of something here that doesn't fit Jesus."

"What is that?" I asked alarmed.

"The third cross symbol does stand for Christians who

have grown beyond the salvation experience, and thus have matured somewhat. But you see, even those more mature Christians will find an occasion to misunderstand you Jerod," Ruben stared at me . . . "simply because they may not have traveled through enough kingdom stages to truly recognize your behavior or intentions of the moment. You will need to stay loyal even when it appears the best of Christian friends or family let you down. And that's not all."

"What can ever hurt more than being misunderstood by those people you count on the most?" I marveled.

Ruben gave an extra-long pause . . . then said, "The silence of God, Himself. Sometimes, God must answer you with silence. You must be loyal enough to listen your way through the silence **and** the problem."

"How can anyone do that? I mean, when I need to feel God's presence, that I'm doing His will in some matter, I need to hear from Him somehow. I mean I need confirmation, don't I?"

"Yes, Jerod, you do, but you will need to learn to receive personal affirmation through silence, as well as other audible means. Just as you have five senses connected with the physical body, you have, at least five senses connected with the spiritual."

"Whoa . . . you mean there are five spiritual senses? What are they?"

"Well, I could mention those, but I don't want to get you off track."

"I've always wondered about that too", Jill chimed, "if something like our dreams were somehow connected spiritually and that we should get more out of them than we do in modern times."

"Very astute Jill. Maybe you should have been my

pupil, but alas . . . you were not the one I was instructed to find." Ruben responded.

Jill smiled her warmest and I saw she felt more involved.

"Hey . . . just a minute." I grinned.

Michael chimed in. "Well she did hit upon one of the spiritual senses which are actually supposed to carry over into the physical world. Dreams are an extension of a person's seeing ability. See, time has no boundaries in dreams. Dreams deal with the sense of spiritual sight. In the physical, dream activities become little dramas put on by the subconscious, designed to give the person insight into the soul. It is just one vehicle through which God can speak to the individual. Sometimes He even must use dreams to breakthrough one's aware realm and get that person's attention. Those you often call nightmares."

I frowned because some doubt moved across my spirit.

"Now, now." Ruben smiled. "Don't get misled here. That doesn't mean every dream or nightmare is a word from God. Sometimes people do things to their bodies causing nightmares. You've also got to remember the negative forces can work in your dreams too. The subconscious will take good or evil because it's not limited by time or space. It is a pure realm of spirit activity."

"Is that why there are Bible examples of dreams influencing people's destiny?" Jill commented.

"You are right again." Michael retorted. "Dreams were used much more basically in the Bible days. The practical use for dreams got changed when science came into being because dreams were not scientific enough to measure. Or at least in the early days, science was not willing to accept someone's dream experience as a measuring tool."

Ruben clamped his hands together like praying hands, laid his head on them and closed his eyes in a motion of lying down to sleep. "In your modern world of technology and some of your dream laboratories, science gives more credence to the dream experience, but you are still not as adapt in them as Biblical characters like Daniel, who could interpret dreams because God helped him. It's too bad Christians today don't use dreams more as guides to living."

Jill darted a look at me.

I shrugged and grinned and continued. "Ruben you've got my curiosity stirring. I still am thinking about the other spiritual senses you said exist."

"Briefly, another one is hearing. God uses the universal penetration of song, poetry and music. Then, tasting helps. God flavors humanity with attitudes and values. Smelling is available. God speaks through aroma, incense and prayer. Touch is the fifth sense. But I'll just elaborate one specific sense."

"I'll mention one, but this is all I want to discuss now. Think of the touch ability. What humanity often calls *creativity* is a result of a spiritual sense connection. It is so because it stays linked to touch, feeling and what you do with your hands." He stared at me like ex-ray eyes and my mouth shut before I could ask another question. An uncomfortable silence followed.

Finally, Jill spoke again. "I can see the physical and spiritual connections, but you got me thinking about what the Bible calls persecution. You know, Mr. Michael, we don't really get outright oppression today in America . . . I mean . . . I don't think anyone is going to put us in jail for our Christian beliefs. How does the 'blessed are the persecuted' actually apply today?"

"Ok . . . good . . . back to the point. That may be one of your gifts, Jill. Ruben nodded toward her and spoke.

"You can see from the warnings of Clarissa's symbols mistreatment might come from her set of circumstances, but you are right they may not be so obvious. For instance, probably no one is going to stand up during one of your husband's sermons and heckle him openly. Such display would certainly be persecution. But they can intimidate him subtly in a thousand different ways behind his back . . . you too, by the way, like some prideful disagreement."

Jill clasped her hands in front, sat up straight and looked at the ceiling.

"Harassment can come in any form, like an attitude. Or an obvious negative can happen, like well-meaning Christians withholding their tithes from church because they disagree with something the preacher may say. Or, people getting you caught up in grievous little annoyances to rob you of time for the more important things. Did you ever waste your time in a useless committee meeting? Of course, the real point is you should make sure you're getting hassled for Jesus' sake and not just something you created on your own without including the Holy Spirit."

"Man, Ruben," I hesitated. "You've covered a lot of territory. It makes me almost paranoid to think I must be on guard all the time. I'm not sure I want to know all this if I must go around looking over my shoulder half the time." I interjected.

"Oh, Jerod . . . Jerod, you must quit being so afraid of shadows. Part of the kingdom challenge is to remind you **when** you are persecuted, annoyed or maltreated. Remember, you have the Holy Spirit's guidance to remind you and the kingdom is in you as well as you are its representative. So, you may respond in the name of Jesus, with love, instead of some off-track human justice. See . . . once again . . . remember, you may be traveling through these smaller kingdoms of the Mount, but you have the overall larger kingdom of God Himself. Living and growing in the larger kingdom of Jehovah stays the greatest kingdom of all which holds together all the rest. It is worth living and dying for."

"Well, I can see how tough this stage is, especially the idea of developing a **willingness** to be misunderstood. Most of us want to be liked." Jill interrupted.

Ruben leaned forward and turned directly in my line of sight. "See how subtle the human mind is. Jill put her finger on one very large dragon—the false need to be liked by everybody. The truth stands: all holy desires tend to grow by onslaughts and delays. If a desire can be easily diminished by delay, then it was never holy in the first place."

"Excuse me?" I flinched.

"Never mind. Enough for this morning. Ponder this one truth: "God's complete vibration quality spreads His true essence beyond any of what a human obtains by His Grace."

With those parting words, Ruben Michael sprang up from his seat and marched out the front door, leaving Jill and me staring at each other, sitting with our mouths open.

Chapter 19

Jill moved to the bedroom for more mundane activities. I was close behind her and wondering what she thought. I watched Jill unpack her traveling clothes, hang them in her closet and neatly put away her shoes. For a while, we did not discuss Ruben's visit.

Finally, she said, "Not much happened at my brother's house. We did go shopping which you know I like there. That state always has something different than ours. But away from home, I thought a lot about my life and our relationship. I've always felt marriage meant much more than some ill-defined comfort for two, since no children graced our house. I truly felt we were full partners in all ministries of the church. At least, we were until now. I'm still not sure how to handle any individual involvement with Ruben. Of course, I do understand better how appealing the whole enterprise is after my short encounter with that mysterious little man. He seems like a wise grandfather."

I realized, in her better moments, she understood why I was drawn toward the man, his wisdom and teaching were spiritually disturbing but in a Biblical and alluring manner. To both of us, Ruben indeed appeared winsome and charming in an unusual spiritual way. Yet,

I also felt her dissatisfaction in the manner which I made her feel left out in the beginning, as if there existed things in life that could not be shared in a marriage. Maybe after briefly hearing Ruben, she'd be able to get past anger and what she admitted to herself was probably some jealousy. Yet, I was concerned she felt a wedge, a small wall between us, as if part of our intimacy was broken. I know she did not like any feeling of distance between us because it made her too fragile about all of life.

Jill started down the hallway and suddenly the hall land-line rang. With automatic reaction, she picked up the phone. "Hello."

"Hi. Jill. This is Gary Butler. By any chance, is your pastor and mine there?"

"As a matter of fact, he is. Just a minute." She looked at me, put her hand over the mouthpiece and shrugged, as if she did the wrong thing in answering.

She whispered. "Jerod . . . Gary Butler is on the line,"

"Oh, no, Jill," I groaned. "You know I was trying to keep from talking to church people today . . . especially since I skipped out on church services. What were you thinking?" I blustered.

She jerked the phone against her chest and with closed fist placed her other hand on her hip. "I guess I didn't think since I'm not used to hiding out in my own home. Are you going to answer him or not?"

I reached for the intrusive instrument and said, "Hi Gary, what's up?"

"You tell me, brother. You sick or something? You need us to bring you food or do anything?"

"Hold on, Gary. I'm not sick."

"Well, we missed you in church today. The substitute

was ok, but not like you. Is there something wrong buddy?"

"No, no . . . Nothing's wrong Gary." I thought to myself: *Man, I don't want to lie to Gary.*

"Oh . . . well, if you can't talk about it." He murmured.

"It's no big thing . . . really. I just . . . Uh . . . needed a day off. You know. All you guys get Sunday off. It's one of my big workdays and sometimes I just need to feel a day off on Sunday."

"Like you want to take a day off from God?"

"No, nothing like that!" I flared.

"Hey, take it easy, old friend. I was just concerned about you." Butler responded.

I thought: *Concerned, yeah right . . . nosy more like.*

"Uh, sorry Gary. See what I mean. I'm a grouch. I needed time off, I guess. I'll be fine tomorrow. Really."

"Hey, I didn't think ministers ever got grouchy."

"Contrary to popular belief, guy, we are human."

"Right . . . yeah . . . ok. Well, if I need to know anything, I mean . . . if I can do anything, let me know."

"Sure, Gary. I'll see you later."

"Blessings on you, pastor."

"Right! Back at you Gary." I hung up and walked back into the living room. where Jill sat, looking like a child might look who was about to be scolded.

"I didn't mean to snap at you, Jill. I was as mad at myself for not making my feelings plain today. I just didn't want to deal with church people if I could help it, especially someone like Gary's inquisitive personality. I should've mentioned not to answer the phone. Let the machine get it. Part of me was still immersed in what Ruben had discussed. He always says something way out, then disappears on me before I have a chance to clarify. He used to say he did that to shock me, to get my attention off the world and onto what he had to teach me. At first, it worked a lot."

I looked at my hands and continued. "Jill, he can do weird things . . . I mean, now don't freak when I tell you this, but he could make things float in the air, make things disappear, things like that. I don't know if he's a magician, doing sleight of hand or what, but it sure got my attention. He said I was too attached to this world and needed jolting to hear the real spiritual message he was instructed to give me. I kept asking 'instructed by whom?' and of course he simply says God does the instructing."

"You say he could make things disappear? Like what?" Jill puzzled.

"Himself . . . for one thing. I could go into a room where he was supposed to be and he'd be gone. Another time he made music come from nowhere and then disappear. Once by a poolside, he seemed to make his dropped sunglasses float back up into his hand. It was very strange at first but I got used to it, I guess. I really hadn't thought much about it lately until today. Please don't think I'm losing it or making things up. I **know** what I've experienced. And yet, even with all that stuff, he opened some of the most profound thinking in me I've ever known, even greater than all my Seminary training. Everything Ruben says seems to head right for my soul and bear witness with my spirit what he says is true. And not just true in the sense of facts, but truth in the sense of eternal application, truth that keeps erasing my exhaustion and filling my empty receptacle; and as he would say, helping to spill over onto others. This guy is something. He makes me want to re-evaluate my ministry, to say the least."

"Well . . . whatever you believe about him," Jill sighed, "he does have a winsome quality. He oozes charm and the kind of magnetism which makes you want to listen to what he says, that's for sure. I found myself caught up in his speech like you do when you get caught up in a song; kind of forget where you are and what you're doing. I can understand why you want to spend time with him, but I'm still not sure why I couldn't be with you on this all along." Jill folded her arms across her chest and looked like some regal judge.

"I admit perhaps I didn't go about the pursuit right," I replied humbly, "I didn't mean to hurt you or have anything come between us. You know me when I get bull headed sometimes. I may have misinterpreted Michael, but I got the impression he just wanted me as an audience. It may have been he wants me to have the challenge to convince everybody what he's teaching, even you. I don't know. I could have been all wrong since he didn't seem to mind your being here this last session. I don't know what that means for the future."

"Well I **was** pretty miffed when I went to my brother's. And I still don't think you handled it right, but I've thought about it. I'm trying not to be petty, but I just don't like the feeling I had, like a wedge between us. I can't stand that. We've always been a strong part together with everything. I did not like the disconnected feeling. It shakes me too much and makes me doubt who I am."

"I said I admit I blew it. Forgive me, ok? I sure don't want a wedge there. Can I make it up to you somehow? I mean, you're not going to punish me, are you?" I beamed.

"Yeah . . . bring out the cat of nine tails!" Jill grinned

an impish smile. "Let me just ask you this. How many more teaching sessions are left?"

"Actually, Ruben mentioned the parchments contained nine of Clarissa's coded symbol messages. This morning's lesson was the eighth, so I suppose there's one more left for sure, but as you saw yourself, he does leave abruptly. He never says what comes next until he surprises me with some connection."

"So, what does he do then?" she asked.

"Well, he usually contacts me and has me meet him in some unusual place. This was the first time he'd been at our house."

"Strange." Jill grunted.

"Not if you'd seen him every day. Strange seems to be his normal. And yet, I wouldn't mind having him around all the time. I don't know what's going to happen when we finish the lessons," I trailed off.

"Ok . . . well . . . change of pace. Why don't we eat a sandwich or something?" Jill blurted.

"Good idea."

Both of us went into the kitchen. Jill took precooked frozen turkey patties out of the freezer and plopped them into the microwave. I dug lettuce and tomato out and started chopping. In silence, we put together two TV trays of turkey sandwiches, potato chips and drinks. Ambling down the hallway to the T.V. room, we sat down and began to eat as we watched our favorite news program.

We stared at the screen, paying very little attention to any details of the program, more lost in our own individual thoughts. I ran through my mind the last few days, trying to remember all the kingdom steps, what Ruben said about each one. I felt like a child at school who might worry over homework, just fearing I would forget all the information if called upon to recite the material. I wished I'd written down many things so I could do easy review, but since that didn't happen, I had to trust my short-term memory, something which tended to make me nervous. In my mental computer, I reran the events of the last few hours.

On the other hand, I could read Jill's facial expressions. She probably pondered more about our relationship, trying to examine her feelings, wondering if anything was permanently wrong, any irreversible damage to our closeness. As I watched, she had the look that said something **did** feel out of place, but wasn't quite sure what. She tended to twirl and pull one strand of hair when she felt any small nagging idea, like wanting to pull out the problem.

Both of us sat with our own individual thoughts and barely heard the front doorbell ringing *Ring, ring, ring.*

Finally, the buzzing sound stirred us both and we jumped up, sat our tv trays aside, and headed for the front door. I hesitated, peeked through the peep hole and stared at a dark blue, white trimmed, uniformed young man, shifting from one foot to the other, whistling some tune. Dumbfounded, I opened the door.

"May I help you?" I asked.

"Are you Rev. Dr. Sellers?"

"Uh . . . yes I am."

The uniform snapped to attention, both hands held out a small, square yellow piece of paper and announced in a booming voice: "**Singing telegram delivery**!" He sang to tune of Old McDonald Had a Farm:

"Once upon a time of glee,

We did meet by an old oak tree.
Now we've come so very far,
Meet me at the Evening Star.
EEii . . . EEii . . . O."

Meet me at 2 o'clock. **Come alone**. *Bring parchment copies. Signed Ruben*," said the uniform.

I gawked. Jill gaped. We both looked at each other and slowly burst out laughing. The uniform stood with a silly grin on his face. I thought it reminded me of Michael himself.

I turned to Jill. "Do you have any change to tip this guy?"

"Not necessary," the uniform spoke, "all taken care of. Have a nice day." The young man handed me the telegram, turned and strolled down the sidewalk, whistling.

I closed the front door, looked again at the yellow paper and put my arm around Jill, leading her back to the living area. Both of us sat on the couch and stared at each other.

"That's one of the neatest things I've ever seen," Jill commented.

"See what I mean. This is mild. One time he had a whole written banner stretched across a room in a motel to announce my arrival. Whatever you say about Michael, he's inventive and interesting. He does these things out of nowhere. Again, he says to throw me off balance and make sure I'm giving him my undivided attention. And another thing, his calls are not always clear. For instance, he says here in the telegram to meet him at the **Evening Star.** I have no idea where that is. Do you?"

"Hey . . . the newspaper office has a big star on its

outside sign, but it's actually called The Star Registry, not Evening Star." Jill rapid fired.

"That's right . . . still and all, Michael might pick something like that and there would be some built-in meaning I'd have to figure out . . . Huumm . . . you know there's that old run-down motel out on highway three that has the flashing neon sign. Remember, it's a large star, although sections of the neon are burned out. That place has been there since the fifties. It's also the kind of place Ruben would pick."

"Gosh, that's right. Are you going to have to think of every star in town and visit them all?" Jill pleaded.

"It looks like it, although, if we think logically about Ruben, there's usually a clue which narrows the field a bit."

"Hey. . . I just thought of another star," Jill injected, "You know the old abandoned drive-in movie lot out east of town."

"You mean the place that sits back from the road and is all grown with weeds and trash everywhere?"

"It's got that huge iron frame star on the back side of the old screen." Jill added.

"Yeah . . . you're right again. That place belongs to one of our church members. He's been trying to sell it for years. It's not a bad piece of real estate, it's just no one knows what to do with it. But you're correct . . . it does have a star sure enough."

"We could go on like this for hours. How are you going to get all done by 2 o'clock? I know, we could split up . . . you take some and I'll take some . . ." Jill hesitated.

I held up his hand. "Wait a minute . . . Ruben has a religious message in his little ditty. I was just thinking.

He talks about *glee* and *far* and *star.* They could all point to the star of Bethlehem. And as we've been talking about the possibilities, the old drive-in movie place is the only one in the East . . . and that's where the star of Bethlehem came from. I believe that's the place I should start. This would be just like him to work out his little game so I'd be very intent on finding him for our next lesson."

"Ok . . . that makes a kind of sense. Let's go." Jill blurted.

"Uh . . . sweetheart . . . you're forgetting something. The telegram said to come alone." I flinched and felt sorrow at the same time.

Jill stood up abruptly, crossed her arms and started to pace back and forth in front of me.

"I guess I just don't get it. He knew I'd see the telegram. He knew I'd want to be a part of this since I've seen and heard him here. It's not like he's some secret agent. I don't care what he says, I'm going. He'll just have to live with it."

"You don't understand, Jill. He means what he says, always. I've seen him do things, remember . . . like the disappearing act . . . he might just do that again if you showed. I'm sorry we can't chance it. I'll have to fill you in later." My eyes pleaded for affirmation.

Jill gave out a deep sigh and fell onto the couch like a disgruntled teenager, wrapping her arms around herself, staring at the floor. The silence followed as loud as an echo chamber and my ears began to ring. I felt trapped but could not think of anything else to do but follow Ruben's instructions to the letter. I certainly didn't want to jeopardize the last lesson, besides Michael said to bring copies of the parchments. Some new development may be in process.

I moved delicately over to Jill's side and kissed her on the cheek. "Stay with me sweetheart," I whispered, "we'll make sense of all this I'm sure. In the meantime, why don't you take a nap? You're exhausted from your trip anyway. And while you're at it, say a little prayer for us. I'll be back before you know it and we can discuss what's next. I'm sorry I don't know what else to do."

Jill stared back coldly, some of her frost melting when I asked her to pray, but she was in no way pacified. Finally, she resigned to the events by being able to admit she **was** tired and did need rest. But I knew in her mind this wasn't by any means over yet. She needed an explanation why a plain stranger could build this wedge between us.

She turned to me and asked, "Can men just do that? Something to do with male bonding? Are you even capable of keeping an undiluted bond with a female, one female, and holding to it for permanent duration? Are all men just looking for the wise older father figure, one that can once again teach them childlike private secrets?"

She sat a moment and finally, she pushed me away gently and patted my arm at the same time. "Go on and do what you have to do. I'll manage as usual."

I frowned and thought: *Why did I feel so relieved? But I do,* as if I'd been given permission for some disgraceful activity or some risky enterprise. The feeling only perplexed me and I could only cope by shoving it down into the basement of forgetfulness. By this method, any confused feeling would not immobilize my actions; I could continue with what I thought my only responsibility.

I moved to the door. I would have to hurry if I was going to find the place Michael mentioned in his little telegram ditty. I glanced at my watch. Not much time before two o'clock. But in my opinion, the old drive-in at the east of town prevailed as a good guess for my destination.

After kissing Jill on the cheek, I got in my car and drove to the old Starlight drive-in movie. The large outside screen sat back off the road of a poorly repaired, two-lane hiway. The old black-top road sprouted grass and weeds of various lengths. The weeds seemed to know that growing along the edges of the road, no black-top shoulder could keep away the stubborn vegetation.

Abruptly, a white gravel turnoff pointed to the entrance. Foot-high weeds stood on each side of the driveway, a forgotten gateway to a once booming era of outdoor movies. It was an era that allowed you to treat your car like your living room. As I pulled into the driveway, I heard myself saying, *just bring your own living room to the drive-in and do what you want.*

About forty feet down the gravel road entrance, an old aluminum gate attached itself to the 100-foot-tall, monolith film screen—a towering, rectangular giant structure of wood, braced and fortified by steel pipe and cables. The screen side of the structure faced away from the hiway so a passerby could not see the film being shown inside. Blazing across the structure, the huge Star of the word **Starlight** was once a bright red, but now faded and cracked paint fell in chunks like dry leaves. The star faced out to the road.

I found the gate unlocked, opened it and drove on through. I knew of this place and had a pretty good idea what I'd see at once. The giant screen looked down upon an enclosed parking lot half the size of a football field. Scattered rows of individual car spaces stood like little rolling hills with each of the black top humps displaying a 4-foot-tall by 3-inch pipe stand to attach individual speakers. The humps were raised and designed so the individual car could pull up at an angle to face the screen in such a way the cars behind would have no obstruction for viewing. Each mound had its own portable speaker stand with a large wire connection. In the past, individual volume controlled speakers hung on the inside of the car by a built-in mount which could fit snugly over the driver side of the car window. All the speaker stands now had only wires dangling, evidence of speakers being ripped away.

As I viewed the abandoned, cracked-ridden parking area, I thought about a time of my own past. The drive-in movie concept promoted several advantages. A whole family, blessed by a crying baby, could come and disturb no one, except perhaps those within the car. Teenagers could pile a vehicle full of companions who could squirm and hoot and talk, yet be entertained by a film. Older people could enjoy the privacy of the auto and still make comments to each other about some actor or scene, never to be overheard by anyone not involved directly in the conversation. Some people came for other reasons, lovers for instance, or those wanting a cheap way to get out of the house, so the film tended to be secondary, and a convenient excuse to spend a Friday or Saturday night out.

Still, there were other designs of entertainment at

the drive-in. In separate buildings, the concessions of popcorn, candy and cold drinks awaited participants. Restrooms were available and even an outside sitting area for the good weather candidates; those that did not want to be penned up in a vehicle. Some people would drive their pickup trucks backwards into a parking space, drop the tailgate, and line the pickup bed with quilts and pillows, thereby having the best of both worlds—the stars overhead and the film screen straight ahead.

From time to time, the theater management would even show a double-double feature, four full length movies back to back. In those days, the films were shorter and the films may not have been academy award winners, but what difference it make when you could spend five to six entertaining hours outside the home in the world of fantasy land. After all, I surmised, these were the days of the **big** screen film, way before the technology of computers and home-bound movies. A wave of nostalgia flowed through me, something warm like the sentimental part of the 'good old days'.

I drove up to one of the old speaker stands and parked, gazing around for any sign of Ruben. I felt searching here was on the right track for several reasons. This would be the kind of place Michael would pick and, that front gate should have been locked. My church member and owner of this place would never leave the gate unlocked unless some realtor showed the place and forgot to lock up. But from the looks of everything, there existed little evidence of anyone around.

Am I in the wrong place? Could there be foul play? I thought. No evidence of that either, besides, what would anyone want to steal? Most of the speakers were gone from their stands, of which no one would want those outdated electronics anyway. Certainly, no one would want the stands because they were set in concrete and only made of inexpensive three-inch pipe. Nothing left to steal really. I got out of my car and walked toward the old building in the center of the lot where once housed the concessions and restrooms.

Suddenly, my body stiffened as I thought I heard voices. Perhaps the place was haunted; after all, a lot of energy and experience permeated this place, lots of emotion packed by thousands of people. Perhaps some part of them stayed behind, like an imprint on time. And under just the right conditions, one might hear traces in the wind or sounds floating on the atmosphere, remnants of events started in the lives of individuals long ago. How many arguments took place at this movie lot? How many individuals might have seen a film which some scene in it changed lives forever? How many couples made commitments in the back seat of a car? How many new lives might have been started there as well? *No question about it*, I murmured, *this place carried great influence.*

I turned the corner of the dilapidated concession building, following the sounds toward the area where people used to sit outside during a showing.

In what used to be rows of wood theater seats, Ruben Michael jumped up and down, pointed to the screen, made jabbering noises, laughed and pounded the backs of old seats.

"What in the world is going on, Ruben?" I begged.

"Having a boat load of fun watching this old western movie."

I glanced up at the large blank screen. "What movie?"

"That movie." Ruben pointed to the screen with his thumb like a hitchhiker. "See, John Wayne riding burnt leather to get away from the bad guys. In those days, the good guys were always the good guys and the bad guys were always the bad guys. None of this wondering who you're going to like in a film. Can't you see them up there? Use your imagination, boy. It ain't over yet." Ruben giggled.

I looked hard in the direction pointed, but saw nothing. Then, just as I glanced away, I thought for one fleeting moment I saw four dirty, scrubby men riding horses across a dusty plain; they seemed to chase one well-groomed, tall, lanky cowboy. I blinked and they were gone.

Michael clapped his hands together and motioned for me to come sit by him in one of the old wooden chairs.

Ruben puckered his lips, scratched under his chin like a man pondering the most important question in the universe. "Well . . . what shall we talk about on this balmy Sunday afternoon? Are you in a DR. SELLERS mood or a just plain JEROD mood?"

"Hold on . . . a second", I stammered, "Did I just see some men riding horses up there?"

"Ah . . . you're in a DR. mood of doubt. I have to get your attention again."

I flinched and felt discomfort through my whole body. I did not like the badgering undertone of Ruben's voice. I knew **that** tone provoked emotional responses which prompted me to run away. Reluctantly, I sat and stilled my mind, forcing small courage to accept whatever came next.

"Don't get too finicky. I just want you to consider something. Look around you at this place." Ruben waved his arm in a wide sweep.

"You mean this old concession building?" I implored.

"No, no, this entire setting, including the idea of the place. Why do you think it ended up old news, passé, and caput?"

"Well, I can think of several reasons, but I don't know how correct any of them are." Uncomfortably I shifted in my seat. "Say, how did you get in anyway? That outside gate is always locked. It didn't look busted or anything."

"Locks only keep people in, they don't keep people out," Ruben admonished.

"What is that supposed to mean?" I appealed.

"Never mind now. Come on . . . name some reasons this place failed. This **isn't** a test. I want to hear your thinking on the matter, besides, it does have a point I want to make about the ninth lesson and last kingdom."

Suddenly, Michael jumped up, imitated riding a horse back and forth in front of me. Just as quickly, he stopped, said, 'whoa paint', raised his leg like dismounting a horse, then sat back down.

"Ok, ok. I'm relaxed now. You have my undivided attention. Nice ride, by the way." I grinned at Ruben who returned his eighteen-caret smile. Then we both started laughing so hard out of control that tears ran down our cheeks. Finally, we ended with little snickering sounds as both of us exhausted our energy.

"I don't know what's so funny, but I felt like letting go. I couldn't help myself," I snickered.

"Nothing like a good laugh. Some will tell you it's better than an old-fashioned enema." Michael blurted.

I broke up one more time. Holding my side, "Stop . . . please stop, you're going to make me sick."

"Right . . . right. Back to the question. Why do you think all this became obsolete?

I rubbed my eyes, gained some composure and responded. "For one thing, they didn't keep up with better technology, like speakers and such. Those speakers were awful."

"What else?" Michael invited.

"I suppose a cultural shift happened too. This idea promoted people getting out of the house and going where the entertainment was. People going to the mountain, so to speak. Then, it changed with home videos. The entertainment movie people brought the mountain to people. People are basically lazy. It's a lot less trouble to stay home and be entertained if you really like the entertainment."

"But a lot of people still go to inside movies, don't they?" Ruben raised his brows.

"Well . . . yes, but that's different I think because the inside experience is more intimate. It's kind of like being in a big living room, but you get the big screen effect. I think people feel safe with the inside thing. Plus, you can do amazing effects with sound. The high-powered, quality sound stuff really promotes the music industry, I suspect."

"All very insightful, Jerod, but as you think through all the various reasons you can think of . . . can you see an underlying principle why the drive-in became obsolete?"

"Well, it seems to me that they had a good thing going here, but they didn't keep up with meeting people's needs. Perhaps they got stuck doing their thing only one way, which means they didn't deal with change very well. I don't know . . . is that more to your point?" I pleaded.

"You're getting close. The truth is, this place and idea

fizzled because those who possessed the resources did not **persevere**."

"You mean they gave up?"

"Something like that. With all the changes happening around them, they did not adapt and stay with their original good idea. One of the beginning ideas for the drive-in proposed having something inexpensive for families to do together. People still like to get out of the house and go to a place worthwhile. People still go to outdoor zoos, outdoor car shows, outdoor swap meets, fairs, all kinds of things. So . . . it isn't the idea that became ancient. It was the lack of prevailing. They did not endure the changes and adjust with new technology and other measures. Christians dropped the ball, again too."

"Huh . . . did you say Christians?"

"Yes Jerod, Christians. Wouldn't it have been a wonderful ministry if churches would have bought several drive-ins and made them places that showed affirming movies. They could easily update the technology, make the places safe and run Christian valued movies. They could have a place where you wouldn't be ashamed to take your kids or your mother. You wouldn't have to listen to bad language or see violence sensationalized. Plus, you could use such a place to have Christian music concerts, dramas, all kinds of cleaner entertainment, promoting values more in line with Biblical truths."

"Man, are you saying I should get my church member to turn this place in that direction?"

"You could do a lot worse. But No, don't get off the point. I'm trying to talk to you about the **kingdom of Perseverance**—the last blessed. Did you bring any parchments with you?"

"No . . . Uh, the originals are still in my safe deposit. I forgot the copies. I could go get them. Is that ok? I know you said bring them. But when your singing telegram came and Jill and I discussed whether she should come, I just forgot. Sorry . . . by the way, your way of sending the gram was a hoot. Jill thought so too"

Michael reached out and gently gripped my arm. "No big deal for now . . . do you remember the last set of symbols Clarissa made?"

"Vaguely." I pictured the copies in my mind. "There appeared to be what looks like a row of people walking somewhere and they were all carrying individual crosses. I figured it had to do with all the Christians being killed in that first century setting."

"Not exactly. The last beatitude says, 'blessed are you when people insult, abuse, or persecute you falsely for Jesus' name sake'. I know some Christian thinkers put this verse in with the one before, concerning the kingdom of Loyalty, so they suggest there are only eight beatitudes, but I assure you, there are nine . . . and this becomes the toughest of all."

"I'd always been taught there were eight as well", I responded.

"I know but that's not what matters now. For you see, many people are stuck either in pride or their old ways that they become like murderers of the soul. They do this by false accusation, subtle innuendo, a rumor here, and a rumor there. When you are in pursuit of true kingdom principles honoring the name of Christ, you will be challenged by those, even close to you, who will insult you by spreading half-truths or untruths about your activities. These people will misunderstand your motives and question your methods every chance they get. When you enter this kingdom of perseverance . . . and you will very soon, you will have to rise above your feelings of being misunderstood."

"How can I do that? You know that issue bothers me more than most. I want everybody to understand me." I insisted.

"The growth occurring through this kingdom creates a powerful assurance; a clear knowledge the suffering of Christ finds a way to conquer pain of all kinds. Those little figures of Clarissa's, carrying crosses, show each Christian moving through all the kingdom principles that will end with his or her own cross to carry."

"See Jerod, you will understand people's shortcomings but be willing for Christ's sake to suffer with them. At the same time, you will be able to confront others with solid Christian values, persistently upholding those values even in the light of being misunderstood. While all of this sounds too tough, the truth is, the Holy Spirit will delight in comforting you and you will rejoice in your future reward because it will be a grand, heavenly surprise."

"I have to be honest with you, Ruben. This scares the socks off me. Something in me cringes when you talk about suffering and pain. My old tendency to feel guilt tries to creep in and I know guilt is not what God truly wants from me. You're going to have to make this clearer to me, especially in the light of my serving a church and all. I hope you're not saying I'm about to be crucified in my church. I don't think I'm ready for that. I'm not sure I ever would be. I suppose I could handle being misunderstood a little, but to have a whole church reject me might be too much. I don't do rejection very well."

"My word, son, most people don't. And I'm not talking

about rejection based on something **you** may have done, although I guess that's possible. I'm talking about rejection for Jesus' sake and **that's** a whole different matter. I see right now, I must clarify a great deal. Don't forget, you will have grown while passing through the kingdom of loyalty such that you learn more how to absorb the anger of others without over reacting. You probably are more afraid now because you've not grown enough through the kingdom of loyalty. You still tend to react to other people's anger with what you think is justice. Again, it's not you would necessarily become disloyal to Christ, but you need more ability to stay loyal to Christ under certain unpleasant circumstances and conditions." Ruben frowned.

"What conditions?" I flinched.

"My role is not to tell your future, Jerod . . . I'm to show principles."

"You mean you know the future?"

"You're going to fall pretty soon, but you won't be hurt badly." Ruben glared.

Panic crossed my face. I felt unsure of myself and glanced around the area for any danger. Then I started twisting and squirming in my seat, looking right and left. Suddenly, a slow creaking sound rose from my seat, then came a ripping **snap** and I fell straight down on the ground. Michael grinned and started whistling the old church hymn, 'Stand Up, Stand Up, For Jesus.' I got up brushing off my pants.

"**Why didn't you tell me this old theater seat was so weather worn**?" I boomed.

"I told you . . . you were going to fall . . . that's the principle." Ruben chuckled.

I started dusting my clothes again, glancing around

to see if anyone else saw me tumble. "But, I didn't know if you meant my fall would be symbolic or literal. You didn't give me enough specifics."

"Sometimes knowing the future simply means recognizing the obvious. From now on, Jerod, you must pay more attention to everything the Spirit offers. Let go of your analyzing so much and depend on the Holy Spirit's guidance. The Spirit can keep you more alert than all the knowledge in the human world. You are going to need **all** your focus from now on, and the truth is . . . for you to have real focus . . . you need to rest more in the Spirit of Christ who can clear out all the useless garbage and harmonize your decision-making."

"Well, I think I've been fairly persistent and persevering with you, Ruben. You have kept me on a roller coaster ever since we met." I shot back.

"Toleration would be a better word, I suspect." Michael looked sad. "And just think, I'm fully on your side and look how I get you riled up. Think of those down the road who are going to stir your blood."

"I know, I know, so you say. I'm still too uncomfortable with talk of pain and suffering and such." I said.

"Did you hurt yourself when you fell on the ground?" Ruben invited.

"No, not really."

"Did you discover anything?" Michael bugged his eyes and wiggled his brows up and down, eyebrows almost touching.

"Yeah . . . don't sit in weather worn, outside theater chairs." I blurted.

Ruben slapped his knees and whooped. "See, boy you're learning endurance already."

I couldn't keep from smiling. It was as if Ruben's

humor could reach out and wrap around me like an old comfortable blanket.

Ruben raised his hands and dropped them abruptly in a gesture of total resignation. "Seriously now . . . one of the hardest challenges as you move through the kingdom of perseverance is this: you need to let go of any desire to defend yourself."

"Wait . . . you mean if someone physically threatens to attack me or my loved ones, I'm supposed to let them do whatever they want . . . not defend?" I demanded.

"Not necessarily, Jerod. You always tend to start your thinking process with the physical. I'm talking about the spiritual quality first. You are to practice getting rid of the need, the actual lust of the soul, to justify your actions for Christ. You see, the true heart of people wanting to blame others for their failures is this built-in desire to pardon or exempt one's own behavior. For example, let's say you propose a true scriptural principle to your congregation, like the act of confessing sins to each other, and there develops opposition who say you should not confess to anyone but God . . . you will need to subdue your desire to argue with them, put them straight . . . simply let the Holy Spirit speak and work the principle in his own way. To do that, you must constantly be on guard and squelch the natural defense mechanisms. Just as God sometimes answers you in silence, you will need to answer with silence. This is the heart of perseverance."

"All right, but what about the issue of violence? We live in such a violent time. Are we not to defend ourselves?" I argued.

"It depends. Jesus certainly defended against those misusing children. He defended the weak who could not help themselves. He defended God's house from those who misrepresented it. There are times when you take a stand, but like Jesus, He never justified his actions by returning either violence with violence or when He was accused spiritually of falsifying God. He did not argue his case as much as He simply spoke the truth and the Holy Spirit worked the work. Remember, His final refusal to defend came at the Cross experience."

"**That** certainly scares me," I shuttered.

"Most people don't go to a literal cross anymore, Jerod. But you do have many spiritual and psychological crosses to bear. There will always be in this imperfect world those who will want to nail you, so to speak, because they do not understand what sin really is. The tragedy in the heart of sin is pernicious evil—the kind of evil that does not know it's wrong and wants to drag everyone down with it. That is Satan's main nature. And that is also why he can never be saved—he truly believes he's right when he's so wrong."

"I've met some church members like that," I retorted.

"Yes, but you are to keep hope for them, not argue with them. They can tie you up and spend your energies on the wrong things. Just answer them in silence, concern and prayer. **Some** will be saved."

I sighed heavily and looked at the ground.

"Let's take a break. Look what I have." Michael moved to a certain old wooden seat and reached under it, pulling out a small portable cooler. He opened it, reached inside and pulled out two soft drinks and two candy bars. Handing a drink and candy to me, Ruben said, "You're favorite I think."

I accepted the snack, amazed again how Ruben knew such things and wondering why I had not seen the bright red cooler, sitting in plain sight.

Chapter 20

After snacking on candy and drinks, Michael and I strolled around the old Drive-in movie parking lot, discussing the changes possible to do something with the dilapidated, ghost of a movie business. The weather stayed mild on this late September Sunday afternoon, with light breezes whipping through the lot. Long stalks of dried brown Johnson grass pushed their way up through the old asphalt paving, evidence of its once vigorous early spring weather.

Both of us wore casual pullover shirts, soft slacks and clean tennis shoes so we looked like prosperous investors dressed for an outing and for a look-see, surveying potential profit. Any onlooker would see the two of us were comfortable with each other and might have thought we'd been in business together for years. Some might even think we were perhaps father and son.

Soon we arrived back to where my car was parked, still inside the fenced lot, close to the giant movie screen.

"Let's sit a spell and enjoy this marvelous weather." Michael sighed as he slowly opened the car door. "You know Jerod; you have the experience of this entire marvelous created world to enjoy in a proper way. One of the most difficult challenges for you remains being in the world but not of it."

"Yeah. . .I remember that is exactly what Jesus prayed in John's gospel for the disciples," I mused, "But I'm not always sure what it means."

"It is profound but simple", Ruben said, "You are to discover how to appreciate the world of things without the need to possess them. You can use what you choose, be a manager of it, but to experience too much comfort in owning a thing is to be tempted to be owned by it. The Creator is the only genuine possessor and can own the world. He wants to own you too, but it's more like ownership with a partnership built in. Jesus is the partner." Ruben took a deep breath; sighing like one tired from a long journey.

"Are you tired, Ruben? It seems your pace and everything seems a little down." I said concerned.

"Things are winding down, actually . . . I should say 'winding up' for I want you to remember something: Nowhere physically is potentially somewhere spiritually."

"Oh no, not again. What in the world does **that** mean?"

"Very soon, in times to come . . . just remember that fact. But for now, I need to give you final instructions. Please do not question these too much . . . there isn't time . . . you see . . . I have to leave soon."

"What? Are you going to do one of your disappearing acts again?" I entreated.

"No, I said *leave*."

"What do you mean, leave? Where are you going? What's the deal?"

"Jerod . . . please . . . subdue your curiosity for now. It's imperative", came Ruben's breathless reply.

As I stared at Ruben, for a fleeting moment, I thought I saw him fading in and out as if he were becoming translucent. I rubbed my eyes, thinking perhaps I lacked sleep. Then I blinked several times and shook my head, trying to feel more alert. I felt tired enough for my eyes to start playing tricks on me and yet I didn't feel the usual drowsiness before sleep. Finally, I forced my vision to focus more clearly on Ruben, who sat patiently waiting.

"Now listen, Jerod. I want you to get a total picture of what I've shown you about the kingdom principles. If you don't get the right view of moving in and out of the kingdoms or their accumulative effect, you will miss the point of our time together, as well as what you're especially called to do. So still your mind to receive the sum of what we've discussed."

"Ok. . . I think I can do that . . . I mean, I'm with you."

"I started by saying you must work your way through the nine kingdoms of growth and it's easier to think of these in groups of three. This journey begins **after** salvation. It is not some way to obtain salvation. And as I said, the first kingdom experience, poor in spirit, is the salvation experience and begins the opening pathway through the other spiritual challenges. So, I set these out so you keep them in mind like a blueprint:

The **kingdom of Need** saves and dispels loneliness.
The **kingdom of Sorrow** fights selfishness.
The **kingdom of Yielding** overcomes pride.

The **kingdom of Appetite** turns wrong into right.
The **kingdom of Kindness** combats harshness.

The **kingdom of Cleanness** conquers jealousy and envy.

The **kingdom of Harmony** displaces and absorbs anger.

The **kingdom of Loyalty** withstands persecution.

The **kingdom of Perseverance** endures joy and pain.

"Burn them into your memory, Jerod, for they are your travels as surely as the sun will shine again. They are your paths for the Christian road of character building and become every Christian's journey for Christ-like growth."

Ruben coughed and continued, "Be ever conscious of how they are used in practical ways in your daily life because they can link together to enhance Christian personality. Remember, the Holy Spirit will keep you alert more than any human knowledge."

"When loneliness invades you," Ruben continued, "think upon your salvation and the passion of Christ. When you find yourself becoming selfish, work to turn your concern toward other's misfortune. When pride tries to sneak in, yield to Christ's love by helping others reach praise."

"When you are confronted by wrong doing, hunger and thirst for God's word rather than some retaliation. When irritation turns to harshness, lace it with mercy and give away mercy instead of judgment. When jealousy and envy creep into the heart, ask forgiveness so God's light may shine more clearly."

"When anger attacks your very being, accept the

peace God offers and calmly receive adversity among people. When unpleasant people and circumstances thrash your existence, absorb the confusion by knowing Christ's ways are worth living and dying for. Then, when you are accused falsely or abused for Jesus teachings, rejoice in your part of furthering the heavenly kingdom on earth, for you are preparing others to be ready for the true heaven instead of just getting people to go there." Ruben gave a big sigh again and paused.

I sat and stared open mouthed.

"And **remember constantly**", Ruben finally boomed . . . "these principles linked together can urge others to live and display the true salt flavor and the clear light of God on earth."

I felt stunned and yet the truth settled into my soul like snuggling down into my favorite recliner. For a moment, all my earlier, doubting questions melted away. At the same time, a feeling of utter completeness embraced me, a finishing closure authored by the Holy Spirit. I felt all Ruben said was somehow true and coming from a divine throne of grace. All the principles we'd discussed seemed to flow through me one right after the other, flushing my system, leaving inspirational residue throughout. My whole body vibrated peace. For once, I truly felt I understood all as I basked in this spirit of awe.

Then just as suddenly came an internal snap and I jerked alert with the sound of Ruben's voice.

"By God's magnificent Grace, for just a fraction of time, you've just now been shown the accumulative ecstasy of Jesus' principles when finished. You may never experience **that** again until you die. But you will have moments of satisfied completeness when you win battles while negotiating the individual kingdoms."

I blinked and felt my old self again. Then I groveled. "But why can't I feel that completeness all the time?"

"That is not for you, Jerod. For you see, you are destined to live out what you must create. Any less would alter the heavenly kingdom among humanity."

"What? . . . How?"

"All I can say is something magnificently new has begun. God has always been creating a new race of people in Christ. You are to give that strategy a boost."

"Wait . . . wait. I'm not sure I understand specifically what I'm supposed to do now?" I pleaded.

"Always the practical one, eh Jerod . . . Two things. First, I want you to arrange to get the original parchments to your professor friend in Fort Worth, Texas. You keep the copies and interpretations. If they want to buy them just so they'll value them more, you set the price. Make it enough but not too extravagant. Then, I want you to keep the money for what you must do later. But, you must tell Dr. Sturgen they may have them on the condition he set up a course of study for the Seminarians. It will be somewhat of a struggle because the parchments, after all, are written by a woman. He may have some difficulty because of the gender issue. Help him all you can."

"How did you know about him?" I pumped.

"Never mind . . . the second thing I want you to do is more important."

"Oh, all right. What's that?"

"I want you to say *goodbye*." Ruben eased out of the car and solidly shut the door.

"Gonna leave on me again, are you? Do I get to see you go this time?" I exclaimed.

"I'm not just going, I'm leaving." Ruben half turned

and looked back at me with what looked like admiration mixed with sweet sadness, and then shuffled away slowly walking toward the big outdoor movie screen which stood some thirty yards away. I jumped out of the car and started after him.

"Hold on . . . what you mean *leaving*?" I begged.

Ruben shouted to the wind. "The lessons are over and you've given me your nine days attention. I'm done. I must leave. The rest is up to you." Ruben kept walking toward the screen.

"But wait," I reached toward his leaving and was stopped dead in my tracks, as if an unseen force constrained me. "Can't we just meet again tomorrow? I know I will have other questions and such?" I pleaded.

"I wish I could . . . but no . . . perhaps we'll meet again," Ruben called over his shoulder and kept walking closer to the giant movie screen.

What happened next, I will always marvel about and wonder, trying to decide what really happened.

There I was beckoning for Ruben Michael to reconsider and he kept walking straight for the giant screen. I felt completely bound like gravity working against me, holding me in position, while Ruben moved away. I could move my arms but not my feet. As I watched, everything seemed in slow motion, as he strolled toward the bottom of the screen, then started walking right up the screen. He kept moving to the upper part of the screen, moving higher and higher, as if walking on invisible stairs. The closer he got to the top, the more faded he became. By the time he reached the 100-foot screen dead center, he turned and saluted me. Then, he spun around, entered the screen itself and faded out completely.

I sagged when suddenly my body felt released, and

then I began to shake. I stood with hands palm up in front of me, imploring the elements for explanation. I glanced right and left, behind, then back at the screen in a gesture searching if anyone else saw what I saw.

A soft, cool breeze struck my face and moved past to rattle the old tin fence that surrounded this abandoned arena of entertainment. A last golden swirl of sunlight dropped on earth as twilight reminded me of reality once again. Small bits of paper and trash swirled around my legs. I looked down and watched them bump along the dirt, feeling a connection with the tossed debris. I stood alone and knew it. Deep sadness and joy flooded my spirit at the same time, like the void when losing a best friend but remembering all the good times to equalize any hurt.

As another breeze stroked my face, I felt a fresh thought and energy invade my thoughts. As puzzling as the moment was I knew I must push on to what lay next. Whatever came I had to persevere.

Chapter 21

Leaving the old drive-in movie, I had to drive around awhile, trying to absorb all that happened. I was in one of those dream states, driving like I was on auto pilot.

Finally, I arrived home Sunday evening. I'd struggled with my sense of loss from two perspectives: one was the leaving Ruben's friendship and the other a kind of sadness, like a melancholy when some enjoyable experience ends.

With the departure of Ruben, somber feelings gripped my spirit. A part of me always dreaded happy times for the reason of feeling loss afterwards. Embedded down deep in my soul, I really didn't trust happiness. It was too fleeting. Yet, there was nothing left for me to do, but return home to seek refuge in familiar surroundings.

I entered my house and found Jill waiting. She still nursed some hurt pride from not being able to share all the experiences with me. For a while, her attitude seemed cool and distant until she began to really hear my summary of all that happened with Mr. Michael.

I told her, we were right about the Starlight Drive-in. I also explained the best I could about my falling in the chair, about Ruben's final lesson, and then, the agonizing unbelievable event of his walking up and into the screen.

She stared with skepticism and wonderment. Then, she softened, I think because in me, she recognized and accepted some of my sadness and confusion. She began to sense my perplexing mood, feeling the significant change in me and the seriousness of my condition, wondering if I harbored depression. She knew from experience, the best approach for me in these moments was a sympathetic, direct challenge.

"Jerod . . . are you telling me Ruben just disappeared in a giant movie screen?" She asked kindly.

"I know it sounds crazy, but that's it."

"Heavens!" Jill sighed.

"Exactly."

"So . . . are we to believe he really was more than a man, like, some kind of angel?"

"What else?" I exclaimed.

"You're sure it's not some kind of trick? Maybe he'll be back again like before. You know he played all these dumb tricks on you and he certainly didn't seem angel-like on many occasions, now, did he?"

"Jill . . . I don't know what an angel is supposed to be like. All I know is what I feel and my gut says he was the genuine article and he's gone!"

"Goodness . . . you need to tell somebody. . . I mean . . . don't you? Of course, the question is...who would you tell?"

"Who would believe me? . . . You barely do." I frowned.

"Maybe you could explain things to Gary Butler."

"Are you kidding? . . . I can't tell Gary . . . especially not Gary or anyone like him. I've thought about things a lot and the whole experience has to come about some other way."

"You mean like living out the principles Ruben taught . . . what a thought . . . taught by an angel." Jill smiled.

"Yeah, right." I huffed.

"Seriously," Jill continued, "I know this has got to be complicated for you. What are you going to do now? I mean . . . are you going to do what he said about the parchments?"

"What else can I do? I can see the wisdom making sure they get into the hands of Professor Sturgen. At this point, I really do feel what I've been taught and the content interpretations are more important than some old ancient manuscripts. Let those who deal in such things handle that part." I lamented.

"You sure spent a lot of time on them just to give them up." She shot back.

"I know. I know. But it's the only thing to do. I guess I could keep them safe somewhere, and yet, Ruben's instructions were clear and he's been right about so many issues. I don't see any way but do as he said. Who knows? Even though he said he was leaving, he might pop back here and check me out. I sure wouldn't want to face his wrath."

"Well, the way you described his last action . . . if it's not some ruse, I suppose he's really gone."

"I'm afraid he is." I slumped in my recliner, crossed my arms and leaned my head to one side.

Jill knew from my body language I would fall deeper into sadness if she didn't do something to prevent it. I needed another challenge to get my thinking working on something besides loss.

"I still would like more discussion why you feel

you couldn't take me with you on all your outings with Ruben?"

I sat up straight. "What?"

"Why did you have to be with Ruben alone?

"I don't know if I can respond to that now. I'm too numb."

"Come on. Put it in gear. Was it a *guy* thing?"

"No . . . No. Nothing like that. It started out as an individual effort . . . I don't know . . . one of those personal, individual things we do sometimes."

"Jerod . . . I've always known there lurked in you a kind of adventurer. It used to always scare me. That part of you seems so distant and untouchable. But I'm not so frightened of your strong pull for things new. I just want to be a part of all of you."

"I suppose, in the beginning, a part of me felt the adventure, but not altogether. You know how there are certain individual actions you like to do that I don't."

"Like what. Name one." She demanded.

"Uh . . . let me think . . . Uh . . . shopping. You know how you like to look for hours and never buy anything. Yet I like to go straight in the store and buy the first item that suits me. Things like that."

"But did I ever make shopping an issue to come between us?"

"Well, no because I let you do your thing. At least, that's the way I see it."

"It's not quite the same is it, Jerod. I really felt left out when you wanted to spend so much time with Ruben. I don't mean I was just jealous, not that, I don't think. I felt you were sharing a part of yourself you couldn't or wouldn't share with me. We've always been so close since we don't have children and I've felt we shared about everything. But this time, I felt replaced. I don't like that feeling. It makes me want to run away and just let you have yourself to yourself."

"Sounds like part of the Adam and Eve syndrome, at least, that's what I call it."

"What does that mean?" She quizzed.

"Are you sure you want to hear this now?"

"Yes, I definitely want to hear it now."

"Let me see if I can explain, although you probably won't like it. At least, this is my perspective. See . . . Adam was alone at first . . . had everything . . . his work in the Garden of Eden, plenty of food, the animals, even walked and talked with God personally. Then he must have seen the animals in twos and got lonely. I believe about then God gave him Eve. Still, it means originally, a part of man has a need to be alone and at other times, needs someone. He may not can stand being alone forever because his psychological fulfillment is still found in the woman, a being like himself but outside of self."

"Eve, on the other hand, never experienced utter aloneness." I continued. "Remember, Adam was made from dirt, basically nothing. Eve was made from Adam—something . . . an ongoing process. When she coupled with man, she acquired a built-in bondedness. So, she naturally feels a stronger togetherness. But her natural psychological fulfillment isn't in the man; it's beyond, in the care giving principle, children or something which receives her nurture ability."

I paused to view Jill's expression. She just stared so I continued. "The book of Genesis says the woman will suffer in child birth and she will cling to her husband. It also says it's a curse. That's the reason women are often more attached to their children than they are their husbands. If a woman has no children as objects for care giving, she turns that energy to something like a career . . . or someone else. You turned your support to me, and I like that, but it also sets you up to feel betrayed when I need to be alone."

"Well, I can see what you're saying, but I like to be alone sometimes too, yet I never feel I'm alone without you. A part of me feels the need to be with you all the time and another part doesn't, yet it doesn't cut you out of my life."

"You've just described what happened after Sin came into the picture. First, understand, I don't blame Eve for the first Sin, not really. I think Sin started to creep in when Adam became discontented. Remember he had everything, even God, and that didn't seem to be enough. In my opinion, something wrong there."

"Anyway," I continued, "Eve did disobey by eating of the forbidden fruit. After that, God told her once her desire was unto God but after Sin, her desire would be unto the man . . . and he pronounced it a curse. So, in a sense, when it comes to relating to a man, you are sort of cursed if you do and cursed if you don't. Part of your desire is for a man; the other part of you knows you could live without a man. You get caught in split loyalties and it plays havoc with your emotions."

"Are you saying there are parts of me that can't live without you and another part that can't live with you?"

"I'm afraid that's the curse." I smiled.

"Well, I'm glad you're feeling better. I'm feeling worse." Jill grinned. "I don't know if I buy all you're saying, but it's an interesting perspective. I like the idea Adam may have sinned first."

"I thought you might." I mused.

"So . . . what does this have to do with Ruben?"

"In the beginning, you know me; I just went out of curiosity. But then, it was as if God sent him especially for me alone. Maybe I was wrong, but even Ruben said as much. He certainly had winning ways and convinced me, although his strangeness threw me and I'm afraid to say out loud what I think about that."

"So, what do you think? Who do you think he really was?"

"Your guess is as good as mine . . . but we **may actually** have been visited by an angel."

"Oh yeah . . . A good one or a bad one?" Jill puzzled.

"Well, I definitely believe he was a heavenly messenger, though strange."

"Why would a good angel cause division between you and me?"

"Come on, Jill, **he** didn't do that, yet I suppose God's truth may seem to cause division. But in the end, it can cause nothing but harmony. See, I feel pretty divided myself, not from you . . . but about ministry. All the old ways I've been doing things don't make much sense anymore."

Jill flinched. "What are you thinking? You're not going to get weird with our livelihood, are you?"

"I don't know just yet what's coming, but I know I can't go back to the status quo. I know something down deep is stirring. I can't quite put my finger on it. And don't get too excited, Jill, I'm not thinking about quitting the ministry . . . nothing so drastic. But I know that profound little man changed my center of feelings and thinking forever. It's like a new path opened for my spirit and, I 'm supposed to follow no matter what. I do feel strong and correct about the change."

I was no longer depressed but reflective, as I stared straight ahead and turned my thoughts toward what the future proposed.

The next day was Monday and Jill and I decided to use my day off to drive to Ft. Worth and hand deliver the package of original parchments with their detailed interpretations. We decided to combine the business at hand with a little pleasure trip, perhaps dinner and a movie. We got the original parchments from our safe deposit, drove to Texas and met with the professor.

In time, Jill and I both explained to Professor Sturgen the request of the benefactor to begin a course in Christian maturity based on the content of the writings. Jill and I agreed on the way down to the Seminary we'd let academia deal with any questions of authenticity or whatever. I kept a copy of the parchments with interpretations and I felt I'd kept much more content in my heart for what truly mattered.

We decided to set a price of $10,000 on the manuscripts but told Sturgen the Seminary could keep the material and pay for them when they felt ready to do so. I did not mention Ruben's strangeness nor who and what we thought he was. I did not want to damage the parchment's chances with any negative bias. Then, we returned home, feeling we'd fulfilled Ruben's wishes, satisfied that part of our mission was carried out.

Still, I felt a gnawing unrest, the kind which lingers just below the surface of awareness, suggesting something forgotten, about to be remembered, something waiting to poke its head up and bring a humbling surprise to remind the consciousness of its imperfection.

And then one day, change became the name of the surprise.

Chapter 22

Two weeks passed since Ruben vanished and I left the parchments of the first century writings, which Dr. Sturgen fulfilled all my requests about buying the works and keeping my name anonymous. But for me, it seemed a lot longer time.

I handled the issue of the $10,000 which was supposed to go to me a little differently. Sturgen was shocked at the small amount because he knew the material was priceless. But, I just assured him everyone was satisfied and I told Sturgen a specific payout plan; put $8000 in a scholarship fund for students, then send me the other two. I felt a couple of thousand was enough for me to do anything through the church, if some specific came up about the use of the parchment copies. I knew my original good faith $100 check I'd given Ruben for the parchments never was used because I had not signed it.

As the days passed, I finally admitted to myself Ruben indeed was gone. Soon, I found myself immersed in the routine duties of the church, pastoral activities kept my body busy, but my mind worried over the unrest of usual ministry methods. My concerns now centered more on what to do next with my own spiritual growth. Ruben's methods probed deeply into my doubt and exhaustion and uprooted any inclination to hold onto past excuse to stay the same. Of course, a part of me wanted to keep the status quo, but then the change in me wanted to go deeper with God as I considered ways to apply the teaching sessions of Ruben Michael.

Sunday rolled around again and I found myself on my knees in the study, agonizing over the sermon for that morning. Most of my struggle and thoughts centered on the last discussion Ruben gave me about the principles being in threes. Erratically, questions plagued my self-talk: *What happened to Ruben? What did all this mean to me personally? What if a group of people in modern day truly committed themselves to the nine little kingdoms?*

Slowly, I rose from my kneeling position, rubbing my forehead where the sinus cavities felt full and swollen. The eleven o'clock church service had nearly begun, so I walked from my study, down the hall to a side door of the sanctuary. Some of the church members nodded and said good morning, but I moved in a daze, giving token recognition to those I met but never truly registering their presence. Music floated in the air as the choir already began the service with an opening anthem: *Praise God from Whom All Blessings Flow.*

I entered a side sanctuary door, moved slowly and stepped onto the platform, making my way to one of the chairs stationed behind the pulpit. A podium stood in the center of the stage as a large wooden cross, fashioned from top grade walnut. I'd sat in this position many times before and always took note of my surroundings, even seeing people I knew and waving or giving a slight nod to those familiar. But on this occasion, all my thoughts were inward and I stayed oblivious to those who watched me.

Of course, the audience saw nothing unusual, recognizing me as their pastor, their spiritual guide and leader. To many, I portrayed a deeply spiritual person and they found comfort and security in a pastor who kept things under control, ran the services competently and led a perfectly timed sermon, allowing most of the people out of service in time to miss the heaviest lunch crowds in the local eating establishments.

Little groups sitting together whispered. Some of the older couples talked louder to each other. Small murmurs came from the crowd. It always amazed me how people would just ignore the excellent music going on and keep visiting like they were in a living room.

As they sat, expecting their usual resourceful sermon, for if nothing else, I excelled as a consistent teacher of the Word. Most of my audience was spiritually well fed, in fact, that was the main reason they came—to sit back and listen. They were a body of believers with as many problems as anyone else, but on Sunday, they put on their Sunday best and came to church in a pious exercise which did very little to change their lives. They were generally content to let their pastor be religious for them, when it came to any practice of God's word. I could visit the sick, the homeless, the downtrodden— that was **my** job. Most were not vindictive about this; they simply allowed themselves to be lulled into subtle complacency. Little did they know of my inner struggle, of my true self-agonizing deep within.

With routine thought, I knew the order of service: Two songs, recognition of visitors, a prayer before the offering, then a special music piece before the sermon.

Finally, a duet sang the special music— the designated punchy performance to get the audience ready for the sermon. It was time for my performance.

I rose slowly and approached the pulpit. I placed my Bible and notes carefully on the podium. My hands were sweaty. There traveled a slight tremble down my spine as I opened the Scripture verse to be read out loud. A mild shuffling stirred the audience as I paused to read the Word.

But then, I paused longer and longer as all eyes rested on me for what usually came next. I looked out among the congregation, first right, then left. I tried to see faces, but only scanned the auditorium. The whole congregation seemed like one mass of unrecognizable people, no individuals registered. As I started to speak, I felt an inner pain, like my physical body was about to shut down. Some dizziness washed over me, but just as suddenly, I felt I could speak.

"For the last few weeks something happened to me . . . and I cannot avoid the experience any longer. . . first . . . I cannot preach the sermon I prepared for this morning." I closed my notes.

Every head in the audience turned to look at one another, then back at me. Shuffling echoed through the auditorium. Never in all their years had they seen me do anything like this. More stirring occurred, then, total silence filled the room as everyone sat staring at me like onlookers at a car accident.

"An event," I continued, "so unbelievable occurred to me recently, I cannot share the details now. But I must say . . . a fresh approach to ministry has come to my attention and I am overwhelmed by its implications. My life cannot be the same . . . I mean I will find no rest until I proceed with what I think God wants me to do."

Then, I saw individual faces, like Gary Butler. I glanced at others. My first impression was the audience must have thought: 'Oh, no, our pastor is going to resign.'

I picked up the pace. "My situation may not be what many of you are thinking. This may seem strange to you, but I want to make a different appeal to you this morning."

I took a deep breath and proceeded, "Some . . . of you . . . I know are concerned, even disturbed, that being Christian in our modern world makes very little difference in everyday life. These days it is hard to tell a person with Christian values compared to those without. However, I do feel some of you yearn for a deeper walk with the Lord. Not only do you want to know Him better, you want to be able to practice His principles in your everyday lives."

"Here's what I want you to do. I want you to prayerfully consider the question: ***what difference does it make that you know Jesus? Let me say again: what difference does it make that you know Jesus? . . .*** Now, then, IF you feel you would like that question answered, that you are one of those who yearn for something more in your life . . . I want you to come to my study, RIGHT NOW, and meet with me in prayer and discussion . . . the rest of the congregation may go. You are dismissed!"

Abruptly, I turned and walked from the platform, out the side door and down the hall to my office. I entered and slumped in a chair, rubbing my temples with index fingers.

I heard later, the congregation sat stunned. Scattered

through the crowd, certain individuals bowed their heads. Many weren't sure they heard what they thought they heard. Buzzing conversations began. Some, like Gary Butler, wondered if his pastor was having a nervous breakdown. Most of the people were surprised, but only shrugged, and felt deep down they'd been given a gift because they could get to the restaurants even earlier. Slowly the crowd trickled away, muttering their individual comments. But over to one side, a handful of individuals made their way slowly through the side door, leading to my study.

Out of three hundred in attendance that day, only sixteen people showed at the door. A solemn hush settled over the group as they eased their way into the room. In many ways, they were strangers crammed in the study, shoulder to shoulder, expecting the next move. But soon, as they settled in, they began to feel a peculiar bond develop, like entering a special place, knowing you are at the right place at the right time.

The Holy Spirit began to interpret to each heart before they knew consciously why they were there. Each person had not felt this genuine warmth for a long time, probably since the days of their individual spiritual conversions. Still, the suspense of the moment produced a strange tension, yet they told me later, they felt peace.

As all eyes rested on me, I looked back at them with compassion, feeling appreciation for their response but also knowing hardships lay ahead. I glanced over the group, looking for Jill. She stood, head bowed, behind the group. Heaving a sigh, I found a rich tonal quality as I spoke. My tone seemed to flow with a new love as this new challenge faced us all.

"Hey guys, I know this seems strange, but you are

here because you want something deeper in Christ. By your response, you've said you are tired of mere church going and you seek to make Jesus a practical reality in your life . . . and so do I."

"With fear and trembling, I want to share with you an experience and a plan that has come to my attention under the most unusual circumstances . . . and please bear with me. Try not to judge because the facts appear mystical to say the least. But I have been challenged to test what I've always thought was sound churchmanship. It may be a new approach, a risk I might add, that will propel us into the mainstream of daily living, calling for abrupt change and some sacrifice. So . . . for the moment, allow God's grace to flow in your spirit as you listen to what I have to say."

A small stir rippled through the little group but all held spell-bound to every word coming from their pastor.

I clasped my hands in front of me and began to relate all that happened to me the past few days. I told of Ruben Michael, the parchments, the interpretations, Ruben's strange comings and goings, then finally his disappearance. I gave a brief sketch of what I thought the commitment meant to those early first century Christians. Then I began an appeal:

"As I thought about what Ruben showed me, I feel it presents a specific strategy for us today. First, the main principle that comes out of the parchments seems to be centered around Jesus' prayer in the 17th chapter of John, especially verses fourteen and fifteen, '*Father, I have given them your word; and the world has hated them, because they are not of the world, even as I am not of the world. I do not pray that you should take them out of the world, but that you should keep them from the evil one.'*

"And so," I continued, "the first principle is an active measure to live **in** the world without being **of** the world, to stay attached to cultural events without those events trapping our free Christian spirits. We need to discover how to appreciate all the things of the world without always wanting to own them. Because when we continually want to have stuff, we get tempted to be owned by those things. It ties us too much to this earth. We must build our lives around a gift economy. When we give stuff away, a free Christian spirit is our true challenge."

"The second special effort comes in the form of a journey for us all based upon the growth stages hidden in the principles of the Sermon on the Mount. There is a definite strategy for us to work, built around practiced love, practiced honesty, practiced right doing and practiced sharing. These exercises of growth become the heart of details shown me and the practical outcomes to which any group of dedicated believers bind themselves together."

"I have not worked these out yet in full detail, but I believe the Holy Spirit will help us work out the specifics . . . And please, don't think I'm off my rocker or wanting to create something like a weird community, doing weird things, isolated from the everyday normal world of living. I'm only asking you to commit with me on this strategy because I feel it's Biblical. We will need each other to hold ourselves accountable, banding together like the early Christians did when they had to meet in homes for fear of their lives."

Each person in the study shifted his or her weight

from standing so long, almost like a wave at a football game. But no one wanted to leave. The Holy Spirit moved strongly in their midst. It was as if they were all tuned to the same frequency, waiting for the next revelation that could only come from God Himself.

After a moment, June Foster, a local real estate agent spoke: "Pastor. . . I don't know if I speak for the group . . . but I feel a strange pulling toward all you've said. A thousand questions rush through my mind, but I don't know if now's the time to ask anything." She slowly glanced at all the others present.

Then Debbie Aldrige, wife of a local car mechanic, chimed in: "I feel it too." She nodded to the others who seemed to nod approval.

Gary Butler made a small harrumph sound and wide-eyed the others in the room.

I felt hot tears burn the corners of my eyes. These were tears of acceptance. It had been too long since I'd felt such fellowship and inclusion with my congregation. I cleared my throat and continued.

"I feel like those people must have felt in the fifth chapter of Acts. I often wondered how and why the Holy Spirit would literally kill Ananias and Sapphira in that first church setting when they'd lied about selling all their property. Now I think I know. In those times, the Holy Spirit must have had complete control of all those present such that He would not allow any sham and pretense or lies to enter their midst. And there was a problem with Ananias and Sapphira. It wasn't that they were bad people or that they were not willing to give something. It was they were asked to give all and they only gave part. So, that little group were bound together with a holy covenant so when falsehood entered the atmosphere, the

Spirit just removed the problem very swiftly. I feel that same power and togetherness among us now."

As I viewed their faces, I knew how scary that sounded, but I also felt without any doubt, we were in the grips of something larger than any one person. Individual personalities may come and go but this was a cooperative atmosphere, the kind of historical awakenings which had changed culture long term. Beaming with confidence, I continued.

"I have asked you here to join me in a specific enterprise, to develop as we can another journey. You can continue your other church activities and concerns but I would like for you to follow a stronger approach for one year and then we will evaluate."

"We will meet once a week as a full group, to hold each other accountable and report the week's activities. We will strive to practice love, honesty, right doing and sharing in the smallest events, not worrying about consequences but trusting Christ to liberate us from those things that tend to enslave us. We will strive to become truly open people and will help all we meet to find liberty and discover how to live in the world without becoming economically or psychologically trapped. As we develop, we will only produce guidelines that help to free-up life and allow Christ's Grace to flow, finding authentic and practical bridges between Law and Grace."

"Wow!" exclaimed Dr. Philip Bigalow, a young university History professor, "those are enormous concepts and I mean this in the right spirit, but I have so many questions. What about this guy Ruben? Or better yet, how will we know just how honest to be in each situation? We live in a culture that has spawned half-truths so long society functions on a kind of dishonesty for their foundation. To advocate total truth to a society that does not even recognize truth is casting the pearls before the swine, is it not? What's going to be our guideline?"

I listened, realizing these were no insincere, simplistic questions. I wasn't sure yet how much I wanted to discuss about Ruben, but I knew the question of honesty would be a genuine concern to everybody and was probably one issue crossing the minds of the whole group. It deserved an answer, yet I also felt I didn't have all the answers. But I responded.

"I am very serious when I say all the answers aren't in yet. What I feel I have are scriptural principles and beginning points. The rest, which must follow, are adventures we will share together somehow. I do know our basic guide has got to be John 14: 16-18 . . . 'I (meaning Jesus) will pray the Father, and He shall give you another comforter, that He may abide with you forever; even the Spirit of Truth; whom the world cannot receive, because it sees him not, neither knows Him: but you know Him; for He dwells with you, and shall be in you. I will not leave you comfortless: I will come to you.'"

Bigalow responded again. "Pastor, does this mean we will all do the same things according to a pledge? Other people might have scriptural definitions of truth as well and their interpretation be different than ours. How will we then know the right direction to take? And please, pastor, I'm not being skeptical . . . I'm really excited about this . . . I just want to know what you've been thinking. I think all of us would. Maybe this isn't the right time for the deeper questions. I was just about to bust."

The group laughed and some of their tension drained away.

"No offense taken", I retorted, "And we really can't cover the questions now, but let me say this . . . at this point, the best I can say about all your questions is we will have to learn how to discern truth in every situation. We must be careful we don't make truth a stopping point, draping it with rules which appear we have all the answers."

"Truth needs to guide us into wisdom and knowledge of our Lord so we never feel we have arrived. Of course, Bible revelation will show us truth and everyone needs to be in tune with the Spirit of Truth, using things like testing the spirit to see if it's really of God. Or, filtering everything we do through a spiritual and relational principle, like what we're about to do, will it glorify God or not. We will literally have to ask any spirit of truth if it accepts Jesus as savior and as the true son of God. If there is a yes answer, then we go ahead. If there is silence or a no answer, then we will have to review our proposed thought or action. We will all have to learn what is too fanatical in action on the one hand, and what too cautious a fear on the other. I believe any action we may take in our individual lives will rise out of Scripture, showing us God's intended revelation and impressing the group with a spirit of unity. So . . . I may be simply saying our task now is to start living the scripture seriously."

Slowly, without another word, I turned around and knelt on my knees, leaning on my chair for prayer.

One by one, the rest of the group followed suit, knelt as best they could. By this action, it was as if all wanted to become a part of the challenge, all turned inward with silent prayer. I was hoping they made a covenant with

God to become modern strugglers and enhancers of the kingdom of God on earth.

After waiting a moment, I began praying out loud:

"Oh Lord, help us to be spontaneous, but not impulsive;
To respond eagerly, but not disrespectfully;
To still be constant in Christ's values,
but avoid haughty justification;

To be aware of true emotions, without emotionalism;
To have true patience, instead of raw persistence.
Help us to be genuinely concerned,
respectfully honest, unselfishly forgiving,
and urgently in agape love
with all other persons with whom we deal.
In Jesus, our model's name. Amen and amen."

It became the prayer for all the members.

■ ■ ■

When the prayer time ended, all the members got up from their knees, ready for some specific action. I waited. No one seemed to know what came next. Finally, Bigalow spoke for the group, suggesting a specific time to meet the following week to make plans. In the meantime, they were to think over all said and come prepared to make any comments or questions about guidelines.

Like smooth flowing water, the group filed out of the study. Buzzing with small conversations, some mingled outside the office, milling around, knowing they should leave but not wanting an end to the deep feeling of togetherness, this unseen spiritual agreement cementing our fellowship.

Quietly, I slipped out of their gathering and walked to my car in the parking lot. I plopped down on the driver's side of my car, reached for a pad and pen, and began to list the people who met with me in the study. I stared at the list and felt intrigued by their diversity:

- My **wife Jill**.
- **Dr. Philip Bigalow**, university professor, teacher of history/ government/ literature.
- **Eva Lambert**, university student, music, singer.
- **June Foster**, real estate; husband Sandy, car sales.
- **Debbie Aldrige**, hairdresser; husband Frank, auto mechanic.
- **Ed Barnes**, church janitor, retired military.
- **Bob and Lucy Sanders**, Starwood Homes Construction.
- **Jerome Fry,** investments.
- **T.J. Holton**, convenience store owner.
- **Alexander Deloach,** accountant; wife Margaret homemaker; daughter Sara, divorced.
- **Gary Butler**, Insurance.

I studied the list a moment, then looked up to the sky, half praying and half talking out loud, and proclaimed: *"Lord, are these the ones to trust with your divine commission? Could you somehow give me some sign, some assurance I'm on the right track? Was the exercise in church and in my study just my yearning? Or, did you speak clearly?"*

I pulled at my ear. At that moment, I realized I had no more heart burn, no more feelings of exhaustion, and no more negative thoughts about ministry. I scratched the tip of my nose and stared at the writing pad. Suddenly, I began to doodle, spelling out the name Ruben Michael . . . Ruben Michael. Then I found myself remembering some of the funny facial expressions that came from my friend. Slowly, I lifted my eyes to heaven and said,

"Oh Lord, something awesome started this morning, didn't it? And by the way, Ruben, wherever you are . . . you did your job. It has begun."

Suddenly, the car door swung open and Jill slid in next to me, smiling.

I looked at her, wiggled my ears, raised my eyebrows up and down, glanced through the windshield to the sky. I started the engine, shifted gears and as we drove away, I started whistling: *Onward Christian Soldiers.*

Printed in the United States
By Bookmasters